HARSH, STRIDENT, COMMANDING, THE VOICE ROSE IN ITS FURY....

Slowly the abbess raised her arms and one finger, pointed accusingly at the sisterhood, appeared to search, then fixed on one of the novices. Haltingly, swaying with fear, the girl stood.

"Take her!" the abbess shouted. Two nuns seized the terrified girl. She screamed and struggled to fight free, but the nuns were stronger. Roughly they dragged her up the steps and threw her on the floor.

"You have sinned!" hissed the abbess, towering over her. "You have defiled the Holy Order. Your thoughts themselves are sins . . . sins of the flesh. You must be punished . . . terribly punished!"

Other Books by
DAVID LIPPINCOTT

E Pluribus Bang!
The Voice of Armageddon
Tremor Violet
Blood of October
Savage Ransom
Salt Mine

DARK PRISM

David Lippincott

A DELL BOOK

Published by
Dell Publishing Co., Inc.
1 Dag Hammarskjold Plaza
New York, New York 10017

This work was first published in Great Britain
by W.H. Allen as BLACK PRISM

Dell ® TM 681510, Dell Publishing Co., Inc.

ISBN: 0-440-11893-X

Printed in Canada

First U.S.A. printing—September 1981

DARK
PRISM

PROLOGUE

Mary-Jo Camero was mad. The Downeys had promised they'd be home by eleven at the latest, and now, dammit, it was almost one o'clock and they'd just walked in the door.

"I'm sorry, Mary-Jo," offered Mr. Downey. "Gee, I'm sorry. But we got hung up, baby."

Mary-Jo knew just how they'd gotten hung up: hanging around a bar with someone. Mr. Downey was the biggest landscape man in town and explained his constant drinking as a necessary burden of his business. Ha. Some burden. Both of them had had too much, and Mr. Downey, in particular, was having trouble putting his words together. She'd told them before they left she had a history test in the morning, and she thought they'd understood. Hiring out as a baby-sitter always leaves your time a little uncertain, but she'd explained that if a freshman at East Orange High flunks a history test, she's in big trouble with Mr. Plankton, who not only taught history but was assistant principal, too. Damn. They'd gone and gotten loaded anyway and come home late, and now she'd be exhausted for her history test and it wasn't fair, not for one minute, it wasn't.

"Look Mary-Jo," said Mr. Downey, sounding a little sulky. "I said we're sorry. We'll give you a little something extra, okay? And I'll drive you home myself, right now. Come on, let's go, Mary Jo. . . ."

"No, it's faster if I go through the lot. Really, lots faster." Speed wasn't the reason. Mary-Jo had been in the car with Mr. Downey once before when he was bombed, and he'd gotten pretty careless with his hands and made some suggestive cracks, and she was damned if she'd get in a car alone with him again.

"But it's so dark, Mary-Jo," Mrs. Downey protested.

"I've got my flashlight, Mrs. Downey. It's a cinch. My house is just across the lot and over the road." Mr. Downey started talking about driving her home again, but there was a funny look in his eyes, so Mary-Jo hurried into her jacket and was halfway out the door by the time she'd pocketed her money.

Mr. Downey stood in the doorway, his voice pleading. "C'mon, Mary-Jo. I'll drive you home, baby. It's not safe wandering around this time of night. . . ."

Safer than riding with you, you bastard, thought Mary-Jo, waving a hand and treating him to her best smile as she turned on her flashlight. Quickly she slipped through the fence and began crossing the big scrub-covered lot.

It was safe enough, but damn, it was scary. She couldn't see a light on in a house anywhere, and every now and then as she played the flashlight across the uneven ground, she'd see some small animal scurrying for cover. She thought she could hear bigger ones, too, further away, but she supposed that was her imagination. Once her flashlight *did* pick out the candescent eyes of a cat staring at her from behind a bush. It made her shiver. You had to be careful where you walked, too; someone had once started construction work in this lot, and when they'd abandoned it, they'd left a lot of deep holes behind that were half filled with water after last week's rain.

The thing that got her rose suddenly from one of these holes with a frightening, snarling rush, its arms spread wide apart like a bat's, swallowing her in an embrace of blackness and screaming something she couldn't understand. Mary-Jo cried out in a terrified panic, but realized that there was no one to hear. She had been knocked flat on the ground before she could scream a second time. Something was jammed into her mouth, and she felt her arms being pinned down. From the little she could see, Mary-Jo knew that the creature lying on top of her was a woman, dressed in a flowing black robe with a hood and wearing something around her neck that clanked each time she moved. She was incredibly strong and her voice was hoarse and angry, a deep, screaming rasp that Mary-Jo couldn't make out.

Desperately, Mary-Jo struggled, straining to tear herself loose, but the woman was kneeling on her and holding her hard. She felt her arms being twisted behind her and her wrists tied together, brutally tight. At the last moment the woman had flipped her over as easily as if she were a sack of new potatoes. The woman turned her over again and suddenly began ripping Mary-Jo's clothes off as if they were made of paper. Mary-Jo's belt and blue jeans only slowed the woman for a moment; they were sliced off her with some sort of long, sharp knife.

She was going to be raped. Mary-Jo had talked about it with her friends; she'd read about it, had nightmares about it; now it was going to happen. Dimly, Mary-Jo's mind began to clear a little. How could you be raped by a woman? Impossible. Or maybe the woman wasn't a real woman at all, but a lesbian. Mary-Jo didn't know anything about lesbians: it was a word girls at school used when they really wanted to insult you. But maybe it explained why the woman was so unbelievably strong and why her voice sounded so funny.

For a moment she was able, pushing her tongue hard against it, to clear the gag from her mouth. "Please, please," she cried out. "What do you want? Why are you doing this to me?" The woman snarled at her in her crazy talk and stuffed the gag back in. Pulling together every ounce of her strength, Mary-Jo squirmed and struggled to a half-sitting position; savagely the woman thrust her back onto the ground. Mary-Jo could feel the burrs and nettles cut into her buttocks, and began to whimper.

From a pocket of the long black robe, her attacker pulled a pair of shears. A second later Mary-Jo realized that the woman had begun cutting off all her hair. When this was finished, the woman produced a straight razor. Mary-Jo's eyes bulged, thrashing uselessly as she waited for her throat to be cut, but the woman simply shaved Mary-Jo's head clean, running one hand over the skull again and again, testing it for smoothness.

Muttering, the woman heaved herself down onto Mary-Jo's body so that she was sitting on her knees. A hand went inside the robe again and came out with a dagger, a strange, twisted object like the end of a corkscrew. Mary-Jo felt her blood freeze. The woman began mumbling incantations, raised the dagger, and brought it down—gently—with its point on Mary-Jo's lower stomach. Carefully, she pulled the dagger upward, cutting a thin line in Mary-Jo's flesh from her naval to just below her breasts. It didn't hurt as much as Mary-Jo would have expected, but almost immediately she could feel blood begin to ooze from the line. A moment later the woman repositioned the dagger and drew another line, this one through the top of the first and at right angles to it, holding Mary-Jo's newly full breasts out of the way to make sure the line came out straight. Even without being able to see it, Mary-Jo knew the two lines formed a crude X.

The woman climbed off Mary-Jo's legs and knelt

beside her; her rasping voice began its curious muttering again. At first Mary-Jo thought she was talking
to herself, but there was a pattern, a cadence, to the
words that reminded her of the prayers they said
at St. Ignatius on Irwin Street. Mary-Jo was praying
herself. She was terrified, she was shaved bald, she had
an X carved into her stomach, and this crazy woman
had her tied up and planned to do God alone knew
what else to her. It was the kind of unreal nightmare
a child might have, waking screaming in the night
and crying for its parents. Mary-Jo wondered what
her own mother and father were doing at this
moment. Probably asleep. As she grew older, they no
longer kept very close track of her—at her own insistence. Suddenly Mary-Jo wished this *was* all a nightmare, a child's dream, and that her family still *did*
keep very close track of her.

From her lowered position, the woman raised her
head and stared at Mary-Jo; Mary-Jo stared back, her
eyes pleading. The black-robed figure stiffened, muttering to herself. Without warning, she threw back
her head and began screaming, a scream that began
nowhere and went nowhere, without shape or form,
but one that tore at the night and assaulted the darkness, ripping open the sky like the cry of a soul in
agony. As suddenly as it had begun, the screaming
stopped, and the woman began fumbling for something in her loose, flowing sleeve.

From nowhere, the dagger tore into Mary-Jo's
stomach. The woman was screaming again, and as
Mary-Jo arched her back in agony, she was finally
able to spit out the gag and begin screaming herself.
The dagger was wrenched roughly out of her stomach
—it hurt, Sweet Jesus, but it hurt—and plunged into
her body again, further up and slightly to one side.
Mary-Jo could hear her own screams as she tried to
twist over onto her stomach, but almost immediately
she felt the woman heaving her right-side-up again.

Mary-Jo saw the dagger raised high into the air and coming down to sink into her one more time, but suddenly everything disappeared behind a bright-red haze and she could neither see nor feel anything.

Her last thought—a peculiar one—was to wonder if Mr. Plankton would think she'd missed the history test on purpose.

CHAPTER ONE

The whole feeling of the place, even the air he was breathing, seemed to change as they drove down Crown Street. Behind them, they left the sordid warrens of downtown New Haven—the slab modern vastness of Macy's, the equally large but rococo mass of O'Malley's, and the endless parade of discount jewelry shops, porno theaters, and unpromising restaurants. Coming off the Connecticut Thruway at Exit 47, there was no way to avoid going through this squalid commercial heart of New Haven, but as they drove further from the center of the city, even the memory of it quickly receded. As if in a fanfare of light, a sudden burst of golden fall sunshine exploded inside the car; they had reached the perimeters of Yale itself.

On either side the pavements swarmed with young people, children poised on the brink of maturity, wearing, like proud badges, the role of student. Alone or in groups, all of them carried the faraway look of people caught in the middle of some weighty, philosophical extrapolation. Chad knew the look was a pose and that their thoughts were more probably focused on either the morning's angry letter from home or the throbbing uncertainties of an all-pervasive libido.

Chad Lefferts had been an undergraduate here himself, back in the agonized, half-forgotten years of the protest sixties. Things had changed. There appeared to be shorter hair and fewer beards than he remembered, and he was surprised to note that even a few ties and sports coats were daring to show themselves— a uniform he hadn't encountered since Groton. Behind him, a raucous car horn sounded repeatedly; his deliberately slow progress along Crown Street was not appreciated by the owner of a fuchsia Caddy. A dark face could be dimly perceived through tinted glass. With a contemptuous stare, Chad waved the man past him. The stare was returned in kind.

"It must be a little like coming home," Lisa said suddenly, and laughed. "Only this time, as the *grand fromage.*"

"An assistant professor isn't all *that* great," Chad answered, although part of him not only accepted her statement, but believed it. Considering, he decided his move back to New Haven *was* very much like coming home. The jumble of irregular streets, the mullioned windows, the reckless mixture of what was basically Gothic interrupted by spasms of Georgian, tugged at something buried inside him, reminding him he had once been theirs and would now be again.

There were so many things at Yale—things large and small, things moving and funny, things serious and whimsical—that he wanted Lisa to see. She should be shown the scattering of buildings that were Gothic on one side, Georgian on the other, built this curious way in the interest of having like face like across the street. There was the hulking bell tower of the main library, rising like a hyperthyroid Chartres, but containing not so much as a dinner bell; it housed the stacks. In time, she should also be exposed to the inscription running around the courtyard of the Grad

School, selected by an architect who believed it to be an early fragment of Anglo-Saxon wisdom, only to have a red-faced University discover after its unveiling that it was an atavistic Old Norse translation of Rafael Sabatini and read "Born with the gift of laughter and a sense that the world was mad." Chad glanced at his watch; they were running late. Besides, he would have ample time to unravel his peculiarly affectionate minutiae of Yale for her later.

They passed High Street, pausing to peer down its gloomy beginnings. On impulse, Chad suddenly spun the wheel and turned down High. Above the street, just beyond where it joined Crown, stretched an elaborate stone bridge, tiered and medieval, connecting the old Art School on one side with Street Hall on the far side of High. Chad drove slowly, shivering a little in the sudden coolness the dense shade of the bridge produced.

If you kept your eyes to the left, you could imagine yourself on a street in some medieval city. The Gothic of the Art School and of Street Hall faced each other across the way; the medieval bridge cast long and dark shadows across the passerby. On the far side of the Art School, farther down High Street, was a forbidding building, completely made of dark-brown stone. Perhaps two or three stories high—it was impossible to be sure because the building was virtually windowless, with only two narrow slits covered with heavy metal grillwork facing out—it was set far back from the pavement. Two large plantings of thick ivy and four low pillars of the same dark-brown stone separated the building from the sidewalk. The building's doors were enormous—black metal of some kind —from which hung a padlock big enough to hold back a tank.

Lisa was puzzled. "What's *that* place? My God, it looks like a tomb."

"Bones. Skull and Bones."

Bones was a peculiarly Yale institution. And a remarkable one—so remarkable that the authors of *Frank Merriwell* and *Dink Stover at Yale* devoted chapter after chapter to it. Equally remarkable in real life is the record of success its members—fifteen chosen each year while still in their very early twenties and not even yet seniors—have chalked up over the years. They include one president of the United States, one vice-president of the United States (the present George H. W. Bush), several Supreme Court justices, countless secretaries of state, war, navy, defense, and treasury, senators and representatives beyond number, governors, ambassadors, generals and admirals, and every conceivable position in the Church except Pope. The man who wrote "There's a Long, Long Trail A-Winding" was a member; so is the author of *A Bell for Adano*. Beyond these, the rolls of Bones bulge with a distinguished platoon of essayists, actors, and writers.

The two men who began the Time-Life-Fortune empire—Henry Luce and Briton Hadden—did their original planning inside its thick, forbidding walls while still undergraduates; the roster of other, more prosaic economic giants is awesome. Who gets elected? The unique selection process used to spot these titans at an early age is as secret and mysterious as the building itself. To Chad, there had always been an almost frightening sense of power to both the building and the organization it housed under the benign corporate pseudonym of "The Russell Trust."

Directly beyond Bones, was a long narrow ally. At the end of this was another Gothic building, perhaps four stories high and of a height equal to the rough stone tower that rose inside Bones's high walls. It had originally been planned as a Bones "hotel" for visiting members by an over-avid Bones alumnus; somewhat rudely, the gift was rejected and given to the university, which for some years used it to house the School of Architecture. At present it is used for

University Administration. Still farther to the left
rose the hulk of Brandford College. To the right the
street grew brighter, where the low buildings and
open spaces of the Old Campus, now a series of dor-
mitories for freshmen, let in a sudden burst of light.

Past the first wing of Brandford, stood the great
stone pillar of Harkness Tower, a disembodied Gothic
finger aimed at the heavens, its only function to house
the baronial carillon that pealed its deafening changes
at noon and at six—or whenever someone could be
talked into playing it.

As they neared the corner of High and Elm, they
passed more of Brandford—cold, austere Gothic—and
then the beginnings of Saybrook College, its lead-
mullioned windows shaped like church arches. Chad
could not escape his initial feeling that High Street
was straight out of the fourteenth century; the
thought, for some reason, sent a shiver through him.

When they hit Elm Street, Chad swore; a large
arrow forced him to go in the opposite direction from
what he wanted.

"What the hell? Elm didn't used to be one-way.
It's crazy."

"New Haven grew, that's all."

"It's a main street, dammit." Muttering, Chad followed the arrow until he came to College Street, then
turned right on Crown again; they were back where
they started. This time, he passed High and turned
right on York. "Here we go," said Chad, glad to be
on a street where he was more sure of his bearings.

"Do we live on this one?" Lisa asked incredulously, staring at the line of enormous buildings on
either side of the street.

Chad laughed. "No, this is the high-rent district.
But I wanted at least to drive you past *Pierson*—and,
of course, Mory's."

"Mory's, *bien sûr*."

Something Lisa had said earlier was beginning to

bother Chad. He didn't want her to expect too much
in the way of living quarters. "You know, Liz, I
wouldn't expect too much of that house they're giving us. When they give him anything at all, an assistant professor probably only rates a hole in the
wall. But, hell, it's free— What did Koerkeritz call
it? Oh, yes. 'A competitive perk.' "

Chad Lefferts's description of how the house happened to be offered was precise. At Harvard he had
held only the rank of senior instructor when his
work in hypothetical physics the previous year produced suddenly academic star-billing. He was as surprised as everyone else when a series of extraordinarily
sophisticated mathematical formulae he fathered un-
expectedly expanded the "black hole" concept originally posited by Einstein. Before Chad's work, it
was assumed black holes could only be inferred within our own solar system; his formulae, along with
the sketchy material available from electronic tele-
scopes, was able to locate and prove that black holes
existed beyond the perimeters of our own solar system, far out in the vastness of galactic space. The
largest of these newly discovered black holes was one
near the constellation known as Omikron Blue, and
was so vast many physicists now hypothesized that
Chad's discovery might represent an entire collapsed
solar system, not just the more ordinary imploded
star.

To those whose lives were devoted to the intricacies
of physics, mathematics, and astronomy it was an exciting breakthrough. Chad's name was mentioned in
a *Time* cover story on the general subject of black
holes, even if only as a footnote.

The Ivy colleges are notoriously jealous of their
graduates who move on and succeed elsewhere, particularly if the elsewhere is another Ivy institution.
Shortly after the *Time* article—Yale apparently read
footnotes—Chad Lefferts began receiving feelers. He

was wooed like a particularly desirable heiress—secretly, but with passion. Dr. Roland Koerkeritz, Chairman of the Yale Physics Department, drove all the way up to Cambridge to lunch with him, although insisting it be at the Ritz-Carlton or Lockober's or anyplace well away from Cambridge. "It wouldn't do, Lefferts," he explained, "for me to be seen with you. What if you should turn me down?"

Gradually, Yale's offer took shape. An immediate appointment as Assistant Professor, unusual for a scholar of only twenty-eight; freedom to explore in any area of any field he might choose; unlimited help in the shape of bright young assistants; a minimum of nonproductive classroom lecturing. Awed by the attention, Chad Lefferts considered.

Harvard matched everything Yale had offered, throwing in minor perks such as special help for Lisa in her own studies—medieval art was with her a consuming passion. (In the interest of sharing hobbies, Chad had once dabbled in it himself, although for reasons he couldn't understand, the subject made him uncomfortable. He abandoned the field to his wife.)

Quickly Yale countered. A rent-free house—choice, they promised. From his own standpoint Chad wasn't sure the house was all that "choice"—in a burst of enthusiasm Koerkeritz had suddenly insisted they go and look at the place—but there was *no* question that it was very large and very different. Chad himself found it ugly, but Lisa, with her passion for medieval art, would love it. Even more, she would love the full-time help Koerkeritz promised came with the house.

Excitedly, Koerkeritz laid more inducements on the line. Lisa could study directly with Dr. Hamilton Pierce, acknowledged dean of the medieval art world, and curator of Yale's Museum of European Paintings. An arrangement with the Llewellyn School dictated that their six-year-old son's tuition be "forgotten."

Dr. Koerkeritz moved uncomfortably in his chair

at the Ritz-Carlton, his eyes enormous behind thick spectacles, widening even further as he dangled the perks in front of Chad. "These indirect—ah—inducements are—ah—the only way we can better our—ah—offer, you see. Otherwise, there would be—ah—mutiny among the other assistant professors in the department—ah—if not the university. We can split the atom in secret; our salaries are the property of every secretary from East Haven to Orange." Chad had accepted.

"There," Chad said suddenly, pointing to their left. They had just passed a long alley giving onto what had been Yale's last surviving fraternity—the Fence Club—and driven past the Baker Workshop Theater, one of the most sophisticated theatrical plants in the country, but housed inside a building with Elizabethan overtones, of red brick and white trim, that managed to make it look like summer stock in the Hamptons.

"I don't see anything," Lisa complained.

"The alley, down the alley." Chad pulled the car over to the left as far as he could and stopped. Between the theater and a blind wall of Davenport College stretched a wide flagstone walk. At the end, Lisa saw two Georgian pillars perhaps fifteen feet high, supporting an ornate wrought-iron arch and a pair of permanently open double gates. "Pearson," Chad announced proudly. "Or anyway, the entrance to it."

Lisa stared. "Well, I can't really tell much from a lot of flagstone and a couple of gates. But that's where you lived?"

"As an undergraduate, yes. Most of the kids were rushing around protesting things; I just wanted to study. It didn't make me very popular."

Lisa looked pensive. "No one ever asked me up to Yale, you know. Princeton, yes; Harvard, yes; Yale, never." She gave a forlorn little sigh. "I wasn't a Yale-type girl, I guess."

"You were probably too passionate for them. In the

sixties, Yalemen took themselves too seriously for stuff like that."

A soft hoot came from Lisa. "I knew some in New York who weren't *that* serious. . . ."

"A laughing lay. Very trendy."

"Shhh." Lisa giggled. "You'll give your son bad ideas."

Chad twisted around in his seat. Six-year-old Robin did not seem apt to have ideas of any kind at the moment; he was still fast asleep in the back seat, his head propped at an improbable angle against the car door.

Chad's stopping brought on a new rash of horn blowing from behind them; he moved on down York, having to pull to the far right when they crossed Elm Street and York suddenly became two-way. Mory's was pointed out to Lisa, who was surprised to discover it was little more than a white clapboard house with a neatly polished brass plate on its door. Chad sighed. There was so much he wanted to show Lisa. It *was* coming home, the return to a place he had loved, the safety of a time when the future seemed endless.

"Now," he announced, "now we go look at that house of ours. I have the keys."

"It's really ready to move into?"

"Skeleton furniture, they said, but habitable. Ours will be coming." A twinge of misgivings ran through him. He had never told Lisa he'd seen the house, at least its outside; he'd wanted to surprise her. The small shudder came again, but Chad wasn't sure whether it came from thinking about his own duplicity, or whether it had something to do with the house itself. His trip down to see Koerkeritz had been filled with so many strange things. . . .

At the end of York Street, they turned right at the Grove Street cemetery. From what Lisa could see of it, the cemetery was a very old one, dotted with a

scattering of brown sandstone mausoleums. Around
these, like fallen soldiers in some long-ago war, was
an army of ancient tilting headstones, their breast-
plates and helmets bearing the cherubs' faces and
small wings typical of early New England. Beneath
each of them presumably would be the deceased's
birth date and year of death, a necrophilic time-
table of arrivals and departures. The vastness of the
cemetery was depressing; Lisa sniffed. "Maybe we
should bring our skeleton furniture out here for a
visit."

Chad didn't groan; his expression amply registered
his opinion of her pun. From far away came the
sudden burst of the noontime bells at Harkness Tower.
The carillon played a complete set of twenty-four
changes, a cascade performed with the medieval preci-
sion required by the *Tintinnalogia*.

"What a glorious sound, Chad. Do they only do it
at noon?" For a moment, he appeared to ignore her,
then: "Oh, noon, six, several other times, I guess."
He drove on down the street in silence. For some
reason he couldn't understand, the sound of the
Harkness bells had sent a sudden shudder through
him, as if a finger in the Grove Street cemetery had
suddenly chosen that moment to point at him. He
shook off the feeling, set his jaw, and continued driving toward their new home. Such superstitions, he
told himself, are not what is expected of an assistant
professor in theoretical physics.

CHAPTER TWO

"My God."

"It can't be. Are you sure you've got the right address?"

Chad pulled the keys out of his jacket pocket and read the number on the paper disc attached to them. "120 DeWitte Street." He looked at the small brass numbers nailed to the post beside the entrance gate. "120 DeWitte. Either this is it, or there are two DeWitte Streets."

Leaning forward in her seat, Lisa studied the house. "Some hole in the wall, Chad. It's as big as that one of yours out by Omikron Blue."

"I didn't tell you, but Koerkeritz drove me by the place when I was down seeing him." Chad shivered; a lot had happened during that visit he hadn't told Lisa about. He couldn't.

Lisa was becoming so excited, she could feel tiny tremulations in the tips of her fingers. From the street, at least, the house Yale had provided them was spectacular. Built of large rough-hewn stones, it careened dizzily skyward, quite narrow, but easily four or five stories high. This unusual height, surrounded by so much empty space, made the house look as if it had expected other houses to be built close on either side of it; perhaps this explained its forlorn look, Stella Dallas waiting for company that would never arrive.

The roof was a sharply sloping Mansard, dark-shingled, and overhung the stonework in front like a pair of angry eyebrows. As with the house, the windows were narrow but tall, made of what appeared to be thousands of small, irregularly shaped panes stuck into mullioning; from the distance, some of the panes looked as if they might be of colored glass. On the front right corner of the house, a circular tower rose from the ground, ending just above the line of the roof. From what they could see, the top of the tower must be flat, for there was a low wall of castle-like battlements running around its upper edge.

To most people the house would have seemed ugly, even grotesque. In fact, no one could argue: it *was* ugly. But Lisa, with her love of the medieval, was enchanted by this whimsical Victorian attempt to look thirteenth century.

Chad was more reserved. "It's big, all right, but it's a little, well—weird, isn't it?"

"I love it!" Lisa's enthusiasm was infectious. By now she was already out of the car, had the back door open, and was leaning inside to shake Robin into some form of consciousness. "Sweetheart, sweetheart," she called to him gently, watching his eyes open sleepily and blink at her. "We're home. Our new home. Come look, darling, look."

Without much enthusiasm, a drugged Robin got slowly out of the car and looked at the house. Following in his father's footsteps, "weird" was his one-word appraisal.

Chad looked at the house again. Number 120 De-Witte was a singular house on an ordinary street; to either side were more conventional homes of more usual shapes, colonials, and federals of white clap-

boarding or weathered shingling. A sharp cry from
Robin made Chad turn.

"Look, look!" said the boy, tugging and jumping
up and down. He had spotted, through an opening in
the hedge to the left of the house, a venerable oak
whose lower branches supported a knotted rope attached to a small swing.

"Robby," began Lisa, but stopped, and couldn't
help laughing. Robin's order of priorities was sometimes bewildering.

"It's okay," ventured Chad. "There's some sort of
terrace there; I can see parts of it." Robin disappeared
like an urgent arrow; less precipitously, Chad and
Lisa approached the house.

The key was fitted into the lock and turned. Pushing hard, Chad finally opened the heavy wooden front
door that was decorated with black wrought-iron
strapping. From inside came a musty draft of air;
this was a house that had not been lived in for some
time.

"Wow," breathed Lisa, taking in with one sweep of
her eyes the huge, square entrance hall. To the right
was the door of what appeared to be the library,
although the "skeleton furniture" consisted of little
more than two armchairs and a sofa, hidden under
dustcovers. That the room was the library they knew
only because, from ceiling to floor, empty shelves
stared out with reproach, pleading to be filled. On
the left side of the hall, double doors opened into
the dining room. It was furnished with a massive re-
fectory table, once highly polished but hidden now
beneath a thick coat of dust that rose in a dark-gray
cloud when Lisa set her Air France tote bag on it.
Around the table sat high-backed oaken chairs with
deeply carved backs, seated sentinels waiting for a
meal that would never be served. Beyond the dining
room, presumably, was the pantry and kitchen, but

Lisa was far more interested in seeing the rest of the house than looking at a kitchen she was sure would be antique, inadequate, and impossible.

As she opened the double doors from the hall into the living room, Lisa's heart stopped and she screamed. Staring out at her was an old woman, her face as expressionless as a rock. Chad had been struggling up the path with two suitcases and stood now in the doorway behind Lisa, blinking.

"I'm sorry, Missus," said the old woman, holding out one hand to grip Lisa by the forearm. "I should have called out when I heard you come in, don't you know." For a moment she studied Lisa anxiously, as if afraid she might have done permanent damage. "I be Mrs. Lafferty," she continued, still staring at Lisa through blank, pale-blue eyes. "Mrs. Lafferty the housekeeper, don't you know. This place be a sight, I swear." Throwing her head back slightly, she gave an unpleasant laugh. "Not that you haven't noticed, I expect. But it's coming along. I gave most of the mornin' to cleaning up the kitchen alone, but it's coming, the whole house. The university shouldn't leave these old places sit month after month, collecting mice and dirt and dead flies. Setting them back to rights is a job, I can tell you."

Lisa held out her hand to Mrs. Lafferty, but the old woman either didn't see it, or didn't want to. "I'm Mrs. Lefferts, Mrs. Lafferty." It sounded like a comedy turn out of vaudeville. "And this is my husband, and my son is playing outside. Are you going to be with us permanently, or—?"

"Permanent, Missus. That is, if you want me." Something appeared to strike Mrs. Lafferty and she stared at Lisa again. "Oh, yesterday afternoon I got the upstairs clean and all, don't you know, and I make up the beds in the master bedroom. I understan' then, from the university, you have a child, but I didn't make up a bed for him. I didn't know which room you'd be wantin' to use for him."

"Fine, fine," Lisa said vaguely, looking for a way to escape from her vaudeville partner. Walking away, she began looking around the living room. It was enormous. Checking the left and right ends, it was apparent the room ran the full width of the house. On the far side from her, the long wall was completely made of open stone, ceiling to floor; the stonework looked exceedingly old, and she supposed some Victorian mason had given a year of his life to making it look that way. In the center of this wall, a fireplace, perhaps eight feet wide and six feet high, glowered at her darkly; a pair of giant wrought-iron andirons with twisted ironwork fronts rose from the hearth. To the left, in a surprisingly modern touch, French doors ran the full width of the room and looked out onto a flagstone terrace. Through thick layers of dirt and dust, she could see Robin. He sat happily in the swing, gently moving it back and forth, occasionally looking up into the branches of the great oak that dominated the terrace.

Walking quickly over to the French doors, Lisa opened one and called out to him so he would know where they were and how to get into the house. From behind her, came a sudden electric whine. Mrs. Lafferty had plugged in a curious-looking flat vacuum cleaner—the base section was about the size of a truck tire—and was using a thick hose to attack the dust that lay heavily over the room. Beyond her, Lisa could see she had pushed furniture, still under its dustcovers, to one end of the room to leave her and her strange machine room to work in.

Lisa stood back for a moment, again studying the stone wall with fascination. Her Victorian mason had done well indeed; if the wall hadn't been part of a Victorian house, Lisa could easily have estimated it to be several hundred years old. Her eyes pictured her collection of medieval paintings hanging from it; to this she could add the pair of repoussé trays of about the same period she'd picked up in Germany. Although from a completely different time, Chad's small collection of Roman antiquities—the legionnaire's breastplate from Pompeii, his cuirasses, and his weapons—would add a distinctiveness of their own. And in one of New Haven's antique shops, she supposed, she could pick up a pair of giant torchères. With a fire roaring in the mammoth fireplace, the effect would be tremendous.

"Jesus!" The voice exploded from behind her as Chad, a new set of suitcases in his hands, surveyed the room.

"Oh, Chad. Look at it. It's a mess now, but when we get our furniture and some curtains and hang our stuff over that fireplace, it'll look like a million dollars. Did you ever see a fireplace like that one? Look at it!"

"That's a fireplace? It looks more like a garage. God, we'll have to cut down a tree every time we want to toast a marshmallow." Lisa gave him an impatient look and started to answer, but Mrs. Lafferty, who had turned the vacuum off when Chad came in, now turned it back on and Lisa and Chad couldn't speak easily.

"What?" Chad bellowed at Lisa. "I can't hear you. *What?*"

"I said I just love it," she shouted, "and I'm so proud of you for rating a place like this, and I'm so proud you married me, because I love you, Chad, my God, but I—"

Lisa stopped, confounded. Mrs. Lafferty had turned off the machine to do something with the vacuum head, and Lisa's last few words bounced around the empty room like a soap opera in an echo chamber.

"What should I do with these bags?" Chad asked, ignoring her embarrassment.

"Upstairs. It's all ready," she answered, tight-lipped. Robin was called in and fed some orange juice from the Thermos she'd brought from Cambridge. She then aimed him at a bathroom Mrs. Lafferty announced was below the main staircase. In the distance, she could hear Chad clumping up the stairs. Lunch would soon be demanded.

The pantry and kitchen provided Lisa's second great shock of the house. Unlike the rest of 120 De-Witte, it was a gleaming modern fantasy, rows of built-in ovens and refrigerators sparkling in their satin chrome opulence. From one wall, two islands of polished Formica held the stainless-steel sinks, counter-sunk blenders and mixers, coffee grinders, ice-makers, and juice extractors. A third island held stove tops and warming ovens.

Lisa was staggered. She might not have been a Yale-type girl when she was younger, but she felt she could very easily enjoy becoming a Yale-type faculty wife if they lived like this. The only cloud on her present euphoria was the thought of their things arriving from Cambridge, of all the unpacking, sorting, and fixing that stared her in the face. It was a small thing. Robin's shrieks as he slid happily across the polished polyurethane tiles quickly chased the concern from her thoughts. She was going to like Yale.

"It's the damnedest thing," Lisa said, swallowing a morsel of sirloin while trying to be dainty about it. The steak Chad had brought home from the A&P was so colossal, maintaining her ladylikeness was not easy. They were having dinner in the pantry, which automatically robbed the meal of some of its pretensions. "I've been over the house from top to bottom now. And there's not a single window on the whole rear side of the house. "I can understand it in the living room—that fireplace wall—but *upstairs?* It

doesn't make sense. It's like whoever built it knew
there was something out there in back no one should
see."

"What's behind us?" Chad asked. He asked only because he knew she wanted him to; the mystery of
a house with one totally blind side was only one
more unsettling detail of a house that for some reason
troubled Chad, an ominous prescience that made him
distrust their new home for reasons he could neither
define nor explain. He could see that Lisa had noticed
his discomfort, but suspected she would not let him
change the subject. She rarely did. The series of
comments that followed from her proved his suspicions
valid.

"I didn't get much of a chance to explore—there
were a dreadful lot of things to put away, even without our stuff here yet. But from what I could see,
nothing. There's a wall—maybe twelve or fourteen
feet high—that comes out of either side of the house,
right where the fireplace wall is. It could even be
part of the same wall; I don't know."

"Maybe there's a house beyond that and they
didn't want people staring in the windows."

"No house. You can see some treetops, that's about
all."

Struggling with his steak knife, Chad sliced another piece of sirloin from the main body of meat on
the platter; with a shake of her head, Lisa indicated
she wanted none. "Well, tomorrow I'll investigate a
little," Chad offered, without any real enthusiasm.
"There's not much I can do on my project until my
computer tapes show up from Cambridge anyway.
Classes—well, they don't start until next week, and
Koerkeritz has given me a damned light schedule of
seminars to run. Our stuff should show up tomorrow,
and you'll want help, I guess."

They had their coffee in the largely empty living

room; it seemed silly, but Lisa had insisted. In the background, the dishwasher rumbled away reassuringly. Lisa suddenly raised her eyes to Chad's.

"Chad, darling, you had another one of those crazy nightmares last night. You screamed and yelled something terrible. Do you remember it?"

"Yes, of course I remember." Chad could feel a wall of hostility rising around himself. Lisa was on a subject he did not want to discuss under any circumstances; until this moment, he thought she'd probably slept through it.

"Well, they're getting worse and coming more often. They're beginning to worry me, sweetheart. You never had them before. Did you used to when you were a child or something?"

No, he hadn't had them as a child, dammit, Chad told himself, shifting uncomfortably in his chair. He hadn't had them until he came down from Boston to see Koerkeritz. He realized Lisa was staring at him, and tried to say something reassuring. "Oh, nothing to worry about. Nothing to worry about at all."

"That wasn't what I asked you."

Chad looked at Lisa with surprise. When she was worried, her temper could flare like a Roman candle. Usually, he could spot it coming; tonight it had caught him by surprise. The area she was exploring was so sensitive, his own temper began to rise; quickly he tried to slide out from underneath it before they became trapped in one of their donnybrooks. "Dammit, take my word for it," he lied. "It's just what I said it was: nothing."

Lisa stared at him. "Nothing, you say. I'm sorry, Chad. I don't believe you."

"If you don't want to take my word for it, that's your business."

"Damn right, it's my business." Lisa struggled and was able to get her temper under control. She would try reason. "Look, Chad. I'm not prying. But night-mares as violent as you've been having, you don't simply kiss off. I'm just worried and want to—"

"I'm not going to talk about it, Liz." He turned and looked at her sharply. "Drop it, dammit."

Lisa still had her temper in check, but the strain was showing. Her voice, even to her, had a pleading, whining sound to it. "Jesus, Chad. We can't even *talk* about some lousy little nightmares of yours? I've told you things about myself I didn't want to talk about, Chad, but I told you anyway. . . ."

"Those two other guys you used to shack up with in New York? You didn't have to tell me—*they* did." The second the words came out of his mouth, Chad could have kicked himself. The comment was gratuitous, snatched out of the air and jammed into an argument where it had no place. Worse, his remark had a self-righteous, prudish ring to it that didn't even sound as if he could have made it; it wasn't like him at all. He and Lisa had known each other too long and too well for that kind of crap.

Lisa stood staring at him, unbelieving. Then her precarious grip on self-control went out the window. "You're a prick, Chad. A bastard, and a stuck-up bastard at that. You kiss the right professorial asses, they toss you a pathetic little title, and pay you peanuts. They give you a house no one else would probably take. But *are* you impressed with yourself! Your name in *Time,* even if it's in a footnote so tiny only mice can read it. Well, I'm not just impressed, Chad, I'm *awed.*"

Chad opened his mouth to answer, but Lisa had left him with no one to speak to; by the time he started to say what he wanted to say, she had disappeared around the corner at the top of the stairs. A moment later he heard her check Robin and then close her own door with a sharp, final sound.

Swearing to himself, Chad went around the downstairs, automatically checking the doors to see if they were locked, enjoying the satisfying hard click of the metal when he found a lock he could turn. One door, in the corner of the library, at first mystified him; it was locked, but no key was inside. Irritated by its independence, he decided the door must lead to the ugly little tower that rose on the front right of the house.

Disgruntled, he slumped into a chair in the living room, listening to the fickle September wind blowing down the chimney into the cavernous fireplace. It is always a mournful sound, but this chimney was so large the sound became amplified, the desolate moaning of a giant in pain.

Elements of the bitter confrontation with Lisa traveled across his brain, angry blips on a radar screen. As it always did when the argument was over, what he'd said to Lisa seemed petty and unnecessarily cruel. To throw her long-ago shacking up with Charlie Whittier and Vic Lacey at her was accurate, but unfair. They were just two of the many painful confidences Lisa had entrusted him with.

Upstairs, at this moment, he knew Lisa was suffering the same sort of recrimination. What she had said about him was just as unfair. Chad could admit being married to an assistant professor was far from glamorous—Christ, he'd admitted it to her often enough—but it was something, just now, she shouldn't have used.

Inside both of them, he knew, was a deep-rooted need to make up. It would take until morning, when both he and Lisa would pretend the thing had never happened.

He hated these battles with Lisa. They were rare, but when they did take place, expertly crafted. At the heart of this one, he supposed, was Lisa's concern with those damned nightmares he'd been having more and more frequently. More than once he'd been on the verge of sitting down and explaining to her what he thought was happening to him these last few months. But he couldn't; he wasn't that sure himself, and anyway, the whole thing sounded too crazy.

Squirming in his chair, Chad stared morosely at the brooding shadows in the fireplace. He didn't know how Lisa had spotted his discomfort with the house; he had thought it was well hidden.

But an uncomfortable, uneasy sensation had struck him the moment he'd seen the place with Koerkeritz, a feeling the house was as mistrustful of him as he of it. The only place he really felt comfortable was the kitchen, gleaming with newness, with the kind of conventional layout you saw arrogantly displayed in *Architectural Digest* or *House & Garden*. Ordinarily, Chad would have shrugged it off or condescended to it.

His whole life seemed to be in a state of flux. This should have been a happy time for him; the new appointment here was more than he could have dared hope for a few months earlier. Yet the insidious fears of an uncertain tomorrow were beginning to intrude into the picture, little gray clouds against a sky of clear blue, crowding the happiness to one side.

Slowly, without any enthusiasm, he walked into his sanctuary, the kitchen, and mixed himself a strong drink. It had been that kind of day, it would be that kind of tomorrow.

CHAPTER THREE

The next day, at about seven in the morning, the furniture and their other things arrived from Cambridge. Chad's computer tapes were still stalled somewhere in Boston, and he was having trouble finding out when they would arrive.

Today he had planned to explore the ugly tower and see if he could get to its top. He had also planned to walk around the block and look at their house from the opposite side, to see if he could discover why its rear side had been so peremptorily blinded. He still had no real interest in unraveling the mystery of the house's blind side, but he knew Lisa was fascinated by it and figured a show of interest on his part would please her. After last night, he had a little stroking to do—and knew it.

But the confusion the moving men made carting furniture around, bumping into Mrs. Lafferty, and driving Lisa wild, canceled both projects. He had had time, however, to discover that at one time, at least, there *had* been windows on the rear side of the upper floors. If you tapped the wallboarding, you could hear where the sealed-off window frames were.

As he expected, Lisa this morning was pretending

to have forgotten last night entirely. Chad saw no reason to remind her.

Looking around the living room that evening, Chad was impressed. Lisa had been right in her prophecy that their small collection of medieval artworks would be shown to advantage against the old stonework of the fireplace wall. The largest of the paintings—on wood, attributed to a student of Giotto—and three smaller ones, twisted and angular paintings from the slightly later *Zackenstil* school, looked as if they and the great stones of the wall had been together since the birth of time. At some distance above these four hung the two large repoussé trays, their intricate scenes of medieval life rendered into three-dimensional beauty.

Standing back to get the full effect of the artwork, Lisa had decided that Chad's small collection—the Roman soldier's breastplate, his cuirasses and weapons —was too much to add to this grouping and had hung it, instead, from the stone walls on either side of the fireplace. To the Roman warrior's shortsword and knives, she added a few items from her own collection of medieval knives and daggers. Chad's one other piece from the Roman period—the marble head of a man, most of his nose lost in some disaster before Christ—was also put to one side, standing on its simple pedestal in one corner. It would take some small art-gallery spotlights, Lisa told Chad, to do the paintings, the armor fragments, and the statue full justice, but she assumed they would be easy enough to come by.

At about eleven, they fell into bed, exhausted. Any remaining bitterness dissolved in some quiet, restrained lovemaking, the product of physical exhaustion, yet peculiarly satisfying.

It was after this that Chad made his only reference to the night before. "Not bad," he whispered to Lisa as he crawled into his own bed. "Not bad, for a stuck-up prick."

He was answered by a gentle giggle.

He could see the feet, the legs above them wearing their gleaming metal cuirasses, marching endlessly in their perfect step. The sound was pervasive—a thundering, rhythmic chorus as thousands of boots struck the cobbles at the same instant.

Slowly, the many feet merged into but a single pair; the sound of marching was replaced by a hammering noise that echoed it, a harsh, hollow *clank-clank* of metal against metal. The feet were no longer clad in armor, but were bare; they no longer marched, but were held awkwardly together at the ankles; the rhythmic *clank-clank* was the sound of a heavy metal mallet driving a thick spike through the feet into a timber behind them. He could feel the agonizing pain of the first blow, and he screamed. . . .

Chad woke, still feeling the pain, and glanced, almost guiltily, across the room to see if his scream had waked Lisa. She appeared still deeply wrapped in sleep. Perhaps the scream had only been part of the dream itself, although he at first had been sure that it was his own cry of agony that had awakened him. Cursing himself, Chad drew the covers tighter around himself. . . .

The night was filled with whisperings, shouted orders in his own and harsh-sounding foreign tongues, and the chorus of metal against metal.

The man with the round leather shield had fixed an eye on him long before he had even drawn close. He studied the barbarian as he raced his huge horse bareback across the plain and could see every detail of his enemy as clearly as if he could reach out and touch him. The man was dressed in the skins of wild animals and wore a pointed helmet from which hung more skins, cut into strips like the festival ribbons that children hung from the statue of Jupiter the first day of Spring. From this distance, the barbarian's face looked full of hatred, and he wondered if the face had been painted, something many of the Visigoths did to frighten their enemies.

Ahead of him, the foot soldiers tightened their lines as the waves of horsemen neared them; they had formed the traditional hollow square of the legion, with him as commanding officer in its center. "Prepare to fight for your lives," he warned the foot soldiers. "These savages will destroy you if they can. Beware of them, I warn you, beware." He was not yet himself worried; the foot soldiers would stop this horseman who had selected him as his personal target long before he got inside. He was stunned when the Visigoth jumped his huge horse over the infantry's heads and thundered toward him with his lance.

The lance was avoided, but the horseman spun his mount and came racing back at him, yelling in his strange language. With all his strength, he slashed at the horseman's bare leg with his shortsword, and as the Visigoth leaned over to grab his leg in pain, plunged his shortsword into the man's side. He had expected him to fall over, but the man galloped his horse a few feet, pulled the shortsword out of his side, and whirled back toward him. This time the lance did not miss. He screamed, trying to escape, as the man pulled back the lance for another—and final—thrust. . . .

Chad again thrashed in his bed. It made no sense; none of these nightmares did. For about a month before he left Cambridge—just after visiting Koerkeritz in New Haven—they had preyed on him, sometimes in fragments, as tonight, sometimes as whole frightening stories. Always they were about this same Roman, struggling, fighting to survive, an officer in the emperor's army. This last fragment, like the one before it, had been short enough—and preposterous enough, Chad told himself—so it did not wake him entirely. What Chad dreaded were the long, extended nightmares that had been coming more and more frequently, filling him with terror, and robbing him of sleep entirely.

With a sigh, Chad rearranged the covers, plumped the pillow, and forced himself gently back into sleep.

"Hoc congri est. Cohors, dessum!"

The third cohort of the famous Tenth Legion, until a few years ago the favorite army unit of Julius Caesar, stamped their feet smartly as they came to a halt on the cohort leader's command. The bright sun of midday Rome gleamed on their polished armor; beyond them, as they stood stiffly at attention, you could see the bustling city going through its daily business; a group of small boys, in their short tunics, stood to one side, awed by the soldiers. Rome might be the Imperial City and always filled with the troops of the Emperor Tiberius, but these boys never overcame their fascination with the soldiers, staring at them, ogling them, and, later, imitating them in their own games.

The Quaedestor—cohort leader—watched as his lieutenant came over, dragging one small boy by the arm, laughing unpleasantly, and pointing out the wooden cross that had broken loose from its concealing cover and was now visible at the boy's neck. Tiberius had many good qualities; tolerance of the Christians was not one of them. Had he not just been himself proclaimed a God? Christianity was therefore treason.

Chad stared at them as the Quaedestor and his lieutenant began to talk, the boy still firmly held by one arm and beginning to cry. Chad could feel his mouth move as the Quaedestor—his name, Chad knew, was Marcus Flavius—spoke. Latin was a language he did not know, yet he could understand every word being said.

"He is a Christian, Flavius. The Imperial Decree says they are to be killed."

Chad could see Flavius wince and felt the shudder of revulsion pass through his own body. "You would not put a small boy to the sword, Caius, would you?" There was a pleading tone in his question.

"Watch." Caius suddenly moved his short Roman sword toward the boy's neck. The boy began struggling and screaming. Caius laughed, slipping the point of the sword under the thong by which the cross hung around the boy's neck, and with a sharp yank, cutting the thong. The wooden cross clattered to the cobblestones. Caius laughed again and stepped on it, shattering the piece. Once again, Chad saw Flavius wince, once again felt himself shudder. He knew he should be fighting this man Caius, protesting and arguing with him; instead, he was allowing all of this to happen without a word. Why was he such a coward?

Shaking the terrified boy, Caius said that while, yes, he'd like to kill the boy—the time to get rid of Christians was before they grew up and started telling their filthy lies—he had a better plan for this one. "He lives near here but won't tell me where. His mother and father must be Christians, who have filled this boy with their poison. Take him to each door with the sword at his neck. When we come to the house where his family lives, they will confess their Christianity to save the boy's life. They, the parents, we will kill as the Imperial Decree demands. Easy, Flavius, easy."

Marcus Flavius dismissed the cohort, and turned to Caius. "Do what you will, Caius. It is not my business." Chad, his lips moving, was as appalled to hear himself give this order as Flavius himself was. It was sentencing the boy and his family to death.

Flavius moved quickly down the street and slipped through the door of a small white-washed house. The plain people there seemed to know him. "Quick," said Flavius, and Chad could feel the man's body shudder in his urgency. "Quick, hide yourselves, hide yourselves; the soldiers are Christian hunting." He pulled the man of the house to the window. "That boy, there. They are going to take him from house to house until they find his family. Then, they will kill them all. Quick, please, Marius Suetavius, get some friends and cause a racket on the street. Stage a fight. Anything—a diversion."

The door to the house came crashing in just as the man, Marius, started to follow Marcus Flavius's orders. They poured into the room, soldiers of the Imperial Guard, their armor encrusted with heavy gold ornamentation, their faces wearing the arrogant expressions these men were seldom without.

"*We* shall provide your diversion, Flavius," shouted the captain of the Imperial Guard, his face furious. "We have been following you for days. Our spies said they heard you were a Christian, but until now, I didn't believe them. Seize him!" the captain commanded, and two of the guards grabbed Flavius by the arms, twisting them behind him as he tried to struggle free. Chad could feel his heart pounding with the fear of it. "The sword is too good for you. You will die the death of a common thief—crucifixion."

There was a struggle and Chad could feel himself screaming as the Imperial Guard dragged him toward the door. Crucifixion was the one death in the world he feared the most. His voice screamed "No, no, no!" over and over again, but the soldiers of the Imperial Guard paid no attention. Struggling and writhing,

Flavius was dragged out of the house into the street. Chad could feel his arms being pulled almost out of their sockets as he fought them, even though he knew it was useless. The soldiers of the guard were laughing now; crucifixion was a sadistic enough execution for any Roman to enjoy, even if the victim in this case was a fellow soldier, although not a member of the Imperial Guard. The captain was also pleased; Tiberius would be grateful that he had uncovered a distant relative of the Imperial family in the ranks of the Christians before the man had had a chance to do any real damage.

"There's a place down this street where we can do it," shouted the captain, and the soldiers of the guard cheered, eager to get on with it. Marcus Flavius renewed his struggling, and Chad felt the sweat run down his body, yelling in pain as his arms were pulled and yanked to keep him under control.

In the crowd by the roadside he saw more Christians he knew and repeated the same warning he had tried to give the others in the house. "Quick, hide yourselves, hide yourselves!" Strangely, Chad felt he was giving the warning as much to himself as he was to the uncomfortable knot of Christians he saw along the road.

"No, no, no," he cried again, as they drew closer to where the captain would perform the crucifixion. . . . "No, please, dear Christ, no!" Behind him he could hear the soldiers laughing again.

Marcus Flavius screamed in agony as one of the soldiers pierced his side with his short sword. "No! No!" Chad screamed, and heard himself try to begin the Lord's prayer. "No! No! No!" he pleaded once more. The soldiers laughed.

From an eternity away, he heard Lisa's voice. She was shaking him, slapping him to wake him up, holding him. He sat bolt upright, leaning far forward from the headboard, the sweat pouring from him, his whole body shaking.

"Chad, Chad! For God's sake, Chad. Wake up, sweetheart. What's happening, what's happening?"

For a moment or two he was unable to answer her at all. Then from somewhere inside himself he heard himself whisper the warning to Lisa: "Hide yourselves, hide yourselves!" He blinked at her, startled to hear the words. From *what*? Slowly, bits of the dream returned to his memory and he could fit the pieces together. Sort of, anyway. It had been one of those terrifying nightmares that had been invading his sleep for the last two months, but it was the first, he thought, in which he'd made so much noise Lisa had had to get out of her bed to calm him.

The dreams were sometimes just terrifying fragments, sometimes as this one, almost complete stories. Mostly, the worst of them seemed to center about this early Roman, Marcus Flavius. He could not have explained why, but he felt this nightmare, like all the others, contained some kind of warning, a warning from Flavius to him. During the dreams, Chad experienced the eerie sensation of both watching Flavius and *being* him at the same time; he could feel himself speak the soldier's words even as Flavius spoke them. It was insanity, and the insanity of the thing was why he had not been able to bring himself to explain the nightmares to Lisa; she had too much respect for the rational.

"Wow," he said, forcing a smile to calm Lisa. "One beaut of a nightmare. They're usually not *that* bad," he lied. Struggling, he tried to light a cigarette. He couldn't; his hands were shaking too much, and Lisa had to light it for him. "Christ, I'm sorry to wake you up like that, Lisa. . . ." He forced another smile.

She didn't smile back, but continued to stare at him, lines of worry etched on her face. "You were screaming in some crazy language, Chad. And your fingers, when you tried to light that cigarette—well, you're *still* shaking. Your pajama top's wringing wet. . . ." Lisa stopped, hearing something down the hall. "My God, Chad, it was loud enough to wake Robin."

She started for the door, but turned to him when she reached it. "These nightmares, Chad. They frighten me. What's happening? Can't you tell me? My God, what's *happening*?"

The crying from Robin's room grew more insistent. With a last agonized look at him, Lisa walked quickly out of the room and down the hall to comfort her son.

Still shaking, Chad leaned back against the pillow and watched the smoke rising unevenly from his cigarette. He couldn't have answered Lisa's question even if he'd wanted to, because he didn't *know* what was happening. He only knew the dream would be back tomorrow, and the next night, and the night after that, torturing him, robbing him of sleep, and eventually, he suspected, destroying him.

By the end of the next day, Lisa, with the eager but uncertain help of Mrs. Lafferty, had the house in a pretty finished state. Still to be done were things like carpeting and curtains, but they would require shopping for and then price-approval by the university, which would be paying for them. Slowly, Lisa was revising her opinion of Mrs. Lafferty. She talked too much and to little point, but she was a willing and resourceful worker; the vaudeville team of Lafferty & Lefferts had contrived to do wonders with the curious old house.

Lisa had been to the Yale Art School and talked to Dr. Hamilton Pierce, the curator of European paintings. Dr. Pierce had been well briefed by Yale on the terms of Chad's contract; Lisa was welcomed with open arms. For himself, Chad spent some time with Dr. Koerkeritz, and was shown his "laboratory," a single large room with all four walls lined with black-boards. The wealth of blackboards was provided to give him space to work out his mathematical extrap-olations; they were the hallmark of any theoretical physicist. Leading from this was a sort of study fur-nished with a leather couch and two deep leather chairs, along with built-in bookcases for Chad's refer-ence books.

Looking around, Chad had to admit that physicists' laboratories were unimpressive to the untrained eye. No bubbling retorts or complicated displays of elec-trical wizardry rose from mysterious, smoky lab tables. The only concession to space-age technology was a computer terminal and printout device waiting in one corner of the librarylike room, within easy reach-ing distance of the farthest leather armchair. He liked his quarters, though; they were far more lavish than anything he had been given at Harvard.

Late that afternoon, he decided Lisa should be given a reward for her back-breaking efforts as well as a respite from cooking amidst shambles. They would go to Mory's and have an early dinner—early enough so that Robin could come with them. Thinking it over, he knew he would rather not have to cope with Robin—Mrs. Lafferty had already offered to baby-sit anytime they needed it—but knew that Lisa would not consider leaving Robin in an unfamiliar house with what to him was still a relative stranger. He would have to be taken along or Lisa would refuse to go. Reluctantly, he called Lisa and suggested the early dinner, including Robin. She hooted with delight.

"You know," Chad suggested halfheartedly, "if we really wanted to, we could probably get Mrs. Lafferty to baby-sit Robin. . . ."

Lisa was adamant, raising the precise set of objec-tions Chad had predicted, and sounding quite irri-tated at him. "I just thought it would be more fun, Lisa, the two of us. It doesn't matter."

"Good, Chad. I couldn't bring myself to go without Robin."

"Okay, okay."

As he hung up the phone, Chad stared at the blank blackboards—actually they were green, a color chosen because it reduced glare and prevented eye strain—and pictured them full of his figures and formulae, written in his neat, yet dramatic hand.

Damn Robin, he heard himself say suddenly. Children were a delight; Robin was not only the issue of his loins, but the apple of his eye. But sometimes . . . sometimes . . . children could be a royal pain in the ass. His fickleness about the apple stunned him.

Laughing at himself, he walked out of his lab and climbed into his car.

Driving to Mory's, Chad, Lisa, and Robin virtually retraced the path of their search for DeWitte Street two days earlier. The Grove Street cemetery was as gloomy as ever, its brown headstones looking even more forlorn in the long rays of the late afternoon September sun. For some reason, the ordered rows of leaning headstones in that particular light reminded Chad of the teams in Yale Bowl leaning against each other in a football game. Robin, behind him, was chattering endlessly, pointing his finger and asking what this was or why that looked so funny.

From far ahead of them came the sudden sound of the six o'clock bell change at Harkness Tower, ringing a half hour later than usual, but as loud and persistent as always. Peal after peal cascaded forth. Chad was slowing down for an unexpected red light, cursing softly. "Oh, that wonderful sound, Chad. I could stay at Yale for the rest of my life just listening to it. . . ." Lisa looked at her husband. He sat transfixed, his face ashen, small beads of sweat gathering on his forehead. "Chad? Chad! Are you all right, Chad?"

Without answering, Chad's head suddenly snapped

far back; his body arched rigidly behind the wheel, rising off the seat and forming a stiffened arc; his lips drew back from his teeth as if he were having an epileptic seizure; saliva ran unchecked from one corner and a strange moaning cry rose from somewhere deep inside him.

The car continued forward with maddening slowness, yet completely out of control. "Chad!" screamed Lisa. "Chad, the car! What's happening, Chad? Are you all right?"

No answer came. Chad's body was twisted and yanked by a series of convulsions that racked his body, making his legs thrash and his spine go alternately rigid as steel and limp as putty.

Broadcast over a great distance from somewhere far below him, Lisa's voice sounded hollow and reverberating to Chad; he had been hurtled into space and was spinning, helpless, around the vast perimeter of the black hole beside Omikron Blue. His work had proved the existence and the reason for this new black hole; now, as if getting even with him for his prying into its secrets, he was being held its prisoner, trapped in a silent gyral void by a gravity field so awesome even light could not escape its crushing force. Distantly, he could hear hollow voices screaming at each other, fighting, apparently over him; his whole being felt as if it were being pulled apart, torn between two powerful forces.

Desperately, Lisa tried to reach the brake pedal; ahead was the busy intersection of Howe and Asthmum with Grove Street. She could see the cars racing past the corner at full speed directly in front of them. By pulling and hauling at the wheel, she'd managed to keep their slowly moving car sneaking past the others stopped on Grove Street for the red light, but if it ever reached the corner and went through the intersection into that onrushing traffic, a frightening accident was virtually guaranteed. Her yelling at Chad continued because Chad's legs kept leaping and thrashing as if they had lives of their own. Relentlessly, the car moved forward. At the last moment, within yards of the intersection, Lisa made the decision she probably should have made earlier; with a sharp yank, she turned the wheel hard over, sending the car off the road and onto the soft grassy stretch beyond its shoulder. They bumped and bounced, still moving ahead, until they ran head on into an unavoidable tree—not really terribly hard, but with enough shock so that Robin, who up until now had only been yelling excitedly, suddenly began screaming in fear. Trying to calm Robin—he'd thought the crazy ride was some sort of game until they bumped into the tree—Lisa found herself shaking like the thin leaves of the Old Campus elms.

"What's wrong with Daddy?" Robin asked suddenly.

"I don't know, sweetheart. He'll be fine in just a minute."

She was still reassuring him when she heard a cough and watched Chad slowly return to consciousness. Chad heard her voice; heard Robin's repeated, insistent questioning, as if from very far away. Slowly, the sounds grew closer and he saw Lisa looking down at him, brushing the hair back from his face, attempting a smile but having great trouble bringing it off. He could see the tears running down her face and the look of absolute terror in her eyes.

"Are you all right, Chad? What happened? Are you all right now?"

Chad came very close to answering her too fully. Shit. It had happened again. Just like in Cambridge, and once before that, in New Haven. But he couldn't tell her that. Any more than he could tell her about the nightmares. She would think she was married to a madman. Savagely he drove his fingernails into the palms of his hands to force himself all the way back into the world. Lisa was still staring at him, trying to understand what had happened, trying to think what she should do. She'd never seen anything like this happen to Chad before. To anyone. Lamely, he tried to reassure her: "I'm sorry. God, I'm sorry."

Pleading, Lisa put her hand on his arm and helped him straighten himself in his seat. "Chad, are you sure you're all right now? What *was* it? Please, darling, tell me. It was awful. Say something, please, Chad. Help me understand."

He couldn't tell her that this was not the first time he had had one of these seizures. He couldn't tell her of the doctor in Cambridge, who had tried to help but was refused by Chad. "Mr. Lefferts," the doctor had said. "I can't find out what the problem is unless we first put you in the hospital for some tests. The EEG I did tells me that it is not simple epilepsy. My suspicion is that the seizures may be psychogenic in nature. But first we have to rule out sugar-level disturbances, glandular irregularities, thymal difficulties, some forgotten spinal injury, perhaps, that has chosen this moment to make itself known. It would not be a long stay in the hospital, Mr. Lefferts—perhaps less than a week. But without it —well, I can't do the kind of tests we need for a definitive finding in my office, you see."

" 'Psychogenic,' you said. That's a polite way of suggesting the seizures are coming from my being slightly off the wall. Swell. Either I am epileptic, foaming at the mouth—like Hitler—or I'm a nut. Some choice."

"An epileptic like Julius Caesar would have been a better choice. And no, it doesn't mean you're nuts. The tests, Mr. Lefferts. The hospital—" The doctor had spread his hands, smiling with appreciation of both the problem and the difficulties of its solution.

"No." Chad's voice had been firm and final. He was due to leave for New Haven in less than a month, and he refused to appear with a medical history that smacked of a disturbed mind. "Isn't there something I can take—for the time being anyway—some pill, *something?*"

The doctor had sighed. Long before Chad answered, he had known what the response would be. He gave Chad a prescription for Dilantin, an anticonvulsant. Attached to it was a long list of cautions about the drug—things that should not be done while under the medication. It had seemed to Chad just about everything except sex was eliminated. They'd be back to prohibit that next, he figured.

Chad had taken the Dilantin religiously, but quickly abandoned it. The side effects—the drug made him feel extremely flaccid—were as unpleasant as they were mysterious and always, to him, unpredictable. He had returned to the drug when, a month before, he had come to New Haven to visit with Dr. Koerkeritz; he didn't want to have a seizure while talking to the head of his department. That night at his hotel, he'd had another seizure—as well as a return of the disturbing side effects—and had given up Dilantin once more.

None of this, he felt, could be told to Lisa; she would worry too much and would insist he do something about them. "It's nothing. Really," Chad told Lisa after a long pause. "I'll see a doctor if I have another one. It's probably nerves or something."

Lisa fixed him with a stare, indicating the tree standing in front of them with a sweep of her hand. "Nothing," she said bitterly. "If we'd gotten to that intersection, we could all have been killed. But it's 'nothing.' Has this ever happened to you before, Chad?"

"Damn it, no." The tone of defensiveness in his voice startled even Chad. As with any man hiding a secret, he was extremely sensitive to questions about it.

"Are you *sure* you're all right, Chad?"

"Christ, yes, I'm sure."

"Well, you certainly don't want to go on to Mory's. We'll go back and you can lie down on the couch while I fix us something to eat, if you feel up to food."

"The hell you will. We're going to Mory's and that's that."

Lisa started to say something but stopped. The defensiveness had not escaped her; this was no moment to begin arguing with him. "I'll drive if you like," she suggested.

"Stop treating me like a fucking baby, Lisa. I can drive."

Lisa closed her eyes as she heard the motor start and felt the rocking of the car as it slowly backed up to a place where they could get themselves on the road easily. She was worried sick, but knew better than to say more; the scab on the wound was still too sensitive. From the rear seat they heard a sudden giggle from Robin. "You were funny, Daddy. Jumping up and down like my rubber spider-toy."

No one else laughed.

CHAPTER FOUR

When Lisa woke the next morning, her eyes felt as heavy as the stonework of the living-room fireplace. Chad had had two more nightmares that night, each of them waking her violently and leaving her too worried to get much sleep. She knew Chad must feel even worse; the ceaseless glow of his cigarette as he thrashed in his bed still haunted her; after the second dream, he apparently gave up even trying to go back to sleep.

Somewhere around five, Lisa figured, she must have dozed off. Looking over at Chad's bed when she woke again, she was surprised to find it empty; the bedclothes looked as if someone had staged a wrestling match in them, one end of the top sheet trailing to the floor, the blankets knotted into an angry ball, and the lace blanket-cover pushed off the end of the bed and lying on the carpet. More surprising, when Lisa hurried downstairs to fix Chad's breakfast, she could not at first find him.

After a little searching and a good deal of calling his name, she finally found him sitting in a chair in the dimness of the living room, staring straight ahead into the empty fireplace. "Chad. Chad," she said softly. "Wouldn't you like some breakfast?"

For a long time, Chad Lefferts didn't answer. Slowly his eyes rose to hers and then returned to the fireplace. "Already had it."

The distant cast of his reply left Lisa bewildered. With a forced smile, though, she tried to make contact. "Sure you did. Coffee. And if you were feeling expansive, maybe toast," Lisa said, forcing a laugh. "Don't you want a *real* breakfast now? Eggs—or, I know what—I bought some frozen waffles. With maple syrup they're damned good. I tried them on Robin yesterday. Chad, don't you—?"

Without looking up, Chad answered dully. "I said I've already had breakfast."

The tone was so cold and distant, Lisa wasn't at all sure what to do next. Leave him alone? Let him work out the problem himself? For a man who a short time ago seemed so immersed in his work, so content with his small family, it seemed strange—even unfair—that he should suddenly be absorbed with strange, disturbing things like escalating nightmares and convulsive seizures. "Chad," Lisa said suddenly, a hint of desperation in her voice. "Chad, I don't know—what I mean is—all of a sudden—these nightmares—that seizure or whatever you had yesterday—maybe you should see someone to . . . well, you know what I mean."

"I've already had breakfast." Chad repeated it as if he hadn't heard anything Lisa had said. She went through the same logic again, this time a little more coherently and specifically.

For a moment Chad's eyes appeared to understand what she was saying and that she was standing there in front of him asking him to do something about himself. The eyes narrowed. "As for the rest of the crap you're muttering about, it's *my* business," Chad noted bitterly.

"The hell it is. Among other things, you're my husband, and Robin's father. I also happen to love you. If you have a problem, I want to help you get to the bottom of it, dammit. *And*, from a brutally frank, selfish viewpoint, this is the second night in a row you and your crazy dreams haven't let me get any sleep. You may not buy the rest of what I'm talking about—you can call it 'crap' if you want to—but Christ, Chad, the sleep—well, that *is* my business."

In a hostile manner unusual for Chad, he rose out of his chair, looked Lisa square in the eye, and unblinking, spoke softly in a measured tone that was deadly. "On that score, you're right. I'm moving into another room, Lisa. One of my own. So you can get all that damned precious sleep you want."

Lisa was stunned. In the years they had been married, the only nights they'd slept apart was when Chad was off somewhere at an academic conference or short trips like the one he'd made to New Haven a month ago to see Koerkeritz, or that one painful time Lisa was so sick with a virus they'd decided it was better for everybody if Chad moved into another room to avoid catching whatever it was. Someone after all, had to be on their feet to look after Robin. Now Chad was suddenly—unilaterally—announcing he was moving into a room of his own. Just like that. "God damn it, Chad" was the best Lisa could manage.

She turned quickly, her face crumbling. At the doorway she stopped. She had expected, somehow, that Chad would stop her, take her in his arms, and tell her everything was all right. Instead, apparently unaware she was still even there, Chad slumped his way out through the French doors onto the terrace. Lisa watched him settle himself into Robin's swing and start slowly rocking back and forth, like a baffled, lonely child. She turned again and went into the house. Suddenly Chad had become a stranger. The

wonderfully close relationship they'd always shared
was disappearing behind a screen of nightmares, convulsions, monosyllabic conversations, and separate
rooms. Lisa was close to crying; instead, she went upstairs and woke Robin. At least she was sure that
Robin loved her and needed her and could let her
know that he did.

That afternoon, Chad mounted a direct assault
against the nightmares; they might be disturbing Lisa,
they were shattering *him*. Each night, the fragments
seemed to grow increasingly violent; mostly, at the
moment, they centered about Rome in the early days
of Christianity, although there were other vague characters from other eras—dim, shadowy voices and
figures that Chad could never remember when he
woke up. The accent on Rome and early Christianity
baffled Chad; he had taken the mandatory four years
of Latin at Groton, but had forgotten almost every
word of it. Always there was the sense of warning.
The most terrifying of the nightmares centered on
someone's being crucified.

Now, if his plan worked, he would exorcize the
nightmares and the Romans and his inevitable alter
ego, Marcus Flavius. Earlier, he had gone to the hard-
ware store and picked up a strange assortment of
electrical equipment. His knowledge of physics made
designing the device relatively easy. It was designed to
prevent REM sleep—a state of profound somnolence
without which dreaming was impossible. Usually, he
had read, it occurred after about an hour of light
sleep: the state was called REM—for Rapid Eye Movement—sleep, because anyone's eyes can track what the
sleeping person sees in his dreams. Without REM,
there could be no dreaming; simple logic told him if
you were prevented from achieving the REM state,
you could not achieve a dreaming state either.

His device was simple. Attached over his eyes from

beneath a thick canvas band was a series of delicate sensors that would detect when his eyeballs began to move. The sensors in turn triggered another device, which rang a loud alarm and would wake him up. Granted, his sleep would have to be taken in short bursts of about an hour each, but anything was better than plunging back into the weird world that occupied his brain when he dreamed.

Lying down on the bed, Chad tried out his invention. He felt both self-conscious and just a little silly, imagining how he must look with the wide white canvas band suspending the sensors strapped around his head and wires running to the second device with its electric bell. If he weren't being so rattled by the nightmares—not to mention the seizures, which at present seemed a totally separate phenomenon—he would never in a million years have allowed himself to wear such a weird-looking gadget. Chad tested the machine, with his eyeballs unmoving. Nothing happened. Slowly, he began darting them from one side to the other in simulation of Rapid Eye Movement.

The bell startled him, even though he had expected it. Reaching over, he had to stretch himself so far out from the bed to shut off the bell, he almost fell out of it. This was deliberate—to prevent him from stopping the bell so easily that he could drift back into an REM state. Chad sat up and removed the band and its sensors; his invention worked. Softly, he put all the machinery into the closet and hid it under some clothes; Lisa would be even more confused if she set eyes upon it.

The thought of the sudden distance that had sprung up between Lisa and himself shocked him. Ordinarily he would have shown her this damned insane machine, and Lisa would have laughed, and he would have laughed, and they still would be laughing together about it later over martinis. But nothing was ordinary anymore. He was hiding too much. Reflecting, Chad was jolted, realizing how much his withdrawn performance this morning about breakfast must have hurt her. He would have to try. The effort would be extremely tough when he felt as defensive as he knew he was at the moment. But the nightmares couldn't be explained to her; neither did he dare tell her that the seizure on the way to Mory's was not his first. To two people so used to being completely close and totally frank, there was something tragic in their present situation. With a shudder, he went into the bathroom and combed his hair—the damned canvas band had made a mess of it; he looked as insane as he was beginning to feel—and braced himself to make the effort with Lisa and Robin to return things, on the surface at least, to some fleeting shadow of normality.

Later that afternoon, Chad began his effort toward normalization with Lisa and Robin. To Lisa, there was something almost as frightening about his trying as there was about his earlier aloofness; the effort was too easily apparent. Robin, on the other hand, accepted Chad back eagerly. As it had his mother, the house—with its mysterious tower, its stone vastness inside, and its overtones of a fairy-tale castle—fascinated him.

"Daddy," Robin said suddenly. "Daddy, you promised you'd take me up in the tower. Please, Daddy? *Please.*"

Something inside held Chad back. He could remember the promise—it was made the day after they arrived—but in Chad's mind, some vague uneasiness had attached itself to the tower. Robin kept begging, and Chad kept putting him off, trying to get him interested in something else, but Robin had his mother's single-mindedness and wouldn't budge. His promise to himself to try to be more giving to Lisa and Robin returned to him; he was going to have to go through with it. "Lisa," he called. "Do you have the key to the tower?"

"Only if you'll set Rapunzel free." Lisa had recovered from her initial shock and, like Chad, was trying to reestablish a normal tenor to things. "She's bobbed her hair, you know, so she's in a hell of a fix."

From the top of the stairs, Lisa tossed down the heavy key to Chad, who let it slip through his fingers and crash onto the slate floor. "Great catch." He smiled at Lisa. "I'm taking Robin up to the top of the tower. I promised him I would when he first got a look at it."

A look of concern crossed Lisa's face. "Chad, please be careful with him up there. It's so far up. Don't even let him go near the edge by himself. Hang on to him when he looks over—hold him by the belt or something."

Chad felt a flash of irritation, but struggled and quickly doused it. "I'll hang on to him like I was a dragon."

Lisa laughed. "Okay. I've got to pull on something and go to the A&P." She disappeared from the balustrade to put on more presentable clothes, listening with new hope to the chatter flowing between Robin and his father. Suddenly the events of the past few days seemed unreal; maybe she was stupid to have gotten so worried . . . maybe Chad's behavior was just a passing thing. Maybe the nightmares were gone for good now and Chad would move back into their room . . . maybe. . . . But the memory of his seizure on the way to Mory's dampened her rising spirits. Maybe she was hoping too much.

As they walked through the living room, Robin raced small circles around Chad's feet, his arms outstretched, alternating airplane *zooms* with cries of "I'm Superman!" With difficulty—the lock was a hard one, seldom used and in need of oil—Chad put the heavy key into the thick, squat door in one corner of the living room. When he pushed the door open, it gave a gratifying squeaky groan that made Robin clap his hands with delight. Quickly Chad switched on his flashlight and looked around. The tower, on the inside, was perhaps ten feet in diameter, built of the same sort of stone that made up the living room's fireplace wall. To one side, a set of circular stone steps ran around the tower's circumference and rose skyward, disappearing into a ceiling of wooden planking far above. Presumably there was a chamber below the tower roof; the stairs would either continue above it to the platform of the tower itself, or there would be a trapdoor giving access to its flat roof.

The place smelled dank. Unlike good gothic novels, no moisture dripped from the rough stone walls, but there was a good deal of moss growing on the stones and Chad suspected that in winter some water, at least, must collect on them. Taking Robin by the hand, they began the long, steep climb up the steps. Increasingly Robin grew more subdued; the wraithlike atmosphere of the place was getting to him. Once Robin stopped climbing and began to say something, but changed his mind. Correctly, Chad suspected that the eerie light of the flashlight, the hollow sound of their feet on the steps, and the haunted atmosphere of the whole place was making Robin reconsider his enthusiasm. "You want to go back, Robin?"

For a second Robin stared at him, his head tilted back in an agony of decision. Then he shook it vigorously. "Of course not, Daddy. This is fun." Chad could not miss the lack of conviction in Robin's answer.

Carefully, slowly, they made their way upward; as the walls of the tower grew thinner, the circumference grew bigger, but the steps narrower. It was a little harrowing, even for Chad.

When they reached the top of the long flight of steps, things grew somewhat less fearsome. They were in a low room—so low that Chad had to bend his head. Its floor was the plank ceiling he'd seen from below. Above them was another ceiling of wooden planking with a trapdoor in its center. Reaching up, Chad pushed at the trapdoor and finally was able to open it. Sunlight poured into the chamber in a narrow shaft. By standing on his tiptoes, Chad was able to raise his eyes above the level of the floor above. As he had guessed, the tower roof was flat, surrounded by the row of battlements—perhaps one or two feet high—that you could see from the front lawn. It was safe enough, as long as Robin didn't go wandering off by himself. He turned to him.

"Look, Robin. I'm going to push you up through that opening over our heads. The hole up there where I just opened the trapdoor. It's safe. Very safe. But I want you to promise me you won't move an inch until I heave myself up after you. Understand? Not an inch."

"Yes, Daddy. I promise."

"And stay on all fours; don't stand up. Understand that, too?"

"Yes, Daddy." Robin's head nodded vigorously each time he answered Chad's questions.

"Okay, Robin. Now, what are you going to do when you get up there?"

"Well, I'm not supposed to move"—a small frown passed over his face as he struggled to get the words right—"move an inch. Right? And I'm supposed to stay on all fours. Like a horse. Until you come up through the hole, too."

"You got it. Okay, now. Here you go. Remember what I said, Robin. Not an inch and stay on all fours." Gently, Chad lifted Robin up through the trapdoor and saw him kneeling safely on all fours. "Everything okay?" Chad asked.

But some sound had made Robin's head turn away from the open trapdoor and he didn't answer. Chad heard the sound, too. And then he started to spin, his mind reeling, unable to focus, out of his control.

As she came out through the front door to climb into her car, Lisa felt better than she had in days. Chad seemed to be on the way back to his normal self. He had been more than pleasant—and a little off-color —with her this afternoon. For him, normal. That part of their lives felt as if it were going to be all right again; he had been evasive about moving back into their room, but Lisa didn't press the point. Inside her, some instinct spoke and warned her that Chad might not be as close to normal as he was acting.

When she opened the car door, Lisa suddenly remembered she had left her grocery list on the kitchen table, and swore at herself, torn between going back to get it or counting on her memory to supply the items when she got to the store.

From behind her she could hear a sudden voice beneath the peal of the Harkness bells. "Hi, Mummy," Robin called. "Look. Just like Superman." Her heart stopped. Robin had his arms outstretched and was balancing on the low battlements of the tower far above her, stepping uncertainly along the wall like a child circus aerialist in his first performance. Through Lisa's mind, a host of possibilities and decisions raced wildly, some of them rational, some of them not. To call out to Robin, to show any great sign of concern, could frighten him and cause him to plunge screaming to the ground. Dear God, it must be forty feet. To let Robin continue his skywalk was just as dangerous; eventually he would slip, lose his balance, and fall anyway. She tried a middle-of-the-road approach. "Oh, that's wonderful, Robin. But I'm not sure I'd do any more of it; it must be very tiring—even for Superman. Why don't you step off and sit down or something. You know, take a little rest."

"I'm not tired, Mummy. It's fun."

That approach wouldn't work. Desperately, Lisa
tried another, one that also had buried in it a question
that was burning in her brain. "What does Daddy
think about it, Robin? Where *is* Daddy?"

"Oh, he got all funny again—like in the car—and
didn't come up. He's on the floor downstairs. Funny
Daddy."

"I tell you what, Robin," Lisa said, struggling to
keep the panic she felt from showing in her voice.
"I'll come up as quickly as I can. Why don't you get
off the wall and sit down on the roof. I'll be there to
watch you in a minute."

She glanced up and could see Robin had no intention of stopping his tightrope walk. She walked calmly toward the house—she wanted to wave to him to
give him more confidence but was afraid that in waving back Robin might lose his balance—until she was
where Robin couldn't see her. Then she raced for
the front door, tore it open, and raced toward the
stairs of the tower. She could feel her breath coming in painful gasps, and her damned shoes kept making progress difficult as she climbed. Violently, she
kicked the shoes off, hearing them clatter far below
her as she again started the agonizing climb at top
speed. Getting up the rough stone steps was easier
without her shoes, but every few seconds she would
bang one of her toes painfully into the stonework.
By the time she finally reached the wood-plank land-
ing toward the top of the tower, both her feet were
bloody, her breath was coming in gasps, and tears
were streaming down her face from pain, frustration,
and fear.

Below the trapdoor, Chad lay, still thrashing in the
last stages of another convulsion. She would get to
him later; her immediate concern was poor little
Robin, balancing on the edge of fatal disaster one
flight up. As Chad had done, Lisa poked her head
through the trap doorway. She could see Robin, still

on the parapet, swinging now from an upright metal
pipe that rose out of the plank floor beside the battlements. As Lisa watched, Robin let go of the pipe and
again began his precarious balancing act, singing softly while putting one foot ahead of the other to move
along the parapet. To call out his name, even softly,
could bring disaster; he had no way of knowing
she was there. The only safe method was to grab him
in such a way that he couldn't be startled and fall;
Lisa was reasonably sure a fall from such a height
would spell death. She waited until his course around
the parapet brought him close to the trapdoor; the
heaving form of Chad became her footrest as she
lunged upward through the trapdoor. Her leg caught
on a nail and Lisa screamed inadvertently from pain
and surprise.

On the parapet, Robin turned to find the source of
the scream, his mouth open in astonishment. Suddenly, his arms began swinging in tight circles as he
tried to regain his balance, lost by the suddenness
of his turn. For a moment he teetered on the edge;
Lisa made a second desperate lunge and brought
him crashing to the wooden floor of the tower roof.

For a second, neither of them moved. Robin's eyes
stared at his mother as if unsure whether she had
saved his life or had failed in some mysterious effort
to destroy him; his face suddenly twisted into a rub-
bery mask and he began crying, a wail of hurt and
confusion in a strange world where his father had
abandoned him and was thrashing on the floor while
his mother suddenly appeared out of nowhere and
tackled him like an enemy.

On the floor below, Chad was just beginning to return to the world. From a very great distance he heard
Robin's crying and Lisa's efforts to calm and reassure
her son. His head hurt where he had crashed to the
floor at the beginning of the seizure. Once again he
had been sent in a motion that felt like he was spin-

ning around the circumference of the vast black hole
near Omikron Blue; once again he had heard the distant voices fighting with each other and felt himself
torn in two by their struggle for his being.

Half sitting, he watched as Lisa lowered Robin carefully through the trapdoor, following herself a moment later. Her look was furious. "Chad, do you know
what almost happened?"

Numbly Chad nodded his head. He could imagine.
"I'm sorry, my God, Lisa, I'm sorry. Another one of
those damned things . . ."

Lisa was wiping the blood away from the cut in
his forehead Chad's fall had produced. "He was balancing on the wall. Like a tightrope walker. If he'd
been killed, dammit, it would have been your fault."

Chad glowered at Robin, who had come over with
Lisa and was staring at him. "Did you?" Chad demanded. "Did you do what Mummy says?"

"I got bored, Daddy. You didn't come up like you
promised. And the kneeling—it made my knees hurt.
I was safe; I was all right, Daddy."

The strain and anger of the last week boiled up inside Chad. He wasn't even aware of it when he did it.
But with the flat of his hand he slapped Robin's face
so hard that the child was knocked over sideways onto
the floor, screaming and holding out his arms to his
mother.

Gathering up Robin, Lisa looked at Chad, her face
dark with pain and confusion. "Chad, I don't know
what to do. But this is it. I feel sorry about whatever
is happening to you, but when you come damned near
killing your own son, it's time to face some harsh
realities. We've discussed it before and you've refused.
What I'm telling you is that either you get professional help—see someone, a doctor, a shrink, an Indian
Guru, if you want—but go and get some help, or I'm
taking Robin and leaving you. I love you. But something's going on inside you I don't understand. And

when that something begins to affect my son, I draw the line. I'm sorry." She took Robin by the hand and turned toward the stairs. "Come on, sweetheart. Carefully, now. Everything's going to be all right."

Chad watched them disappear down the long, winding stone steps. He couldn't believe what Lisa had said, and yet, he supposed she was right. He didn't know what was happening to him, and now that it had thrust Robin center stage, he owed it to his son to find out. But he couldn't. It was impossible. He wasn't even surprised when he found himself crying, his head in his hands, sitting alone in that weird dim room at the top of an insanely designed tower.

CHAPTER FIVE

Sulking, Chad Lefferts sat in the living room, staring first into the dark of the fireplace, and then through the French windows onto the terrace as the last of the day's light changed unnoticed into darkness. Upstairs, Lisa was putting Robin to bed. She had fed him early and was sitting on the edge of the bed reading him a story, making sure he was thoroughly calmed down after his doubly traumatic experience of the late afternoon: being thrown to the rooftop by Lisa, and the sudden slap by Chad. Earlier, Chad had tried to make up with him, but while Robin might say it didn't matter and admit that, yes, a new derrick truck to add to his collection of Corgi toys would be nice, really terrific, there was a look in his eyes that made Chad realize it was going to be some time before he fully trusted his father again.

"He's already half asleep," Lisa announced, coming into the room. There was a grimness to her voice that let Chad know she still had plenty to say. "This afternoon is going to take a while for him to get over. Provided you don't manage to kill him first. Which brings us back to *you*, Chad."

Miserably, Chad twisted in his chair. "Lisa, I'm

sorry. God damn, but I'm sorry. I didn't mean to have one of those fits up there—it just happened."

"I didn't say you meant it to happen. But it did. And what I said up in that crazy tower still goes: either you start finding out what the hell is going on with you, or I take Robin and move out."

"Shit, that's the only thing I *can't* do, Lisa."

Lisa looked startled. "What do you mean '*can't*'?"

"Look. The only decent doctors in this stupid town are connected with Yale–New Haven. Yale–New Haven is the medical school's teaching college. Most of the doctors there are connected to the university. A lot of them are professors in the school of medicine on the side. Can you imagine me walking in with a story like mine and telling it to another member of the faculty? Sure, they're not *supposed* to talk about their patients, but because it's a teaching college, they do. And with me the new boy on the faculty, Christ, they'll have a field day with the story. 'This new hotshot assistant professor—what's his name? Oh, yes, Lefferts—well, anyway, lemme tell you, this Lefferts is one big flake. Jesus, *is* he!' " That's what they'll say. In a couple of days it'll be all over the campus. Koerkeritz said that people were going to be jealous of me anyway. The rank at my age, the special arrangements, all that crap. I'll be crucified."

Lisa's voice never wavered. "I'm sorry, Chad. But the ultimatum sticks. There're so many things suddenly gone haywire with you, I don't even know where to begin. The nightmares—bad enough so you have to move into a separate room. Some crazy gadget you build with wires sticking out all over the place. What's the damned thing supposed to do? Give you an orgasm without having to bother with me? And then there're the seizures—"

That was as far as she got. Chad was on his feet, his face twisted with fury. "What the fuck were you doing nosing around in my closet, dammit? Shit, Lisa, you've become a snooping old bag, going through my stuff to see if I have any dirty pictures. You've got one hell of—"

"You wouldn't know what to make of a dirty picture, Chad. The people in them are too real for you to understand. All you do understand is the formulas and numbers and hypotheses you have tattooed on your groin instead of a prick. Big deal."

"You goddamn whore—" Chad began the statement to an appreciative audience of no one. Lisa had already spun after her last snipe and run up the stairs; there was some question whether she had even heard Chad's final explosion. He suddenly hoped she hadn't. By now, he was accustomed to the thrust and parry of their quarrels; both of them, he suspected, in an odd, perverse way, enjoyed them. But today's encounter was different.

For one thing, there was no question but that Lisa was right. Chad had difficulty explaining to himself how a man as immersed in the scientific approach as he, could blind himself to his need for some sort of professional diagnosis and treatment. His rationale about the medical community at Yale–New Haven's talking to other faculty members was a sham; it was correct, but only as far as it went. If that had been the real sticking point, there were other doctors in New Haven not affiliated with the medical school's teaching staff. Or he could put himself into some sort of special category and make a Yale-affiliated doctor/professor solemnly promise him secrecy. Inside, he knew the real reason he was avoiding help was that he was afraid of it. Particularly if it was going to lap over into the area of psychotherapy. Chad wasn't exactly antipsychiatrist, but close to it, and always had been. It smacked too much of the medicine man with his rattles and beads and whoops. Yet even Lisa was

now willing to suggest it might be where the solution
lay—and, up until now, she had always been as anti-
shrink as he.

The whole complex of events left him bewildered.
The nightmares. Could they be medically caused or
was something like that bound to have psychological
roots? Why were they increasing? How was it they
could affect him so profoundly he would go to the
lengths of building that crazy Rube Goldberg machine to avoid having them? He had given loss of
sleep both as the reason for moving into a room of
his own and for constructing the gadget; exhaustion
was only part of the problem. Far more important
was the effect deep inside him this escalating series of
dreams was having. Chad kicked the chair in front of
him in frustration.

The seizures. Lisa was right about them, too. No,
it wouldn't be a matter of endangering Robin again—
he would plan things so Robin wasn't ever in a position where one of his seizures could affect him. But
there were other people to consider. Suppose he had
one while driving his car someplace, and instead of
merely bumping gently into a tree, as he had last time,
ran headlong into an oncoming car, killing the people inside? Or a bus. Or through a school crossing
teeming with children not much older than Robin.

Chad shuddered. The memory of the spinning feeling shot through his mind: a terrifying journey to a
frightening yet somehow familiar place, one made
unwillingly, thrust upon him by angry, powerful
forces determined to tear him apart. Another shudder
ran through Chad. He could not talk to a doctor
about either the nightmares or the seizures any more
than he could to Lisa; he would be considered mad.

From nowhere Lisa's ultimatum returned to haunt
him. It was difficult for Chad to imagine her really
taking Robin and moving out, yet, like himself, she
was afraid of what might happen next. Whether he

would injure Robin or her or even himself by avoiding the treatment he himself could admit he had to have. But something inside Chad—a determined pair of hands clutching him desperately, holding him in an iron grip, refusing to let him do what he knew must be done—held him back. He could not go. At almost the same moment as he made that decision, Chad began to waver again. It wasn't fair to Robin. It wasn't fair to Lisa. It wasn't, he supposed, even fair to himself.

Disgusted, Chad fled to his refuge, the kitchen. He mixed himself a strong drink and put together a leathery sandwich from the refrigerator. Slowly he went upstairs to his bedroom to face what he knew would be a long night of agonizing. Chad already knew what his decision would be, what it *had* to be.

"Yesterday, I almost killed my eight-year-old son. I *think* it was accidental." Chad's answer had come from somewhere deep inside him, surprising him almost as much as it did Dr. Oeschlee.

At first Dr. Oeschlee's only response was a curious look, then: "I'm not a psychiatrist, you know, Mr. Lefferts."

"I don't want—or need—a psychiatrist," Chad snapped. His answer had been too fast and too vigorous, and Chad knew it. He tried to temper its tone. "That is, maybe everybody needs one, I don't know. But what I'm trying to say is that my problem is a purely medical one, not psychiatric."

"Tell me about it. The complaint, I mean."

Haltingly, Chad told him of the seizures—the first one while still in Cambridge, the two recent episodes here in New Haven—and described how Lisa and others had described his behavior during the episodes. Edited out was his feeling of spinning in the black hole near Omikron Blue, as well as any mention of the nightmares. He had come intending to include them, but Dr. Oeschlee's remark about not being a psychiatrist had made Chad too aware of where the doctor's diagnosis would come out if he included either of those two pieces of information. The bastard already had him pegged as a flake as it was.

Chad was here unwillingly, yet the decision to come had been his own. The one thing in the world he didn't want was to hurt either Lisa or Robin. Seeing a doctor, then, was his only alternative. On top of this, while the device he designed had worked efficiently the first night—the onset of REM sleep had been effectively halted by the insistent ringing of the bell—by the second night, the device was still working but no longer waking him. He stepped up the loudness of the bell, but with no success; he had become inured to its ringing. The nightmares descended on him worse than ever, as if resenting his efforts to avoid them. Chad's eyes could barely stay open most of the day; his nerves were so stretched and taut, a loud sound from the street would cause him to jump violently. He could not put a word to it, but simple exhaustion was reducing him to a near catatonic state. His excuse for not being at his lab had, until now, been the absence of his tapes from Cambridge; they had arrived, and Chad knew he would have to start showing up or Dr. Koerkeritz would become first curious, then agitated.

In spite of his earlier excuses to Lisa, Dr. Oeschlee was a member of Yale–New Haven's staff, and a fully accredited professor in Yale's school of medicine as well. The doctor, considered one of the country's leading diagnosticians in the tricky field of internal medicine, had been hand-picked by Dr. Koerkeritz. Without explaining the nature of his problem, Chad had asked Koerkeritz for the name of someone to see, and Koerkeritz, almost without having to pause for thought, had not only suggested Oeschlee but expedited Chad's first appointment with him. The head of the Physics Department had undoubtedly been curious, but one look at the deep lines in Chad's face and the sallowness of his color made it clear to the physicist that something was very wrong with his brilliant new addition, Chad. "I hope it is nothing serious," was as far as Koerkeritz went in exploring Chad's illness; it was an invitation to Chad to tell him more, but one that he wisely did not press.

At the end of his story of the seizures and a cursory examination, Dr. Oeschlee came to very much the same conclusion that the doctor in Boston had. "The decision of course is yours, Mr. Lefferts. But I don't even know where to start—I wouldn't essay even the beginnings of a definitive diagnosis—without an extensive series of tests. There are too many possible variables. Blood-sugar levels. Metabolism. Brain sugar. Electrical discharge patterns of the brain. Evidence of prior spinal injury. Insulin levels. Potassium implosion rate. Psychological input. Psychogenic background. Physiological and psychogenic family/hereditary considerations. That doctor you saw in Boston was quite right, you see, in suggesting the seizures could be the product of false—or as I prefer to call it —psychological epilepsy. But first we must rule out a late-developing case of petit mal and other possibilities. That is what the hospital tests can do for us. It would not require a long stay—a week at the outside. But it is central to anything I can accomplish. In my opinion, it would be extremely unfortunate if you could not see your way clear to such diagnostic hospitalization. If you are concerned about money, Mr. Lefferts, I hasten to remind you that for a member of the faculty the group insurance program covers virtually all of the expenses. If you have private health insurance of your own on top of this, there *is* no expense. I must urge—I don't mean to frighten you—

but I must urge you, Mr. Lefferts, to follow this course I recommend. Without it, I can't be responsible for what may happen. . . ."

Chad studied Oeschlee. He seemed a nice man, even a kind one. Earlier—and with a certain graciousness—he had accepted Chad's insistence that any communication between them be kept out of the normal teaching-school discussions, thus guaranteeing, he assumed, Oeschlee's silence. The doctor seemed to understand his position about it completely. The idea of being hospitalized, however urgently, so early in his career here, appalled him, and Chad's first instinct was to refuse. He hated doctors, he loathed hospitals. He always had. But in the back of his mind was one simple fact: he had no choice. Without getting at the root of his problem, he could end up damaging the two people in the world who meant the most to him —Robin and Lisa.

He would be admitted tomorrow, Oeschlee said cheerfully, adding that the tests were not painful, only unpleasant. "Tomorrow, please, Professor Lefferts, no breakfast. I shall initiate the testing program as soon as you are admitted. I realize how anxious you must be to get this over with."

Chad nodded. It was already beginning. Rule: tomorrow, no breakfast. There would be more—many, many more.

On his way out of Dr. Oeschlee's office, one particular event from the encounter remained in his mind. Up until he gave in to Dr. Oeschlee's request, he had been repeatedly addressed as "Mr." Once he had surrendered, he was suddenly metamorphosed into "Professor Lefferts."

He wasn't sure why the distinction should be so important to him, or even why it was drawn. The mysteries of modern medicine preferred to remain inscrutable, much as Omikron Blue did.

* * *

The tests, coming at Chad day after day—unbidden, preprogrammed, accounted for only by a grim army of nurses invoking the doctor's name, "Today, Doctor wants you to . . ."—were never explained and rarely even named. Dr. Oeschlee appeared infrequently, doing little more than sticking his head inside Chad's door at night to ask how he felt. The question was ridiculous. How did Oeschlee expect him to feel, punctured by what seemed a thousand needles, undergoing unpleasant proddings and explorings for reasons that were seldom spelled out?

Some of the equipment was quite extraordinarily sophisticated from an electronic point of view and ordinarily might have fascinated Chad, but he was so depressed by his present situation, he virtually ignored them; a pliant lump of flesh on one examining table after the other, pushed this way and that without either complaint or interest.

It was a young senior resident named Peter Loening who finally brought Chad out of his lassitude far enough to take an interest in what was being done. Loening was bright, blunt, and, on the surface anyway, totally frank. He appeared to be about Chad's age—twenty-eight—and perhaps because of their closeness in age or their similar views on life as a whole, Chad found Loening easy to talk to, the first such person he'd encountered at the hospital. It was Loening who appeared in the X-ray area and explained the chattering machine moving slowly back and forth across Chad's midsection, doing what Loening said was a liver scan.

"You see, Professor, earlier you were injected with an isotope solution of gold, and for reasons no one quite understands, gold tends to collect in the liver and spleen. This scanning machine moves slowly back and forth across your viscera, recording on film the various concentrations of gold it encounters. From this we can get a picture of sorts of the size and shape of both your liver and spleen; it's made up of hundreds of tiny lines that are etched on a drum as the scanning head travels back and forth across your body—rather like a radiophoto."

"At this point," Chad noted sourly, "the gold you shot into me is probably worth more than I am." The young doctor was talking a language he could understand, and Chad, his expertise as a physicist added to his small-boy's fascination with electrical engineering, was reluctantly becoming involved with the medical profession's weird devices. After Chad had spoken, Loening looked at him sharply.

"Well, Professor, we have lots of people in this hospital who feel sorry for themselves. Many of them with good reason. But it's a shock to find one of the country's most noted physicists wallowing in self-pity over what so far seems very little."

The rejoinder stung; Chad knew he deserved it. Letting down his elaborate network of self-defenses was going to take time.

Dr. Loening was apparently quick to forgive. That afternoon he wandered into Chad's room just before they began administering the glucose tolerance test. "Nothing to it," he said. "You drink a glucose solution. We take blood samples every half hour to see how long it takes for your blood sugar to return to normal, and what sort of curve the drop forms. From that we can tell if your seizures have any relation to your insulin production. As an added bonus, if there *is* a faulty insulin production rate, you should have a seizure when the blood sugar is at its high—a sort of controlled diabetic coma, as it were."

"That's a *bonus*?" Chad asked incredulously.

Loening didn't laugh; he rarely did. "Not to you, to the diagnosis. I'll be here and will be able to study the patterns of the seizure; we can learn a lot from them. It's nothing to worry about; I can give you a shot of insulin if you start going too deep into diabetic shock. It can kill people, you know."

To Chad, it *was* something to worry about. Loening was pleasant enough, but this couldn't conceal the deadly earnestness of what the doctor was here to do.

"Here we go," said Loening, handing Chad a glass of syrupy, cloudy liquid the nurse had given him. "Drink it all down; it's not too bad. But so damned sweet—well, it makes you want to throw up."

Every half hour either the nurse or Dr. Loening would come and take a blood sample; Chad lay on his bed fretting, waiting with dread for the seizure that would hurl him spinning, orbiting, out of control. It never came, a fact that appeared almost to disappoint Dr. Loening.

That night, Chad's system made up in nightmares what the day lacked in seizures. He had four separate body-wrenching dreams, one so severe that his shouts produced the night nurse, worried that something terrible had happened to him. All of the nightmares except one were laid in ancient Rome, with Flavius issuing his perennial warning to other Roman Christians—or perhaps it was a warning to himself—"Hide yourselves, hide yourselves!" Flavius was, as always, just one step ahead of the Imperial Guard, who appeared determined to crucify him. In the nightmare that was so violent that it brought the nurse, the guard was dragging Flavius toward a crude cross set up along the Appian Way; their spikes and hammers were at the ready, and Chad began screaming as Flavius did.

The one dream that wasn't set in Rome was in some part of the world Chad couldn't identify. The people in it were speaking a foreign language Chad had never heard before; he got glimpses of great torches blazing from heavy stone walls, men and women in long black cloaks of some sort, and heard an incessant chanting that was finally drowned out by a cacophony of bells. By morning, he was emotionally drained.

Along with his breakfast, the always-cheerful Dr. Loening appeared in his room. "How did you sleep, Professor?" he asked brightly.

"Lousy." Loening raised his eyebrows. "No, I'm not feeling sorry for myself, Doctor. I just didn't get much sleep."

Dr. Loening looked down at his clipboard. "Your chart indicates you'd had a nightmare, so I wondered. But one nightmare shouldn't cost you a whole night's rest. You had more than one, perhaps?" Dr. Loening asked.

Chad felt his defensiveness suddenly rise again. "Yes." He said it sullenly, and without any suggestion that he would be more forthcoming.

"Have you had them for long? Do you have them often?"

Chad shrugged; he would go no further into the matter. Dr. Loening was straying into areas that were not his concern.

"Well, we've got something to take your mind off them," Loening said with one of those smiles Chad had come to dread. "I wish I could say it didn't hurt, but I'd be lying. A spinal tap is on for this morning. It's to see if there was any possible previous damage to your brain or spinal cord that doesn't show up in our X rays. What we do is withdraw a quantity of cerebrospinal fluid through a hollow needle, measure the pressure difference, and then study the fluid we've withdrawn to see if it is clear. If there is damage, it will be cloudy; if not, clear. They'll use a local, but I'd be completely dishonest if I didn't say it's painful and thoroughly hair-raising."

Shortly after, Chad found himself being wheeled into a small operating room. He was turned on his side, his short hospital gown unceremoniously pulled from his body, and a small needle inserted between the lower vertebrae of his spine to administer the local.

"Christ!" Chad yelped. The small needle hurt like hell going in, as did the pressure created by the local's being injected. The actual tap was to be performed by a resident surgeon, who showed up after Dr. Loening had scratched Chad's bare spine several times with a pointed instrument and gotten no reaction.

Suspiciously, Chad watched the surgeon reach for a needle. He felt himself grow slightly dizzy; the needle was several inches long—hollow presumably, so the liquid could be withdrawn through it—and seemingly big enough to penetrate the hide of a horse. At first Chad felt nothing, but as the needle was maneuvered into position between his spinal vertebrae, he experienced a wave of sharp, shooting flashes that ran through his entire body, from the tip of his spine to the base of his skull. At times it was as if someone were scratching on the lining of his brain; at other times it felt more like the diffuse pain one feels in the roots of a tooth when the dentist's probe strikes a nerve. All in all, the tap was unlike anything Chad had ever felt before.

"There," said the surgeon, leaning back and pulling slowly and steadily on the syringe's plunger. The container was them emptied into a small vial that was kept well out of Chad's line of vision.

"It wasn't too bad, was it?" Loening asked, turning Chad over onto his back and pulling up a sheet to cover his nakedness.

"The sight of that needle. Jesus. And a lot of crazy shooting pains. I almost passed out."

"I didn't pretend it wouldn't be painful," Loening reminded him.

"Can I ask you something, Dr. Loening?" Chad fastened his eyes on him, noting that his face was set in a deliberately noncommittal expression that made

Chad suspect his question would not be answered. "Was the fluid clear or cloudy?"

Loening hesitated, then: "That, I'm afraid, you'll have to get from Dr. Oeschlee."

It was the first time Loening had resorted to the traditional doctor's ploy of medical ethics, and Chad found himself irritated by it. "Oh, for Christ's sake, come on. You can tell *me*."

"The hospital doesn't allow it. Not my rule, theirs." Loening abruptly glanced at his watch and shortly after, left.

For a long time after he had been taken back to his room, Chad lay stewing about the test's outcome. He grew progressively convinced that the cerebrospinal fluid must have been cloudy, and that this not only explained the seizures, but possibly the nightmares as well. It also, in his present state, promised him a rapidly dwindling life in a wheelchair, topped by a seizure of such violence he would become unable to breathe and, in consequence, smother to death.

Chad didn't have to concern himself with nightmares that night. He barely slept.

CHAPTER SIX

Chad was not alone in having trouble with his sleep. For the last forty hours Lisa had found the long nights devoted to thrashing, turning, and worrying, instead of sleeping. For each of the five days Chad had been in Yale–New Haven, she had dutifully paid him a visit every evening, leaving Mrs. Lafferty to sit with Robin. In the best of circumstances, hospital visits are strained; the patient is anxiously trying to make his guest comfortable, although suspecting it to be impossible. The chairs are always unsittable, and at too great a distance from the bed to make normal, easy conversation viable. The unnatural surroundings, the sights, sounds, and smells of a hospital, put the guest off. There are long, strained silences while both patient and guest grope for something to say. In normal surroundings, nonstop conversation is not necessary; when someone is being visited in a hospital room, the guest feels he is duty-bound to entertain and divert.

In Chad's case, Lisa found that added on to all the normal distractions was his almost hostile, indrawn attitude. He defied her, it seemed, to say something that would interest him, challenged her to be amusing;

twice he suggested that coming here was taking too much of her time and perhaps she should come only every other night.

Lisa could not hide the hurt. She knew all of this must be terribly hard for Chad, and she was even more worried about the seizures than he was. But she had not expected him to draw so far into himself that she could not even communicate with him. To her, at times it seemed that Chad must somehow be enjoying his misery. In spite of his suggestion, Lisa continued to show up every night; she knew it would be difficult, she knew she would receive more hurts, she knew her only reward would be a continued apparent uninterest in her existence by Chad. But she loved him, and whatever he was going through, she wanted to do everything humanly possible to try to help him. With a sigh, Lisa kissed Robin good night, tried to evade Mrs. Lafferty's questions about Chad's condition, and headed for the hospital.

"Do you know what they want me to do?" Chad thundered. "Can you guess what they're telling me the problem is?"

One look at Chad's face as she walked into his room had warned Lisa that something happened today that was going to make tonight's visit more unpleasant than usual; she wasn't quite prepared, though, for the violence he was displaying. Settling into a chair and trying to appear relaxed, she looked at him and spoke quietly. "No, Chad, I can't guess. Why don't you tell me?"

"Son of a bitch! That bastard—that cock-sucking bastard Oeschlee—wants me to see a shrink. *Me,* for Christ's sake. Says there's no other goddamn explanation."

At different times since the convergence of nightmares and seizures upon Chad, the possibility of some psychological explanation had occurred to Lisa. Always, though, she had dismissed it: it might explain the nightmares, but the seizures were physical happenings that she assumed stemmed from some organic problem. And, as is so often the case, she rejected any implication that Chad might be unbalanced; it reflected too much on her. She struggled with herself, trying to make it make sense.

"But all those tests. Didn't they show anything?"

"The tests," Chad said bitterly. "A lot of painful, unpleasant nonsense. The tests showed exactly nothing. The whole damned raft of them—zilch. All of them 'within normal limits,' that jerk Oeschlee says."

Lisa had been dreading the results of the tests, imagining everything from a brain tumor to a slow disintegration of the nervous system—everything under the sun except *nothing*. Now she felt herself beginning to panic. "But he can't just say there's no explanation for those seizures, he just can't."

"Oh, he's got an explanation all right. False epilepsy. Or psychological epilepsy. Take your pick. Jesus."

Lisa was confused and said so. Chad had been equally confused when Dr. Oeschlee, after explaining that the tests had indicated nothing physical, had tried to explain to Chad what false epilepsy was and the mechanics of how it could produce the kind of seizures he was having. "You see, Professor Lefferts," Oeschlee had said, "sometimes young people—usually younger than you, but twenty-eight is not *too* unusual an age for it—have buried within them a complex of anxieties they cannot face. Conflicts. Sexual, parental, or moral conflicts. Hidden pressures, work and personal. A variety of neuroses can express these. In some instances, however, the person is unable to face them at all; the brain—an electrochemical instrument when you come to think of it—suffers an impossible load of brain-wave activity. In the reverse of electroshock treatment, the brain relieves the overload by a massive discharge of electrical energy. The result is very similar to genuine epilepsy, with the characteristic convulsions of a massive epileptic seizure. The only difference is in origin; instead of the physical roots of genuine epilepsy, false epilepsy is entirely psychogenic. Get at the roots, and the patient is cured. As you can be. In that you are lucky," Dr. Oeschlee had said with a wan little smile indicating he knew his patient did not at the moment consider himself in the least bit fortunate.

"Chad, aren't there pills or something?" Lisa asked, knowing how desperately prejudiced against therapy or analysis Chad was. It was the same question that Chad had asked Oeschlee that afternoon.

"Yes, there is medication that can offer some relief," Oeschlee had said. "That doctor in Boston gave you Dilantin, which is, in general, an effective anticonvulsant. You said, however, it caused unpleasant side effects, which you never quite explained to me." Oeschlee had looked hard at Chad; the side effects were not a usual phenomenon of Dilantin.

"There is, of course," Oeschlee had added without apparent enthusiasm, "another possible area of medication: phenobarbital. It lessens brain-wave activity. However, with most people, it causes a high degree of continual drowsiness, and I should think in your kind of work, an exact science after all, you would find that unacceptable." Chad had agreed, imagining himself standing in front of his blackboard, trying to work out complicated extrapolations while in a semi-drugged state. He edited this suggestion of Oeschlee's out of his answer to Lisa.

"No pills. No shots. Nothing. Except seeing some bastard shrink. Which I'm damned if I'll do."

Lisa was torn. She could not go back to the way things were before her ultimatum had forced Chad into seeing a doctor and putting himself in the hospital. Yet she shared much of Chad's mistrust of psychiatrists and generally hooted at the concept of therapy. She could understand and sympathize with his statement that he was damned if he'd go see one. In the end, though, it was the thought of the danger the seizures held for both Robin and even for Chad himself that made up her mind.

"I know how you feel about psychiatry, Chad. Usually, I feel the same way. But if this Dr. Oeschlee says that's the only way to go, then you'll have to go that way. Hell, Chad, it's not as if Oeschlee had suggested brain surgery or something. If they can't find anything wrong medically and if they haven't got any little magic pills to stop the seizures, well, what else is left? Something is bound to work, and if it isn't one psychiatrist, we'll find another. It's just too dangerous for poor little Robin—not to mention you yourself— to do anything else *but* what the doctors say. I mean, psychiatry can't be all that bad, Chad. Maybe you'll find out why you married a kook like me in the first place."

In spite of himself, Chad had to smile. When he had first asked Lisa to marry him, her answer had been an astonished "You're crazy, Lefferts." Chad's face had fallen; he could remember thinking what Lisa had really said was that believing she would marry *him* was so absurd he had to be crazy even to ask. She hadn't, and quickly let him know it. "I mean for you—an intellect like yours—a tremendous-looking man—a coming giant in whatever that crazy work you do is called—to want to marry a second-rate dowdy frump like me, hell, Lefferts, you'd have to have a screw loose somewhere."

Lisa had been encouraged by the sight of Chad's smiling; she could guess what he was probably remembering and thought it a good moment to press her insistence. "Anyway, Chad, if psychiatry is what the doctors recommend, silly as you—and I, too—may think it is, I guess you've got to string along with it. I'll help you all I can."

"The hell I will. No two-bit medicine man is going to go poking around in my head. I'm as sane as the next guy." Chad's defensive mechanisms suddenly produced an ugly reaction. "Is this some kind of shit you and that bastard Oeschlee cooked up between you? For Christ's sake, I wouldn't be surprised to find out Oeschlee was a new lover. You've had them before; there's no reason to expect you to change."

Lisa was stunned. It occurred to her that over the last couple of months, his stance was taking on an increasingly self-righteous tone that was all out of keeping with Chad. He was back to his favorite accusation —that she had a lover stashed somewhere. The temptation to answer in kind and let it disintegrate into one of their artfully crafted bitter arguments seized her, but Lisa struggled and fought it down. Too much was at stake. Besides, looking at Chad, his angry face lying against the pillow like an outraged little boy's, she felt a surge of sympathy for him. She ignored his remark and glanced at her watch. "Wow, I've got to run. Mrs. Lafferty gets withdrawal symptoms if I don't get back on the dot so she can go home." Lisa knew the lie was transparent; she could see that Chad knew it, too. Kissing him on the forehead as you might a distant uncle, she told him to cheer up and that she'd see him tomorrow.

Chad didn't even answer.

About half an hour later, the night nurse came in and gave Chad his night's ration of pills, staying to make sure he took each of them. She had been surprised to find him lying not *in* the bed, but on top of it.

"Why don't you get under the covers, Mr. Lefferts? You'll be more comfortable. Is your bed all right?"

"I'm lying on top of the bed because I want to. Is that all right with you, or does this damned hospital have a rule about that, too?"

"No, I was just trying to make you more comfortable."

"Well, don't bother. You couldn't in a million years."

The night nurse was used to this sort of performance. After a few days, any patient not in pain or feeling sick grew bored and irritated by hospital procedure, inevitably taking it out on the staff. "Just don't stay up too late, Mr. Lefferts. You need your sleep."

"I need a hell of a lot more than that." Chad watched the night nurse go out the door, shrugging her shoulders and apparently immune to his unpleasantness. Chad was sulking; he knew it, now the hospital staff knew it, too. He stared at the ceiling, he stared at the blank television screen opposite him, hung high on the wall so that enraged viewers could not easily put their fist through the screen. Twice he went to the bathroom—sheerly from nerves. When he got back the second time, he sat on the edge of the bed, fidgeting and restless. Outside he could hear the hospital becoming quiet as the night wore on. There were fewer muted rings of the paging bells, there were a diminished number of footfalls outside his door. The hushed family conversations and louder doctors' discussions of daytime had fled before the grim hospital quiet of night.

Abruptly, Chad stood up and walked over to the closet. His clothes were still there; his wallet was still in the night-table drawer; his car was still in the hospital parking lot. The idea of playing hooky had crept up on him slowly and then suddenly overwhelmed him. He had no particular place to go—certainly not home—he just wanted to escape this claustrophobic little cell and the entire grim hospital atmosphere. To see people—strangers—enjoying themselves, outsiders not worried about kidneys, hearts, blood counts, livers, or spleens.

He stuck his head out the door. The only person in sight was the head night nurse, ensconced behind her semicircular desk reading a paperback. Looking down the corridor in the other direction, he spotted what he was looking for: a small, dimly lit red sign that read EMERGENCY EXIT. Fully dressed, he slithered down the hall and slipped inside the heavy steel door beneath the sign. As he'd expected, it was a bleak cement stairwell, but one that promised him his freedom. For a while anyway.

The car hummed along I-95, heading west. Chad already felt better; the enforced boredom and deadly routine of the hospital world was shed like an extra, unnecessary skin. He found excitement in the lights of the outside world, in the clatter of traffic, and in the thought that behind each pair of headlights were live, breathing people with their own lives to lead, free to do as they wanted and not answerable to a suffocating array of regulations, programs, and schedules.

After he had crossed the West River, Chad turned off at the next turnpike exit and headed for the old Boston Post Road. As he drove along this venerable highway dating back to pre-Revolutionary times, he saw on his left the cheerful lights of a country inn, just beyond the township of Orange. Ordinarily Chad would have scoffed at such a place; but tonight it held some special magic for him, comfortable, relaxed, and inviting. Chad was not the kind of man who would usually welcome the thought of drinking with strangers, but this evening the idea appealed to him enormously; a few drinks in warm, congenial surroundings while making idle conversation with people he'd never met before and would never meet again.

The inside of Smugglers' Hole was curious. The walls were paneled; heavy, time-scarred beams were set in the lowish ceiling above him. Yet the rest of the bar and dining room was garishly modern, not in quite the shattering poor taste of a Howard Johnson's, but austerely functional, filled with Formica and incandescent lighting. From concealed speakers, somewhere beyond him, old show tunes repeated their soft instrumentals and made Chad suddenly feel sentimental.

He took a seat at the long mahogany bar—this remained untouched, the reminder of a time when Smugglers' Hole had been a higher species of inn—and looked up to see the bartender.

"Scotch and water," he said automatically, then changed his mind. "No, make it a double Scotch on the rocks. I need it."

The bartender made no comment, just smiled and poured the drink. A sudden voice from beside him did not startle Chad. He had seen the man when he walked to the bar and had fully expected him to strike up a conversation. "I haven't seen you in here before," the man said pleasantly.

"Just passing through."

"Not a bad place, the Hole," the man continued. "I come here a lot when I'm on the road. See, I'm a salesman."

"I've never been through this way, but you're right, it's not a bad place at all."

"What's your line?"

"Line?" asked Chad, puzzled. Then he remembered the man's saying he was a salesman and realized what he was asking. "Well, I don't have a line exactly. I teach. I teach in a college."

"Not *Yale*? No, that wouldn't make sense; you wouldn't be passing through. Bunch of stuck-up rich kids there, anyway. So where *do* you teach?"

"Some place worse. All rich kids, *all* stuck up. I teach at Harvard," Chad lied.

The man laughed. From the concealed speakers,

abruptly Chad heard a sentimental rendition of "The Bells of St. Mary's," with wonderful old Bing Crosby milking the lyrics and an orchestra made up of what seemed largely to be church bells playing the melody behind him. Suddenly the music seemed to be coming from very far away. Chad was on his second drink, but it couldn't be getting to him that fast.

The man beside him spoke, but it sounded as if he were shouting down a funnel at him. "Fella, you okay? You look awful pale all of a sudden. Hey, you sure you're okay?"

Chad couldn't speak, but nodded his head in a signal that he was all right. It was a lie. He slapped some money on the bar and raced out, just getting inside his car when it happened. He had known it would from the moment the stranger's voice took on its strange, distant sound. His back arched stiffly—so stiffly it seemed something must break—his feet thrashed against the floor, and he could feel the skin of his face draw his lips away from his teeth. From somewhere he could hear a distant jumble of voices, some talking, some shouting, some screaming. To him, it sounded as if they were speaking the same strange language he'd heard in his nightmares, not the Latin of Marcus Flavius's Rome, but the nightmares in which the torches flared against stone walls and great bells shattered his eardrums. The great swelling sound of a choir enveloped him; he could feel his body suddenly hurled into the vast reaches of space, far beyond the galaxy of which earth was a part, and into black, unknown space.

A few seconds later he felt himself shooting around the limitless perimeter of the black hole beside Omikron Blue, spinning helplessly, a prisoner of its frightening gravitational field. As always seemed to happen during the seizures, the unknown woman's guttural voice was screaming at some equally unknown man; Chad could feel the whole force of their battle in his body, pulling on him from opposite directions, tearing at him as if his life would belong to the winner. Somewhere in the distance a young boy screamed in agony, but he was unable to locate exactly where the voice was coming from. For a moment he wondered if it could be Robin's.

An overwhelming roaring in his ears finally drowned out the voices and he could again feel himself hurtle through infinity. As the seizure subsided, the sound diminished and was replaced by the traffic noises and blowing horns of the old Post Road. But he could not move. His eyes would not open. Chad assumed he was back in the front seat of his car, but wasn't sure and was helpless to find out. Part of him was still a prisoner of Omikron Blue a star system so far away in space, it took its light six hundred and fifty-one years to reach earth.

At five A.M. the night nurse—the same one who earlier in the week had recorded Chad's nightmare—looked into his room. Professor Lefferts was having no nightmares tonight; he was in a deep, stuporous sleep, something Chad could have told her almost always happened following one of his seizures. The nurse was curious to find his wallet lying on the floor outside the clothes closet—he was wearing pajamas, not clothes, in the hospital, and it didn't make sense—but replaced it carefully on Chad's bed table without comment. In the night nurse's book, she recorded, "Prof. Lefferts, Room 305, sleeping like a baby."

From the hospital's standpoint, their patient, Professor Lefferts, had never been anywhere that night except in bed.

CHAPTER SEVEN

"Do you have—um, um, do you have—any sevens?"

"No. Sorry. But I don't."

"I doubt you."

Lisa turned her pair of sevens around sheepishly. "You shouldn't doubt everything, sweetheart," she noted, watching the look of annoyance creep across Robin's face.

"You're cheating, Mummy."

Leaning back, Lisa gave Robin a displeased look across the card table. Whenever he lost, he accused her of cheating. The possibilities of "Go Fish" were about exhausted anyway. It would be good for him—not to mention herself—when his school opened in another week or so. The game broke up; Robin went sulking off to find something new to pester her with.

Boredom was not an emotion exclusive to Robin. Lisa had run out of things to do to the house on De-Witte Street herself. Curtains and carpets were still due to come, and she still had some slipcovers to have made for their furniture in the library. All their pictures were hung, and even Chad's one antique artifact was mounted on the heavy stone wall beside the fireplace. The piece was of great importance to

Chad, and had been as long as Lisa could remember; she herself considered it ugly—dark, battered, and stained with almost two thousand years of being buried beneath the soft ashes of Pompeii. Technically, the Roman soldier's breastplate had been stolen. Many years ago, some Italian workman had discovered it while helping in the disinterment of Pompeii and spirited it off for himself. Later, he had sold it to someone, and Chad had run across it in a small shop near Firenze. Because of the impossibility of providing papers that would legitimize the breastplate, the vendor sold it cheaply; Chad had used his official position at Harvard to declare it a fake—something he well knew it wasn't. This minor fraud allowed him to get the breastplate out of Italy and back to the States. The attraction it held for Chad baffled Lisa; he was not given to interest in antiques of any kind, and this was a particularly unattractive one to boot.

The idea that had been possessing her again crowded into her mind. In spite of her worries about Chad, the mystery of what lay behind their house still fascinated Lisa. There must be something there that was extraordinary indeed to have caused its owner to seal off all the rear windows of their house and make seeing it impossible. She had wanted to wait until an unwilling Chad could be talked into going with her; she had wanted to go without Robin. At the moment, neither was possible, and over the last few days she'd found the mystery consuming.

The hell with what she had wanted; she would go today and take Robin with her; Mrs. Lafferty was downtown shopping for her, so there was no readily available sitter.

"Darling," she began saying to Robin, "how would you like . . . ?" By the time she had finished Robin's eyes were wide with excitement.

"Soooooperman!" shouted Robin, and began tearing around the room in small, tight circles, making the zooming sounds of an airplane in a power dive.

"You'll have to promise to be very good and do just what I tell you, Robin," she cautioned. Robin promised. Fifteen minutes later they left the house, Robin ecstatic, Lisa pleased that at last she would get a look at the mysterious place that had cost her house all of its sunny rear windows.

Walking around the block until Lisa guessed they were coming close to a spot opposite their own house, the exact place became suddenly easy to locate. They had come to a high wall, crumbling in places, that appeared to surround the entire property and run all the way up to their own house. Every few feet, there was a sign nailed into the stonework of the wall warning that the property inside was private and that trespassers would be prosecuted. These were signed with the printed name "George Oliver, Esq."—a signature necessary to have posted land legally protected. To Lisa, the name was not new. Mrs. Lafferty had mentioned that their own house, before its purchase by Yale, had been owned by someone named Oliver, a name easy to remember because of Oliver Twist.

Because of the walls, Lisa could see nothing. The short patch of what had once been lawn that stretched toward the street in front of the wall had long since been taken over by weeks and scrub growth. Earlier, Lisa had tried the bells of the houses on either side, but no one answered. Going along the wall for the second time, she found, almost hidden by some tall bushlike growth in front of the wall, a narrow opening where the stonework of the wall had crumbled and fallen inside. By squeezing past the bush—Lisa wasn't certain, but thought it was probably a wild sumac tree—she was pretty sure she could slip inside; Robin, of course, would have no trouble. Lisa wasn't too fond of this idea, but the only other entrance was a heavy pair of steel gates farther along the wall; they

were firm and solid, fastened by a gigantic padlock
that was a caricature of an old-fashioned lockbox.

"Come on, sweetheart," she said to Robin, and took
him firmly by one hand. Slipping through the break
in the wall wasn't quite as easy as she had thought;
more of the same sumac trees that grew outside the
wall also flourished inside. Before she could squeeze
herself through, she had to force the bushes on the
inside back to give her room. Robin followed easily,
laughing at how simple it was for him to do something that reduced his mother to muffled swearing.

It was a strange place. Perhaps it was an overactive
imagination, but the moment Lisa stepped inside, all
the clattering sounds of New Haven's traffic seemed
to disappear, as if this ruin of what apparently had
once been a garden belonged to some other time
and place. Lisa couldn't hear a sound. More realistical-
ly, she knew the sudden silence was due more to the
sound-absorbing qualities of the dense undergrowth,
the height of the ivy-covered wall, and the muffling
qualities of the gnarled old trees and twisted bushes.
The grass came to slightly above her waist; once, she
guessed, it had been lawn.

Seeing any distance ahead was difficult. Formerly
well-pruned shrubs and bushes had been allowed to
grow wild, taking on grotesque, tortured shapes. In
some places, they had grown into each other, forming
a dense, thick screen that made seeing beyond them
completely impossible.

Slowly, carefully, they moved forward through the
tall grass, Robin making a game of it, enchanted to
be maneuvering through something he couldn't see
above. Robin's sudden scream galvanized her. Calling,
Lisa hurried to him, only then realizing how far she
had allowed him to stray. It was easy to see why he
was so frightened. Rising out of the tall grass ahead
loomed a sun-bleached wooden statue of an unidentified figure, one hand raised as if in benediction.

She comforted Robin, telling him please not to wander so far from her next time. Robin, still frightened, was only too happy to agree; when he first saw the statue, he had thought it was a living figure, not a statue, its ancient sun-bleached wood as pale as any ghost.

To Lisa, the statue remained utterly fascinating. It was a primitive prie-dieu, the kind placed alongside the early roads of medieval Europe so that the traveler could rest and, kneeling before the figure—usually one of the saints'—implore God to protect him on the next leg of his always hazardous journey. Carefully she studied the figure.

All of her study and knowledge of medieval art failed to place the prie-dieu in time or country; Lisa had never seen anything like it anywhere. There was a strange beauty in its very ugliness, in the rough way the folds of the long gown the figure wore fell, in the thousands of tiny wormholes with which time had riddled it.

To the modern eye, this kind of primitive statuary appears almost stylized; its mournful eyes were as enormous as they were unseeing, disproportionately long in relation to the face, which had a stylized beard of some sort. One hand, the fingers extended, lay flat against its left shoulder in a rough approximation of a blessing. First from one side, then the other, Lisa continued to study the statue, absorbing its details, memorizing its features. Angrily she cursed herself for not bringing her camera; she would need all the help Yale could provide in identifying, dating, and placing it. Robin was becoming bored and kept pestering her, pleading that they start going ahead again or that they go home; he needed to go to the bathroom, he was hungry, he didn't feel good—all of his usual ploys to get his way were unsheathed and used without success.

Lisa was so absorbed in her examination she didn't

realize at first that Robin, irritated when his pleas were fielded without apparent effect, had wandered off again through the tall grass, carrying an imaginary machine gun in his hands and making dead soldiers out of occasionally resistant stalks of tall grass. Because she wasn't aware how far away Robin had gotten, his new screams of fright at first confused Lisa. Smiling to herself, she decided he'd probably run into another statue and was as terrified of it as he had been of the first. "Coming, Robin. Where are you, sweetheart?" All Lisa could see was the gently waving field of tall grass; Robin was only visible when you were right on top of him in this field, anyway. She smiled again as she heard him scream a second time, a little amused at how easily children's imaginations can play tricks on them.

But there was an intensity in Robin's screams that began to upset Lisa; his cries had become genuine shrieks of terror, erasing her earlier amusement; something more than a statue was terrifying him. She began yelling to him as hard as she could, hoping an answering shout might help locate him. She heard him shriek again, but the sound seemed to come from nowhere; it was a cry without direction, muffled and hollow. Lisa found herself running through the tall grass, shouting Robin's name, trying to keep the fear out of her voice for Robin's sake, but aware that she was not succeeding. A sudden soft spot in the ground made her gasp; as she fell, she realized she had turned her ankle.

Sitting up, nursing her ankle, she called to Robin again. Robin's answering cry seemed very close to her, yet he continued invisible. Crawling painfully to where she thought his voice was coming from, she noticed the eerie echoing sound his shouts and screams held; it mystified her. The explanation came a second later. Ahead of her, she saw the rotted wooden planking of some curious structure that lay flat on the ground; there were pieces of fresh wood, brighter than the rest and looking strangely new, where the planks had been broken by someone falling through into whatever it was that lay beneath.

On all fours, Lisa advanced and peered down through the decaying planks, calling to Robin in a calm voice that did not reflect the growing panic inside her. In the dim, murky light that filtered down through the holes and cracks, she could see that he had fallen through the rotting boards of an old well-cover. He had been lucky enough to land on a small, flat outcropping that protruded from the steep stone sides of the well itself; if he had not, he would have plunged all the way down into the water she could see shimmering blackly below.

It took all of Lisa's self-control to preserve her calmness, but she knew that if she allowed any sign of panic to creep into her voice, Robin would pick it up and probably panic himself. Children are famously good at reading these nuances in someone's voice. Panicked, he could easily lose his balance and plunge off his hazardous perch.

"Robin, darling . . ." Lisa began very softly. At first Robin didn't seem to hear her. He was terrified by the sights and the sounds of this terrible place and, his arms outstretched, was hugging the stones of the well for safety, crying miserably. Finally he seemed to hear his mother. The sound of Lisa's voice—its reassuring promise of rescue and safety, and a return to normalcy—coming from so close above his head, was too much for him. He spun around, letting go of his grip on the stones, and looked up to see if his mother was real. In that terrible instant, Lisa saw him begin to teeter back and forth on the edge of the outcropping, his arms making little circular movements as he tried to regain his balance. With a lunge that almost carried her into the well herself, Lisa broke through the wooden cover with her body and grabbed at his outstretched hands. Robin shrieked. Painfully, holding on to his wrists as tightly as she could, she began pulling him up the wall. Instead, without the outcropping to support him, he fell even farther down, until his body was half in the water and his small arms stretched out as far as they would go. It took Lisa's last reserves of strength to drag him through the water and finally pull him out.

For a second the exhausted Robin and Lisa lay in the long grass. Robin was crying and Lisa wasn't far from it. "It's all right, darling," she repeated over and over again. She pulled off his drenched shirt and wrung it out before she gave it back to him to put on; at least it was a little drier. She did the same with his khaki trousers; his shorts were taken off and thrown away. As Robin climbed back into his still wet clothes, Lisa looked around her again. At the far end of the garden, backed up against the stone fireplace wall of their own house, was a long, elaborately columned arcade, medieval arches of some kind, under a slanting slate roof, a little like the cloisters of some ancient abbey. Again she felt the same surge of excitement she'd experienced when she saw the priedieu. It was something she would have to come back and investigate at some later time. But without Robin. The entire place was far too dangerous for a child; God knew how many child-traps like the old well lay concealed in the long grass.

Lisa dried Robin's hair with her hankie and tried to think of what else she could do to make him warm; the day was fortunately a sunny one, but there was a chill in the September air that even the clearest day couldn't hide. Like his jockey shorts, Robin's socks were discarded. He still sloshed when he walked, but there was nothing she could do about it; his sneakers had absorbed a great deal of water during their brief immersion in the well. Once they were out of the curious garden, the sneakers too would be removed;

Robin's bare feet on the warm pavement would be warmer than in the sneakers. His chatter was returning as the fright began leaving; it was rapidly becoming an exciting new adventure to add to his recital of *Captain Robin Lefferts and His Close Escapes from Death*. Ahead Lisa could see the opening in the wall they'd come through; she moved Robin along quickly, not really listening as he jabbered excitedly away.

As she struggled to push the sumac bushes back to let herself through, a dark shadow seemed suddenly to fill the opening. Going through, holding back the bushes, and pulling Robin behind her, she felt her heart jump wildly as they were confronted by a large man firmly planted on the sidewalk outside the opening. Lisa felt her heart stop jumping and begin pounding against her ribs. The man glared at them. Lisa could not put her finger on it, but there was something hostile, almost sinister, about the man's expression, an air of police-force belligerence, as if she and Robin were trespassers he'd caught trying to steal something. "Doing a little sightseeing, eh?"

"Please," Lisa said, feeling herself beginning to come apart.. "Please—my son's soaking wet—fell into a well in there—we live just back of here—Professor Lefferts—that place in there is dangerous—please. . . ."

"The old Oliver place? I could tell you a thing or two about *that* house. But my manners, I'm sorry." The man's whole manner had changed once he'd discovered who they were and where they lived. "I'm Richard Thomas. I live down this street just a little way. I thought I heard someone inside and came down to wait for you on your way out. We've had a lot of trouble over the years with vandals there, you see."

Lisa found that the shock of Robin's plunge down the well was only catching up with her now. Numbly she shook Mr. Thomas's hand. "Do you have any old clothes I could put on Robin—he's soaking wet—I thought he was going to drown—that place should be better protected—poor little Robin was terrified. . . ."

Mr. Thomas was suddenly sympathetic, holding out a hand to steady Lisa. "No children, no old children's clothes. But we can certainly dry him off or, well—how about a good hot bath? Then, I can drive you home—wrap him up in a towel, you see. As for you, Mrs. Lefferts, I think you could use a good stiff drink. Experiences like that are hard on the nerves."

Gratefully, Lisa took Robin's hand and followed Mr. Thomas up the street, turning in at a house just on the other side of the grim stone wall. It was one of the houses where she'd rung the doorbell earlier and gotten no answer. Robin was put to soak in a hot tub, and Mr. Thomas brought him a cup of hot chocolate to warm up his insides. Lisa was given a stiff Scotch on the rocks.

She learned from Mr. Thomas that he was a widower, that he was retired, that he'd been in the oil distribution business in New Haven, and that he'd lived in this house almost since he could remember. "I haven't met Professor Lefferts yet," he added, "which is a little unusual. I was a trustee of the university for some years and still go to most of their functions. Maybe I missed the one he was presented at, I don't know." Something suddenly seemed to occur to Mr. Thomas. "Oh, wouldn't you want to call him and tell him where you are and that everything's all right?"

Lisa floundered. "Chad is not here. . . . What I mean is, he's at a meeting—in Chicago. I call him every night."

Mr. Thomas studied his shoes for a moment, and when he spoke again the subject had changed completely. "I just thought he might be worried. How do you like living in the old Oliver house, Mrs. Lefferts? It's a fascinating place. Eerie, but fascinating."

"My son calls it weird."

"It is, it is."

Lisa leaned forward and suddenly looked Mr. Thomas square in the eye. "Mr. Thomas, can you tell me something? Why does our house have all of its rear windows sealed off?"

Mr. Thomas smiled, as if he'd been waiting for her to ask that question since they'd met. "Ah, the sealed rear windows. That's quite a story, Mrs. Lefferts. Is your drink all right? The sealed rear windows . . ."

To Lisa, it seemed that old Mr. Thomas was a lonely man and that her asking that question about the house had given him an excuse to have someone to talk with. He answered at length. By the time he was finished, Lisa knew the history of the Oliver house virtually from the day it was built, from the first beams put up by a sea captain in the early 1700s, through several restorations and remodelings, to the present. There was nothing frightening about the story, nothing sinister, nothing that didn't make some rough kind of sense. The story, like the house, was merely peculiar. Or as Robin would have put it— "weird."

CHAPTER EIGHT

"No, I didn't screw my sister either. For one thing, I didn't *have* a sister."

Dr. Peter duBrul was used to this sort of assault; psychiatrists have to be. He was not used to the skill with which his patient, Professor Lefferts, could mount his assault, nor had he expected it to happen during this first, very tentative visit. Usually, it took longer, after transference had taken place—unfortunately, in his own case, most of the time a negative transference.

DuBrul was an unusual man, part psychiatrist, part teacher at Yale's Medical School. He was an affable but distant man, and it was his inability to conceal his basic detachment from his patients that caused him to wind up at a college instead of in private practice; patients interpreted the detachment as indifference to their problems and, except in the enforced environment of a place like Yale, would never have chosen him as their doctor if they'd had a choice. This was unfair, really—the unfairness was something du-Brul himself recognized, but had to accept. He knew, as did his peers at Yale–New Haven, that his insights were truly exceptional. He just wasn't much of a salesman. He raised his eyebrows at Chad Lefferts, another brilliant man, he decided, who was no salesman either.

From the moment Oeschlee had described him, Peter duBrul was fascinated by Chad Lefferts. There were always a certain number of faculty members undergoing therapy—and more that should—but none with the brilliance attributed to Lefferts. The seizures, too, intrigued him: a physical manifestation of deep conflicts, something refreshingly different from the undergraduates' usual vague, whining complaints about being unhappy or frustrated or not being appreciated. When he added to this the mysterious nightmares Oeschlee had tipped him off to, Lefferts's case became a handsome challenge. Here was a man, a supposedly stable, highly rational man, a theoretical physicist of all things, subject to violent seizures for which there was no physiological explanation, and plagued by nightmares about a man who lived during the zenith of the Roman Empire. Fascinating!

"Let's get back to the nightmares," duBrul suggested.

"Why?" snapped Chad. "I have to *live* in them. You're nothing but a goddamned voyeur, Doctor, peering out from behind your frilly lace curtains and peeking into my dreams. A fucking Peeping Tom spying on my psyche."

In spite of himself, duBrul had to smile; he'd never heard his profession put quite this way before. The description was so imaginative, in fact, it seemed out of character for a physicist, and the thought crossed his mind again: perhaps this Professor Lefferts was a multiple personality, a particular specialty of his. One personality a superbly down-to-earth physicist, a second personality living inside it and possessed by nightmares, seizures, wild thoughts—and one that could express itself very colorfully. But stacking it up against Chad's other facets, it didn't jell; he would reluctantly have to dismiss the inviting thought of multiple-personality disorder. DuBrul sighed and went back to work.

"I'm not asking you to go into the nightmares in depth this time, Professor. I just have a couple of general questions. Would you say the nightmares are more frightening to you than they used to be, say, a month ago?"

"Yes."

"Do you feel more a part of them today than a month ago?"

"Yes."

"You mentioned this person Marcus Flavius. Have you studied a great deal of Roman history of the early Christian period?"

"Damn it, no."

"Does this Flavius, as a person, seem more real than before?"

"He *is* real. Look, Doctor, let's get off this crap. It's a waste of your time and mine. I can't explain why the nightmares are about this man most of the time, and no, I've studied damned little about the period. All I know is that what's happening to him is very real—to me, anyway."

From the exhaustion in Chad's voice, duBrul knew he'd reached the end of productive talk for the day. He tried to lighten the atmosphere before pointing out that their time was up. "Perhaps you're a reincarnation of a Roman soldier named Flavius. . . ." It was intended as a joke; the reaction was spectacular. Chad shot to his feet and began yelling at duBrul as if he had just robbed him of something.

"What the fuck kind of game are you playing? Reincarnation, for Christ's sake! You're a nutcase. A blind, blithering idiot. He's a dream that's all . . . just a dream. . . ."

As Chad slumped into his chair with a defeated expression, duBrul tried to explain himself. "Professor Lefferts, I made that remark as a little joke. I didn't expect you to take it so seriously. Reincarnation, you see, has been used by some patients I know of as a device to avoid facing their present problems—it's far easier for someone with problems to worry about what happened to his other self, say, two thousand years ago, then it is to accept the problems he faces today. The evasion is classic. I can't say I have much faith in reincarnation, of course, although at a place like Yale you'll find those who believe in it implicitly." Dr. duBrul studied his hands sadly. "That and many things even stranger."

"Crap."

DuBrul rose from behind his desk, and Chad automatically got to his feet. "I see our time is up, Professor Lefferts. There is someone outside waiting to take you back to your room. We'll be seeing each other again."

"I don't know why. Oeschlee seems to think I'm nuts and need a shrink. With you on that reincarnation kick, I think *you're* the one who needs treatment."

DuBrul merely smiled. Chad Lefferts was not going to be an easy man to treat. As Chad reached the door, duBrul called after him. "Professor Lefferts, one final question from this professional madman. I've noticed, throughout our session, that you wince whenever you move your left arm. Is something wrong?"

"I pulled a muscle somehow."

"It's not on your records anywhere so it must have happened last night. From the pain you evidently have, the muscle must have been severely strained. Would you care to tell me whether it happened during a nightmare or another seizure?"

Chad looked at Dr. duBrul with near loathing. He had waked this morning well aware that something was very wrong with his left shoulder, a shooting pain every time he tried to move his left arm, on top of a constant ache in the muscles of the whole shoulder.

Damn. Last night's seizure must have been an exceptionally violent one—so violent its writhings had somehow torn the muscles. A physical manifestation, as it were, of his feeling that he was somehow being torn in two during the seizures. He assumed it had happened in his car outside Smugglers' Hole, although he found the dirt of fresh earth on his clothes and a series of inexplicable scratches on his body. He had also assumed he could successfully hide the injury from duBrul this morning.

Finally, Chad answered duBrul's question. "No, I wouldn't care to tell you."

The night was touched with the sudden September cold that can descend without warning on New England. To some in New Haven the temperature came as a shock; to others, as a pleasant harbinger of the long golden fall to come. Nils Lee capitalized on the sudden change in weather by lighting a roaring fire in the large fireplace set into the handsome paneling of his office in Davenport College. It would give his guests, mostly high faculty members like himself, a pleasant surprise, adding a cozy touch to his first cocktail party of the season. If he'd known the weather was going to be this chilly, he might even have served mulled wine; there were certain self-consciously intellectual faculty members coming who doted on such things as mulled wine, obscure poetry in abstruse languages, and early examples of Japanese movies without subtitles. Most of them, he thought with a small sigh of relief, were concentrated in the English Department, not his own; he invited them purely in the exercise of Yale's Byzantine faculty politics.

Nils Lee was a full professor, holder of the well-endowed Pittman Chair, as well as head of the History Department and executive director of the Institute for Far Eastern Studies, a field which was his particular specialty.

The room filled quickly; there was another party being staged by Professor Greenwald, head of the Institute for Metaphysical Research, in his office at Saybrook College, not far from Davenport. The guests there were dreary, Nils Lee had heard from several people, and Greenwald himself had a gift for making everyone uncomfortable, so an increasing number of his livelier guests were drifting over to Lee's party after putting in a token appearance at Greenwald's.

Coming across the room, working his way through the other guests, Lee saw Dr. duBrul heading toward him. DuBrul was a favorite of his, and the psychiatrist relished Lee's offbeat interests in the psychic. He also considered duBrul a little eccentric, but was aware there were few of the faculty who weren't; Nils Lee simply made no effort to hide his eccentricities.

"Hi, Nils," said duBrul, shifting his glass from one hand to the other so they could shake. "Don't tell anyone. I'm a refugee from Greenwald's. You'll be seeing a lot of them here, I suspect."

Lee laughed. "For a shrink, you certainly have a gift for compliments. What you're saying is that no one would be at my party if there wasn't an impossible one going on up the street."

"Your booze is better. That bastard Greenwald was only offering—can you believe it?—mulled wine. Dreadful stuff. So dreadful, the only defense was to drink too much of it, which I did."

Nils Lee became suddenly glad he'd discarded his fleeting notion about the wine. DuBrul was right: dreadful stuff.

"I don't know," Lee added with a slight smile. "Metaphysics and mulled wine sort of go together."

Something seemed suddenly to occur to duBrul. "You know, I had a crazy experience this afternoon that should appeal to your interest in the psychic. Young professor—new here—can't tell you his name, of course—is in the hospital. They referred him to me.

Seizures and all sorts of things got him tied up in
knots; but what interested me particularly was a series
of nightmares he's been having. Driving the poor man
to distraction. Dreams he's a Roman soldier and is
about to be crucified for being a Christian. Has all the
details of first-century Rome down pat, although he
denies he's ever studied anything about the period.
Down to the smallest details. The nightmares are so
real to the poor guy, he's afraid to go to sleep anymore.

"Well, Nils, we weren't getting anywhere, so as a
joke—just a little livening up of a pretty deadly session—I asked him if he didn't maybe think he was a
reincarnation of that early Roman. Told him, after
all, it's easier to worry about what you did wrong
in another life two thousand years ago than it is to
worry about what you did wrong today. The man
became wild. I mean *wild*—eyes bulging, shaking all
over, the works. Accused me of everything he could
think of. I honestly thought he was going to slug me.
Damnedest thing I—"

For the second time today, duBrul's little joke about
reincarnation backfired. He looked up with amaze-
ment as Nils Lee, his eyes quivering with interest,
stared at him. "Peter, I want to meet that man. I
have to meet that man. You can set it up. . . ."

"Damn it, Nils. I shouldn't have told you as much
as I did about a patient. But I knew you were hung
up on reincarnation and that stuff and I thought it
would give you a laugh. Jesus, Nils, I—"

"I *have* to meet that man, Peter. I understand the
ethics and all that crap. But now that you've told me
as much as you have, you owe it to me to tell me the
rest. His name, anyway; I'll take it from there."

DuBrul didn't know what to do. The last person
he wanted to consider him stuffy, a psychiatrist hiding
behind the venerable shield of confidentiality, was
Nils Lee. But his trade had its rules, some of which

simply could not be broken. "Christ, Nils, I just can't. I'd like to, but I can't."

Nils Lee looked at duBrul, wearing an expression calculated to embarrass, choosing precisely the right words to wither. "I didn't think you were that stuffy, Peter. But, hell. I can find him for myself. There can't be that many new professors who are patients at Yale–New Haven. You'd have just made it simpler."

"Damn it, Nils. If you start poking around, I'm in all sorts of trouble. Look, I—"

Further discussion had to stop when they were joined by two more refugees from Greenwald's party. The discussion turned to generalities, and Nils Lee quickly became bored, drifting off to take care of his other guests. The matter, however, was not in the least diminished in his mind. DuBrul's patient was someone he wanted to meet—and would.

Nils Lee was a remarkable man. His standing as head of the history department was generally considered more than deserved; his position as executive director of the Institute for Far Eastern Studies had grown out of a universally accepted brilliance in the area that was his specialty: Asia. And there was another side to Lee—the side that fascinated Dr. Peter duBrul: his deep interest in the psychic, something that had developed naturally, he supposed, out of his study of the East.

To look at Nils Lee, it was sometimes hard to believe he was a man who would hold such beliefs, common enough in the Eastern World, scoffed at in the Western. He was a tall man, still slender, with a penchant for Harris tweed jackets and suits that would have seemed more at home at Cambridge or Oxford than at Yale. His short gray hair made him look more like a military man, but his posture and gait—a slumping walk that matched his bent shoulders

—quickly shattered that illusion and labeled him an academic. The only thing Nils Lee lacked was a large pipe; instead he affected—he had admitted it was an affectation to duBrul and a few other close friends—Balkan Sobranies, a Turkish cigarette with so pungent an odor anyone could tell when he'd spent even a short period in a room. "I want them to know I'm around," was Lee's explanation. "Frankly, they smell so dreadful sometimes they overwhelm *me*."

Even given the size of Nils Lee's office and the number of people who filled the room; the variety of pipes, cigarettes, and cigars being smoked by his guests; and the bitter smell of the fire, the sweet pungent odor of his Sobranies was impossible to escape. DuBrul, who showed increasing signs that gin and tonic did not sit well on top of mulled wine, made his way over to Nils Lee a second time. "Do you know who just arrived, Nils?" He giggled. "Greenwald. Couldn't stand his own party, I guess. First bright decision he's made in years."

"Peter," began Nils. DuBrul set his face.

"No, dammit. I won't give you his name."

"All right, then, just some more information about the nightmares. Does he only dream about this Roman?"

"Well, he says there *are* other voices and fragments in some nightmares, but he never can remember who they are when he wakes up." DuBrul stared off into space for a second. "As a shrink I shouldn't overlook what a patient *can't* remember from his dreams, I guess; but then, as a shrink I shouldn't be talking about him to you either."

Nils Lee knew he was on the verge of winning; duBrul was beginning to crumble. "Well, as I said, Peter, it won't be hard for me to find out who your patient is. I'm not going to shake him up or anything; it's just that I have reasons to want to talk to him. You understand, Peter. Come on, be a real friend and give me his name; it'll mean less poking around through university channels."

DuBrul gave a long, low sigh and looked at Lee with sadness; his last argument had a concealed threat in it. "Oh, shit. I never *have* been able to say no to you, you bastard." He took a deep breath and watched his ethical canons disintegrate around him. If Nils Lee started a search for the man, his own name would surface as his psychiatrist. Should there be trouble, questions might be asked. With a sigh, he surrendered. "Lefferts. Professor Chad Lefferts. He's a theoretical physicist, believe it or not. But look, damn it. The man's in trouble, big trouble, as it is. If you do anything that upsets him further, I'll kill you. Just listen, don't talk. He's being discharged from the hospital tomorrow anyway, and I'll only be seeing him as an outpatient. Sometimes you infuriate me, Nils. The way you get around me. Polite blackmail. For Christ's sake, never tell him where you got his name. Frankly, I think he's going to look at you like you're crazy. I don't want to know anything about it."

Lee took duBrul's hand. "Thanks, Peter. I appreciate that you're not supposed to do what you're doing. I won't tell anyone. And I'll do my damnedest not to upset the poor guy. A theoretical physicist, eh? Pretty unlikely candidate for nightmares about early Rome. Pretty unlikely candidate for anything except a blackboard full of squiggles proving the solar system is about to explode. *Very* unlikely. . . ."

A pained expression crossed duBrul's face. "Jesus, Nils. Please. I don't know anything about it, okay?" He shrugged and fled into the crowd.

The party continued for some hours, about par for one of the first faculty parties of the year. Greenwald got drunk and became abusive, still smarting over the exodus from his own affair. DuBrul, already well on his way when he arrived, grew progressively more morose and avoided Lee as much as he could.

Nils Lee remained dead sober. His mind was racing, excited at the possibilities—improbable as they were— the piece of paper with Chad Lefferts's name on it being crumpled and uncrumpled in his jacket pocket.

CHAPTER NINE

At around six o'clock the next day, Chad Lefferts came
home from the hospital. His shoulder still hurt, but
he had successfully managed to hide it from both Drs.
Oeschlee and Loening at the hospital; only duBrul
had been astute enough to notice how much pain it
gave him. In one final meeting with Oeschlee, he had
agreed to continue seeing the psychiatrist; originally,
he had planned to ignore the treatment as soon as he
could bail out of Yale–New Haven, but a couple of
things Oeschlee said during the meeting just before
he was discharged changed his mind.

"I know," Oeschlee had said with a faint smile,
"the temptation will be strong for you to break off
treatment with Dr. duBrul as soon as you are returned
to your home environment. It's only natural—particularly with someone as opposed to therapy as you are."

"It crossed my mind."

"Let me point out a couple of things, Professor
Lefferts. All of our tests indicate absolutely nothing
wrong with you organically. Frankly, I wish I myself
were in as good physical shape. But these seizures—
these ugly manifestations of false epilepsy—simply
have to be stopped. They can destroy you—as well as

hurt any number of other people as well. When you first came to see me, you mentioned having 'almost killed' your son the day before during one. That, in spite of any efforts you make to protect him from situations where a seizure could cause damage, can easily happen again. And you cannot always count on being so lucky.

"There is also your wife to consider; surely you don't wish to endanger her. And strangers. The hazards of your driving an automobile. Swimming. Being alone anywhere. In addition to the possible damage you could inflict on yourself, you have to consider others, too, Professor Lefferts. But your prime consideration must be yourself. I can't believe you wish to put yourself in the position of damaging yourself during one of the seizures in such a way that you would be crippled for life. Existence in a wheelchair is bearable, I suppose, but for someone of your age to expose himself to confinement in one for the rest of his life through unwillingness to undergo therapy—repugnant as the idea may be to him—is not the act of even a marginally intelligent man."

"I didn't ask for the damned things." Hearing himself, Chad was surprised at how petulant he sounded.

"No, but unless you continue therapy—we have no alternative treatment—you are acting just as if you *had* asked for them. As added inducement, therapy continued over a period of time should, in the process, clear up those nightmares of yours; I can't believe the two sets of symptoms aren't related. If you don't like Dr. duBrul, of course, there are others . . ."

Chad had said nothing. He was concerned, certainly, for both Robin and Lisa; the idea of somehow damaging them during a seizure was something he had agonized over many times. The idea of damaging himself was relatively new, and Dr. Oeschlee's description of him tied to a wheelchair was a shattering one. But the key factor, the one on top of his concern for Lisa and Robin that finally made up his mind, lay in Oeschlee's casual remark: "It should clear up those nightmares of yours, too."

"What I meant to say," Chad had explained, bending the facts liberally, "was that yes, it had crossed my mind—discontinuing therapy—but that I guess I don't have a hell of a lot of choice about it. I don't want to hurt anybody; I don't want to hurt myself."

Chad left the hospital late that afternoon after calling Lisa, partly so she wouldn't arrange for Mrs. Lafferty to stay to baby-sit Robin, partly because—he at first dismissed the notion as ridiculous—he wanted someone to know where he was in case he had a seizure and became involved in an accident on the way home. The chances of such a thing were minuscule, he told himself, but so had been the chances of the episode two nights ago at Smugglers' Hole. The fear of the seizures was becoming worse than the seizures themselves, and Oeschlee had fed that fear.

Inside the house on DeWitte Street, he discovered Lisa had planned something of a celebration to mark his return. "No one's coming, Chad, don't look so appalled. It'll just be the three of us. A little champagne, a little special dinner."

Chad tried. "I figured you'd asked half the faculty to show them your husband rolling on the floor and foaming at the mouth. It's the new 'in' thing for parties."

Lisa tried. "I'll take lessons and roll on the floor with you. Or under you. Maybe we can hire ourselves out to a salesmen's burlesque. Foaming at the mouth will be optional."

Both of their efforts collapsed. The mention of salesmen reminded Chad of the drummer at Smugglers' Hole; his face went grim and the smile faded. Lisa's was shattered by Chad's expression; it was a familiar one to her now, one of worry, defensiveness, and defeat. Almost as she watched, she could see him withdrawing inside himself.

After dinner—lobster, steamers, corn, and champagne—they sat in the living room listening to Robin upstairs singing himself to sleep. It was a happy sound, yet there was an undertone of the forlorn to it. For no reason, Chad suddenly remembered the young boy's voice that he had heard during that same seizure outside the Hole, the boy screaming in agony, and remembered wondering if it could somehow be Robin's. His mood grew darker.

Lisa tried again. "Did anything they did in the hospital help? I mean, you always leave a hospital thinking you should feel much better; usually you feel worse."

Once again Chad tried, too. "You got it. Waste of time and money. By now, Koerkeritz must think I've fallen into Omikron Blue."

"No, he called a couple of times to see how you were; he seemed genuinely concerned."

Chad stiffened in his chair. "You didn't tell him—hell, that is, well, you know—why I was there?"

"Only the juicy parts." Seeing his alarm, Lisa moved quickly to counter her flippancy. "Of course I didn't, Chad. I'm not crazy."

"No, that's my bailiwick."

"What *about* the shrink? Did he help?"

"Crazy himself, like all psychiatrists. But pleasant enough, just bats. Anyway, I can't believe he'll do much, but old Oeschlee talked me into keeping on seeing him a couple of weeks. So that's settled."

"Good."

"Lousy."

It seemed strange to him, but for the first time he became fully conscious of what Lisa was wearing. It was a hostess gown he'd never seen her in before. He couldn't explain—even to himself—why the dress made him so uncomfortable. It was beautiful, simple and classic, smooth and black, the kind of dress he would ordinarily have flattered Lisa for, its simple classic lines setting off her tall slimness. "Where'd you get the dress?"

"Oh, a little store down the street from Macy's. I've been looking for one like it for years." She'd noticed something ominous in Chad's way of asking his question and struggled to relieve where she thought the problem lay. "It was damned cheap, Chad. Really. In Boston or New York, you'd pay a fortune for one like this."

"No, no, no, it's fine. It looks great on you," he lied. He couldn't place the dress; he'd seen one like it somewhere, but couldn't place where. The associations were bad. There was something frightening attached to the dress, something evil and violent, something terrifying. But no amount of effort would place where he'd seen it.

Chad went into the kitchen and mixed himself another drink. He continued to worry about why the dress held such sinister overtones for him; it was a perfectly plain, simple sheath of black, the kind Lisa loved, the kind he loved her in.

"How about the nightmares, Chad?" Lisa asked as he sat down again. "I hope they're gone so you can come back and sleep in our room. You snore a little, sure, but I miss what went with your sleeping there more than I mind the snoring. By a long shot."

"They're not gone, dammit. I'll have to keep shacking up with my pillow."

Later, stimulated by the drinks, he stopped off on his way to his own room to "visit" with Lisa. She almost tore the clothes off his body, devouring him hungrily. "Oh, Chad, darling. I've missed you so much. I can't even start to tell you how much. I didn't know what was going to happen. It's stupid, I know, but honestly, Chad, when you left for the hospital that day I wasn't sure if you'd ever come back. It was horrible."

"I'm back." Chad kept feeling waves of sensation sweep across him as they lay naked on the bed, wrestling with each other, but for the first time he could ever remember in his life, nothing was happening. He kept trying to think of other things—he'd read somewhere years ago that one of the roots of impotence was the fear of it—but nothing seemed to work. Lisa was as expert as ever, but his prick, which should be soaring and straining, remained as limp as a thawed fish. He tried to pretend he didn't see the puzzled look slowly descending across Lisa's face; in his own puzzlement, he kept trying to tell himself—and Lisa—everything would be all right in a minute. It never happened.

"Chad," Lisa began.

"Oh, Jesus." He began to cry and Lisa began to cry and they lay there for what seemed like hours, wrapped together, sharing a mystery that neither could even begin to understand.

The next morning, Chad decided to go to his laboratory. It was not just a matter of how long it had been since he'd been there, or that he desperately wanted Koerkeritz to know he was back on deck and functioning; the fact was that he couldn't bear to look Lisa in the eye any more than he had to. To rob a man of his potency is to steal one of the fundamental elements that make him a man. Prep-school boys make jokes about it; later, they run across the same jokes in *Playboy*. Last night had been a final crushing blow to Chad's dwindling reservoir of self-confidence.

After he had said good-bye, keeping his eyes moving so he did not have to face Lisa's, he had just reached the door when he heard Lisa call after him. "Chad! Chad! It's a telephone call for you."

"Who?"

"A doctor—a Doctor Nils Lee. I think he said."

"I don't know any Nils Lee." Chad shrugged and walked over to pick up the phone. "Yes?"

"Professor Lefferts, this is Nils Lee. I'm an associate of Dr. duBrul's." Lee, sitting in his office winced as he said it, knowing he was going far beyond what Peter duBrul expected him to say, or what was the truth. "Dr. duBrul and I have been talking, and your name and the difficulties you've been having with dreams naturally came up. DuBrul and I often work these things out together." Nils Lee winced again at the lie.

On the other end of the phone, Chad was doing his own version of wincing. That damned duBrul—he had made him solemnly promise his case wouldn't be discussed with anyone, and already, after only one session, the promise had been shattered. "I wasn't aware," Chad said bitterly, "that Dr. duBrul was going to make me the subject of public discussion."

"It's nothing of the sort, believe me," said Lee, giving a small laugh to show Chad how ridiculous the idea was. "It simply is an area—nightmares like yours —that I specialize in. Think of it rather as a consultation. The information goes no farther than myself."

"That's what duBrul said, too."

"In this highly particularized area, the way to consider me is as an extension of Dr. duBrul. Your confidences are just as safe with me." Nils Lee gave Chad a moment to absorb the meaning of his statement, wondering what he would do if Professor Lefferts suddenly told him to get lost, then: "What I'd like to do, Professor Lefferts, is to have you visit me in my office. Or if it's more convenient, I can come to your home. In any case, I believe if we work together for a while, I can do much to alleviate your problem with the nightmares. I've done it before."

Through Chad's mind a great number of conflicting emotions were doing battle. Basically, he had first gone to see Dr. Oeschlee out of his concern for Robin and Lisa's welfare. The fear of what he might do to them during a seizure—along with Lisa's ultimatum —had driven him to accept a process repugnant to him: therapy. That part had been basically unselfish; he had loathed—and still did—every minute of therapy, but Chad had had to agree with Lisa about the dangers the seizures presented for herself and, in particular, Robin.

The nightmares, to Chad, had always seemed a far more private agony; no one was endangered by them, and now that he had moved into a separate room, no one was even affected by the nightmares except himself. But the lack of sleep, as evidenced by last night's disaster, was definitely taking its toll. On the other end of the phone was a doctor promising relief from them; he was an associate of Dr. duBrul's; no new faces would have to be brought into the picture. "Well, I don't know," Chad said into the phone. "I have to get to my laboratory on a more regular basis, so time's a little tight. . . ." A sudden recollection of the Roman Imperial Guard trying to drag him to his crucifixion raced through his mind; what Lee was offering began to grow on him. "In any case, if I should decide to see you, it would *have* to be at your office; I don't want to add any more worries here at home. . . ."

At that moment, Nils Lee knew he had won; he had him. "How about nine A.M. tomorrow?" he asked, as if the matter were already settled. "That should leave you plenty of time for your lab work."

"Well, yes, it would. I guess, well, sure."

It never occurred to Chad to question whether Nils Lee actually was an "associate" of duBrul's; his mind was too absorbed with the other facets of his problems. He was not even too surprised when he looked up Lee in the University Directory and discovered his office was not at Yale–New Haven, but was listed as being in one of the grander faculty suites at Davenport. The way Nils Lee was carried in the Academic Directory also bothered him only momentarily—head of the History Department and Executive Director of the Institute for Far Eastern Studies—many of the doctors attached to Yale–New Haven had exotic titles within the regular university roster.

The main point consuming him was that this Nils Lee had dangled in front of him the hope of relief from the nightmares; to Chad, such a hope was far more important than the minutiae of title or assignment.

Timmy Owen whistled as he ambled through the woods watching the intricate play of light and shadow the tall trees cast upon the leaf-carpeted ground. It was about four o'clock (later, he would tell people the thing happened at 4:05 on the nose; his father had given him a new watch for his thirteenth birthday and Timmy made any excuse he could think of to show it off).

Owen wasn't supposed to be here—everybody's mother had gotten cranky and possessive after the disappearance—but his mother was off visiting her cousin this afternoon and Timmy had slipped out of the house. In the distance he could hear the cars and trucks roaring along I-95, racing to New York City or Boston; he'd like to go to New York someday; living in Orange, Connecticut, your whole life could get a guy down. Boston they could keep; he'd been there once with his class and it stank.

He almost stumbled over it. A new tennis shoe, lying half hidden among the dead leaves on the ground. There was something familiar in the thought of this nearly new tennis shoe, but Owen couldn't place it; he did know that a new tennis shoe sure as hell was a crazy thing to find in the woods. As he looked around to see if he could find a mate to it—the shoe looked as if it might easily fit his own feet—he noticed a bright flash of color that was out of place in the muted tones of the forest. Whatever the color belonged to seemed to be under a fallen tree branch, its leaves brown and dead, and Timmy pulled the branch aside a little, still looking for the other shoe.

It was Ronnie. Sweet Mother of God, it was his friend Ronnie. He was naked except for white sweat socks, and there was something all wrong with where his head had been. Ronnie had been missing for three days now, and it was his disappearance that had made the mothers around there so tough to put up with. Now he had been found, and for once Timmy could have wished anyone else but himself had done the finding. Automatically, he pulled the branches of the tree limb back a little farther. A pair of eyes stared up at him dully. It was the head.

Timmy Owen screamed; he was still screaming when he'd finished the half mile to his own house and collapsed inside.

If Ronnie Cosaro could, he would still be screaming, too. Three days earlier he had gone to the weekly meeting of Troop B of the Boy Scouts, in the basement of St. Theresa's, about half a mile between his home and the exit ramp of I-95. It was a great night for him because he had gotten elected a pack leader; Timmy Owen had wanted the job, but he was a friend and in the end had gotten behind him to beat Diggy Schulz, whom they didn't like at all. At about ten o'clock—9:53 his buddy Timmy had insisted, always showing off that damned new watch of his—the meeting had broken up, and everybody started to wander off, some on bikes, some on foot, some picked up by cars.

His mom was originally supposed to have come and driven him home, but had had to beg off because his

younger sister came down with a bellyache. Damn
brat. He'd have to walk; his bike was as sick as his
sister. He said good night to the kids that were left
and gave Owen a special thump on the back for helping him get elected, then turned and began trotting
down the road toward his house. As he got to the corner, Ronnie Cosaro had to make a decision; the short
way ran through the little forest, the long way was
down the road that skirted it. Ronnie stood for a second trying to make up his mind, wanting to take the
shorter way, but a little afraid of those spooky woods
at night. Hell, he was a troop leader now, wasn't he?
He was too big to be frightened, he told himself, having to repeat the thought several different ways before
he could convince himself. Ronnie turned into the
woods, noticing a sleek new car parked on the shoulder of the road, pulled off most of the way and almost
into the woods themselves.

Lovers, he told himself, come into the woods to
screw; he wasn't too sure exactly how screwing worked,
but the older boys were always talking and laughing
about it, and if he got a good look at the couple doing
whatever they did, he'd have a real story to go with
his newly elevated status in the world.

Perhaps a hundred yards into the woods, Ronnie
thought he heard something ahead of him and began
to put his feet down very gently—"to stalk game," the
Boy Scout Handbook said, "place each foot down carefully, first the toe, then the heel, so as to avoid anything beneath your feet making a sudden sound and
frightening off your prey"—hoping to get a good look
at the screwing pair. He came to a little clearing, but
it was empty. They were somewhere else. Damn. Leaning forward against a tree, he strained to hear the
sound again; if it was loud enough, he could get a fix
on it and know just where to go look.

A sudden hand was clapped over his mouth, and a
strong arm slammed his back violently against a knee

and sent him crashing to the ground. Ronnie had been
so intent on listening to what was in front of him,
he'd never heard the thing moving up from behind.
The woman was all over him, pinning him tightly to
the ground, screaming in an unearthly voice something that made no sense. He struggled and twisted,
but this woman—Christ, what the hell was she wearing? It looked like a long black witch's dress from
Halloween—was as strong as a Samurai, and Ronnie
found he couldn't even wiggle. The crazy woman was
talking to him the whole time in a language he'd
never heard, and didn't pay any attention when he'd
get a brief second to come out from under her hand
long enough to speak. Suddenly, the hands grew
busier. One by one he felt his clothes pulled off him,
tossed away as if he'd never need them again. Even
his new Adidas went sailing into the air, everything
but his sweat socks, which the frightening lady didn't
bother with.

He was flipped over onto his stomach and felt his
hands tied behind him, then turned over onto his
back again. The crazy woman shouted at him in her
strange tongue and pulled a twisted-looking dagger
from her sleeve, holding it high in the air. Ronnie
screamed and cried, twisting and writhing beneath
her, but it didn't even seem to slow her down. There
was no one for miles to hear, and Ronnie knew it.
Christ, they always told you to stay away from strangers so you wouldn't be something called "molested,"
whatever the hell that was; but he hadn't had a chance
to stay away from this savage woman; she'd crept up
behind him and introduced herself with a wrestling
hold. She held her knife in one hand and his thing
in the other and made a couple of attempts to cut
it off, but gave up. Instead, she raised the knife in
the air again and pushed its point into his stomach,
drawing something in his flesh with it, for Christ's
sake.

Ronnie didn't have any idea what it was and really didn't care; all he wanted was to get away from this hugely strong woman and haul ass home. With a sudden pull on his knees upward, he caught her off balance and sent her crashing to the ground. Ronnie sprinted and got a little way into the woods, but it was damned hard to run with his hands behind him—he kept losing his balance without the arms to steady him, and fell down twice—and he could hear the woman running behind him. For a second he lost track of her. Suddenly from behind a tree, she stuck her foot out and sent him sprawling onto the damp leaves of the forest, then picked him up as though he weighed nothing and threw him over her shoulder. With a savage grunt she dumped him onto the ground of the clearing once again.

Looking down across his own nakedness, Ronnie saw her tying a rope to each of his legs; she spread them apart and tied each leg to the trunk of one of the trees at the clearing's edge. Ronnie kept yelling and screaming, although he wasn't sure why; he knew no one could possibly hear him, unless it was that pair of lovers who'd left their car at the edge of the woods, or maybe, Jesus, there weren't any lovers and the car belonged to this woman with the incredible set of muscles and the crazy language and the twisted dagger that looked like his Dad's corkscrew.

She was kneeling beside him instead of on top of him now, tying another rope around his neck and head. Ronnie tried to figure if she planned to hang him or what, but that didn't make any sense because his feet were already tied to the two trees. None of it made sense, damn it. The rope went under his chin and around behind the back of his head, back and forth like an insane cat's cradle, making almost a web around his head and neck. Then the woman stood up and walked over to another corner of the clearing; he turned his head as far as he could—the web around it made it tough to turn it very far—and could see her tying the rope to a sapling that she'd earlier pulled over so that it almost touched the ground, held down by a short piece of rope fastened to a stake.

Ronnie's heart sank. He'd been taught something a little like this in Indian Lore, one of the tests he'd had to pass to get his Merit badge. He knew what the Indians used the bent-over sapling arrangement for—springing traps—only now he was the game and this lady was about to do something far more savage than the Indians had ever thought of. Ronnie raised his scream to a shriek, but it was no longer a futile effort to attract help; it was the sheer terror of knowing what she was going to do to him.

For a moment the lady knelt beside him, mumbling and waving something in the air. From her long, flowing sleeve she produced another knife—a flat one—and went back to the stake holding the sapling down. He could see her cursing to herself and saw the bent-over sapling tremble, then suddenly spring upward with a roaring whoosh. Troop Leader Ronnie Cosaro never saw the sapling become straight again and was torn into too many sections to really care.

CHAPTER TEN

New Haven Police Chief Raymond d'Attollo stood at the edge of the clearing marked "Crime Site" and fretted. They had been able to keep Mary-Jo Camero's bizarre murder out of the papers, afraid that, as was so often the case, her killing would inspire other unbalanced people to imitate the ritualistic sidelights of her murder. The silence was easy because her body had been discovered by a state trooper; Mary-Jo's family were relieved not to have to tell the papers the grisly details of what really happened. To her classmates, to her more distant relatives, to the inscrutable Mr. Plankton, her death was explained as an accident. She was walking home from a baby-sitting job, you see, when she fell into one of the holes that dotted the empty lot behind the Downey house. Nothing much in itself, but sadly, she had hit her head on a rock and drowned in the shallow rain-water that still filled the hole. Sad. Tragic. Unavoidable.

This story even gave the police plenty of leeway to rope off the lot while they searched for clues; the official explanation was that they were searching for evidence of negligence on the part of the contractor who had abandoned the lot. There were some rumors that the story was rigged, of course, but that was about all. Her classmates showed up en masse and provided her with a stirring funeral.

Now, d'Attollo groaned to himself, it had happened again. He could not keep it out of the papers; this time the boy's body had been discovered by a friend and classmate, Timmy Owen. By the time young Owen called the police, half of his neighborhood already knew what he had found. Ronnie Cosaro, a Boy Scout troop leader, an honor student, a highly popular boy in his class and voted the most likely to succeed, had been brutally murdered—and in a shocking manner.

This was the part that really bugged d'Attollo. Like Mary-Jo, there was a cross or an X carved on his stomach. Like Mary-Jo, he had been trussed up and stripped. Like Mary-Jo, he had not been sexually molested. Well, yes, someone had tried to emasculate him, but had failed and given up. D'Attollo wasn't sure if that was sexual molestation or not; if whoever it was had succeeded, the emasculation would have somewhat eliminated the purpose of the molestation, wouldn't it? This kind of problem he would get to later.

Unlike Mary-Jo, Ronnie's head had not been shaved, but like her, he had been killed—in a bizarre fashion. D'Attollo shook his head. The manner of killing him was sickening. When the sapling had snapped upright, the force had literally torn his head out of his body; his legs, tied to the two different trees, had received the same sudden force, splitting his body partway up the middle.

There wasn't even a passing question as to whether it was the same person; it had to be. The question that was driving d'Attollo up the wall was *Why?* Neither killing made any sense. Both were ritualistic, both were brutal. Even more pressing, from the police chief's point of view, was another question: Would the killer keep on murdering teen-age children of either sex? He was afraid so.

"I found a little something," said d'Attollo's lieutenant, hurrying into the clearing. "There's a lady lives up the road—a Mrs. Klefak—who may've seen something. See, she was driving home that night just a little after the scout meeting broke up. Coming down the road along these woods, see, and a car comes shooting out of them right in front of her. Almost a pile-up. And this car, it goes partway in the ditch and a woman jumps out and starts screaming at the Klefak dame. Man, Mrs. Klefak swears the lady was wild. Hair all down over her face—dark, she says— and wearing some kind of long black dress that goes straight to the ground. 'Flowing' is how the Klefak woman described it.

"Well, she was so scared—the wild woman screaming at her—she can't remember what the dame says because she can't understand a word the woman says— Mrs. Klefak, she says she steers right around her and hauls ass for home. Last she saw of the woman she was waving her arms at her and screaming. Mrs. Klefak thought of calling the police, but couldn't figure out what she'd say. So, she didn't." For a moment, the lieutenant considered something; then, shyly, he offered an idea that had been running through his head ever since he'd talked to Mrs. Klefak. "It sounds like that same screaming dame someone spotted near the Camero girl's killing."

D'Attollo nodded unhappily. "It's sort of too bad they *didn't* have an accident. We might know who she was. And if she's the one doing these things we'd have a license number, at least." For a moment, d'Attollo studied the opening in the trees above their heads, thinking. "I never figured it to be a woman, damn it. Christ, she must be strong. This Klefak woman—can she describe the wild lady's face? What I'm getting at, could she pick her out in a lineup?"

The lieutenant slowly shook his head. "She was too damned scared to remember much except the long dark hair. And the spooky dress. Also, remember, she only saw her in her headlights."

"Didn't get any license plates, I guess."

"Hell, Klefak's a little old dried-up prune, y'know? And scared shitless. She can't even remember what color the wild lady's car was. She probably wouldn'a told anything, except we was making that house-to-house canvass."

"She didn't hear anything when she got home?"

"Negative."

"Okay. Well, tell her I'll be around to talk to her. I don't know whether her 'wild lady' is the killer or not. It sure sounds like it. But, Jesus, a woman, she says. . . ."

The lieutenant hurried off to take a formal statement from Mrs. Klefak and to tell her that Chief d'Attollo would come by later. D'Attollo stood for a moment, again seeking help from the stars visible above the clearing. With a resigned sigh, he turned and began walking toward the newspapermen and television crews gathered just beyond the rope near the edge of the road. It was going to be an exercise in evasion.

"Just keep looking at the light over your head . . . the pulsing light . . . your eyes may hurt a little, but force them to keep looking at the light . . . the pulsing light. . . ."

Chad felt self-conscious, but forced his eyes to keep staring at the tiny light that kept going on and off. It was too high to look at easily, and he could feel his eyelids fluttering as the strain of keeping them on the light became more pronounced. Like most people the idea of being hypnotized seemed silly to Chad; it was surrounded by centuries of myth and superstition, pictures of men with their hands outstretched sending waves of command out of the tips of their fingers, of bogus magicians, and of names like Merlin and Svengali and Mesmer.

But he had immediately sparked to Nils Lee. The man was hugely intelligent, but in no way pompous; he had an easygoing way that Chad found a distinct relief from the professional double-talk of Oeschlee, Loening, and even duBrul—although he had to admit duBrul (surprisingly for a psychiatrist) did not surround himself with Freudian jargon or vague analytical statements that declared him in possession of the truth and everyone else a hapless ignoramus. Nils Lee had gone into the nightmares with him and, unlike the rest, had not tried to underplay the effect they could have on him. He had seemed genuinely interested in the details of Marcus Flavius and particularly fascinated by Chad's feeling that somehow, in the dreams, he *was* Flavius, that he could speak his language, feel his emotions, and share his terror of crucifixion.

Even with all of this, though, Chad hesitated when Nils Lee had first asked him if he could hypnotize him. The prejudices swirled around him; the process sounded silly.

"I think most people are a bit skittish about it," Nils Lee had said. "There have been so many magicians and charlatans associated with hypnosis; at times it's been downgraded to the status of a parlor trick. But it can be highly effective. As I'm sure you've read, dentists and doctors are beginning to use it in place of anesthetics; childbirth is often made easier by using hypnosis rather than a local. I know it's hard for you —for anyone—to disassociate hypnosis from its old associations with sorcery and witchcraft and all that nonsense. . . ."

"No, no," Chad had assured him, in what was not quite a true statement. "I can get past that part easily enough." He thought for a second and finally fastened his eyes on Nils Lee's. "What I'm not sure I understand is why you should *want* to hypnotize me."

For a second Nils Lee had seemed to search the air. "I guess the best way to put it is that we need to find out why such an unusual dream should be repeated to the point of possessing you. Dreams don't just happen. Like anything else, they have roots. That root is what I'm looking for. Find it, and we should be able to eliminate your nightmares." Nils Lee had not been sure, even as he said it, if his answer came anywhere near to the truth.

But it had been enough for Chad. He was having growing difficulty in forcing his eyes to stay open; the positioning of the light was straining them more than ever; at the same time, its pulsing seemed to make him grow sleepier and sleepier. From a great distance he heard Nils Lee's soft voice speaking very slowly. "Try to keep your eyes on the pulsing light. . . . It's hard, I know . . . your eyelids are so heavy . . . so very, very heavy . . ." His voice seemed even farther away than it had before; Chad could still hear him talking, but barely. Almost without realizing it, he let his eyelids slowly close to cover his eyes; he seemed to be floating somewhere a million miles away from Nils Lee's office.

Nils Lee kept on talking, even more softly now, until he believed Chad was really under. For a moment, he stayed in his chair, watching the slow, rhythmic rise and fall of the man's chest. To make absolutely sure, he took a chromium probe and scratched Chad's palm with it; no response, not even a flicker of the eyes.

Reaching behind his desk, Lee turned on the Ampex; the tape machine was arranged in such a way that while no microphone was visible, it would pick up every nuance of every sound. Fumbling in anticipation, he flipped another switch, starting the videotape cameras; one was focused on the chair Chad sat in, the other gave a general picture of the room. With this he would be able to preserve each session in pictures as well as in sound.

"Chad. . . . Chad Lefferts . . . can you hear me?"

Chad's voice was at first indistinct and muddled. "I didn't hear you, Chad," Lee noted. "Can you speak more clearly?"

"Yessir," Chad's voice finally answered. "Yessir, and yes, I can hear you."

"Good. I want to ask you a few questions, Chad. Questions from your life in the nightmares. Do you understand me, Chad?"

"Yessir."

"Good. For instance, as Marcus Flavius you were living in Rome during the first century, A.D. Right, Chad?"

"Right." Lee noticed the subtle change in Chad's voice; the tone he used to give his answers was growing increasingly crisp and military.

"For instance"—Nils Lee had to refer to some notes Professor Kline of the Archaeology Department had given him—"can you tell me—I'm confused, you see—if I turned left from the Temple of Venus and Rome, is the Arch of the Emperor Titus on my right or my left?"

"I know of no one named Titus, and certainly there has been no emperor of that name. The Emperor Tiberius, even though a commoner by birth—Gaius Octavius—is a god. I am distantly related to Tiberius—he is my great uncle. I would know of such a thing, sir. There is and was no emperor named Titus."

Nils Lee stared at Chad for a moment. He had passed the trick question with aplomb; Marcus Flavius would not know of an emperor named Titus because Titus hadn't been born yet. Even more interesting to Lee, Chad's voice and manner became that of a soldier; he had stiffened in his chair and sat rigidly straight with his arms tightly folded across his chest.

His accent was changing, and an occasional lapse into Latin was noticeable.

"You certainly must have studied your history and geography of ancient Rome very closely," challenged Lee.

"I have never studied it, except what the tutors of Tiberius's household taught me."

"Not at Yale, not at Harvard, not at prep school?"

Chad looked confused, as if Nils Lee were talking of things and places he'd never heard of before. "I am sorry. I do not understand you."

"Well, let's move on to some other questions." One after the other, Nils Lee questioned Chad on the streets, the buildings, and the temples of first-century Rome—some of them quite obscure. Chad had an intimate knowledge of the city, but his language was growing increasingly a mixture of Latin and English; Nils Lee realized he should have someone with him who spoke the language. He shifted his approach. "Now, what I'd like to do"—he no longer addressed Chad by his name; twice, during the earlier questions, Chad had ignored anything that began with "Chad," at one point saying, "My name is Flavius"— "is to go back with you into one of your nightmares and have you talk about them as we go. . . ."

Nils Lee saw Chad stiffen; there was a great resistance in Chad, even under hypnosis, to exploring this area. "Let's see, you said you were related to the Emperor Tiberius. . . ."

"My father was sister to Agrippina, Tiberius's wife. My father was killed in the Battle of Alexandria, so, as is the custom, I was raised in Tiberius's household."

"I see. With such a background, how could you become a Christian?"

Chad shifted uncomfortably; the Roman soldier's pose faded before that of a nervous supplicant. "It is difficult to explain. The materialism and corruption of the empire troubled me; I thought there should be a return to democracy, as there was under Julius Caesar. In Jerusalem as a courier, I met a man named Simon. He talked to me. There were other Christians around him, and I felt suddenly I had found what I had been looking for all my life. But I know it is dangerous. Since Tiberius himself is a god, how can he allow a religion to exist that believes in only one god? . . ."

"And you know you will be, as you so fear, you will be crucified if the Imperial Guard finds out about you? I always thought Christians were put to death in the Coliseum by wild animals, not by crucifixion."

Chad had turned pale. He sat back down in his chair, the soldier vanished behind a man terrified for his life. Doggedly, he tried to keep talking to Lee, but his words were becoming a jumble of Latin and English, and Lee was having great difficulty understanding him. "I have never heard of a coliseum except at Rimini. Or of death by wild animals—terrifying thought—Christians are put to death for treason—if they believe in one god, that is treason against the Emperor—put to death by crucifixion, like all traitors and common thieves. . . ."

The sudden earlier shift in Chad's tenses had not escaped Nils Lee. When he started, he was speaking in the past tense. Now, he spoke in the present, as if at this moment he *were* Marcus Flavius. It was a profound change, and one Nils Lee had never witnessed in the hypnotic trances he had produced in many, many individuals. He was also fully cognizant that Chad had passed by another trap laid for him. The Coliseum was not started until the year A.D. 69, under Flavian, and was almost twenty years in construction. Flavius, then, would not have known of it during the early first century because it had barely been planned; using wild animals as the final solution to the Christian problem did not become a general practice until some time after the structure was finished. Shuffling through his notes, Lee took his eyes off Chad briefly. A sudden sound made him raise them again.

Chad had gone so deeply into his role as Flavius that, to himself, he had *become* the Roman; he was literally acting out events he felt happened to him some two thousand years earlier. The sound Nils Lee heard was Chad knocking over a chair. He was hiding behind it, whimpering in his strange mixture of Latin and English—now mostly Latin—holding one hand in front of his head to protect himself from the Imperial Guards he apparently saw advancing toward him. The whimpering became a scream. Turning his head sharply to warn others behind him, Chad suddenly yelled, "Hide yourselves, hide yourselves!" A terrible sound came from Chad's throat as he threw himself on the floor, trying to disappear behind the overturned chair. Shaken, Nils Lee clapped his hands loudly to bring Chad out of his hypnotic trance.

"I don't understand," Chad said, blinking his eyes and having some difficulty in shaping his words. He looked at the turned-over chair at his feet and absently reached down to turn it back upright. "I don't understand," Chad repeated, his expression one of deep bafflement. "You were going to hypnotize me . . . there was that crazy light . . . then . . ."

Nils Lee laughed. "You *were* hypnotized. Professor Lefferts. Believe me."

"I wasn't. All I got was sleepy"—a trapped smile appeared—"or is that what everybody feels?"

"More or less. Would you care to sit down in your chair again?"

As if realizing for the first time, Chad saw that he was clear across the room from where he had started. He hurried across the office and took his chair, as if he'd been caught doing something illegal. "Wow," he breathed, amazed by the whole experience. "You know," Chad added, "it's a little spooky, but I must have been talking about Flavius when I was"—he groped for the right set of words—"well, 'under,' or whatever you call it. I can always tell because I wake up feeling that Flavius—both in the nightmares and just now, again—is trying to warn me about something. I don't know what, but that's what I always feel."

Nils Lee knew this was really the time to excuse Chad for the day; hypnosis leaves many subjects unconsciously exhausted, and because of the violence of Chad's reaction, Lee had had to bring him out of his trance without having the usual time to reassure him of how well he would feel upon awakening. On the other hand, he wanted to bring Chad down slowly, and he still had more questions he should ask. "To move on to the seizures for just a minute, do you think there's any relation between the nightmares and the seizures?"

"No, they're completely separate, I think."

"Well, you must remember *something* after them. . . ."

Chad began to talk; he wasn't sure why, but the period under hypnosis had made him trust this man Nils Lee implicitly. More than any of the doctors at Yale–New Haven, more than Dr. duBrul, more, for Christ's sake, than Lisa. He could not explain it, but although he had never told *them* what he thought during the seizures, he was willing—even wanted—to tell Nils Lee. "Well, first of all, I always feel like I'm going back to someplace familiar . . . I hear voices, very faraway voices, and sometimes, other things. I always have this strange sensation that I'm being spun around inside the black hole near Omikron Blue—it's a place I sort of discovered, you see, first through mathematics, then backed up by astronomers working from my calculations—anyway, that's where I feel I am, and when I'm there, there's always this wild, screaming argument going on. A man and a woman, I think. And while they're in the middle of their terrible fight, I get this crazy feeling that I'm being pulled at from opposite directions, you know, that I'm damned near being torn in half by these people. Last time there was a little boy, too. Jesus, he was screaming. It sounded like he was being tortured. And then there are some—"

"Did it sound like your son, perhaps?"

"That crossed my mind, but I don't think so."

"And there's no relation at all, you think, between the violent things that happen in your nightmares and these feelings?"

"None."

Nils Lee wasn't at all sure that Chad was correct. He doubted he was lying; rather, he suspected the connection might exist but that Chad was unable to remember it at the moment. Casually, he planted a seed. "You're probably right, Professor Lefferts. However, it's something to consider. Your subconscious mind might be working out a problem. Maybe somewhere in your figures on Omikron Blue's black hole you can find something that would link the characters from your nightmares and this black hole together. . . ."

Chad looked bewildered. "Link them together?"

"Well, I use that little word 'link' somewhat loosely. But, as a mathematician, I'm sure you reduce everything to numbers anyway, one way or another. The period of Flavius's life can be reduced to numbers; certainly you have already reduced Omikron Blue to a whole series of them. . . ."

"It's possible, I suppose."

"Will you try, Chad? It could be of great help."

Chad nodded, still looking somewhat baffled.

To Nils Lee's surprise, it was Chad who suggested having another session. Huddling over engagement pads, it was set up for two days from now. For a long time after Chad left, Nils Lee sat in his deep red-leather chair, staring into the dark of his fireplace. It was true. What his first casual conversation with Peter duBrul had made him suspect was slowly turning into fact. More important, Chad might provide a verifiable example. He thought for a moment of Chad Lefferts and the effect this strange thing must be having on him. Certainly the man was moving into an area he would never have imagined existed.

Going to the Ampex, Lee played each section of the tape (he had not told Chad he was being recorded) that included a specific reference to a place, a building, a street, or a person's name. Tomorrow he would check these out with experts in the field. He could already guess what their answers would indicate: every fact Chad Lefferts had mentioned would turn out to be accurate.

CHAPTER ELEVEN

For several minutes Chad studied the yellow chalk equations on his blackboard. To him, what he had written was simple; to someone not schooled in the outer reaches of sophisticated mathematics and physics, the writings would appear strange, almost cabalistic.

To a physicist: $\Gamma = \sum\limits_{a_n}^{0 \times \infty} = \dfrac{(z-a)^3}{(m+n) \pm (V-m_n)}$

might represent the interaction between the relative energy of mass after Einstein's bending principle was applied to the gravitational torque; to the layman, it looked as if its writer had plunged deeply into grass.

Nils Lee's offhand suggestion—or was it so offhand? Chad wondered—that he perhaps try relating the black hole near Omikron Blue with the content of his nightmares had not escaped him. "Of course," Lee had amplified, "you will expect to find no actual physical correlation. However, it is accepted that dreams come from the unconscious. In *your* subconscious, a complex of mathematical formulae must also be present. Somewhere in your mind, there is a link, Professor Lefferts. Somewhere, I further believe, is a link between the nightmares and the seizures—also products of the unconscious."

At first it had seemed a mad idea to Chad. But quickly it grew on him. He could accept that after all of his work on Omikron Blue, the equations that had proven the black hole's existence must all be rattling around, preserved on the nonerasable recording tape of the unconscious. He could accept that. He could also accept that the terrifying nightmares—down to the last detail—were still rattling around inside his brain. And since false epilepsy was the agreed-upon diagnosis for the seizures, and the roots of the false epilepsy had always been explained to him as psychological, the reasons for them must be in the same tape bank, as it were. Find one, you'd find the other.

So far, the equations on his blackboard had produced nothing. The material he put in the equations was being fed him from the computer terminal. In trying to make a match, he had fed the computer a wealth of facts: dates, vector coordinates of places, geographical coordinates, names of people, his own personal statistics—anything he could attach a number to. No matter how he did the equations, the answer was always the same: 6.51 02. With 6.51 as the mantissa, raised to the second power, this was the higher mathematical expression of 651. To Chad, it made no sense. Ordinarily, when one varied an equation, one got a different answer, as would be expected. But no matter how he varied his, the computer kept feeding 6.51 02 back to him.

Omikron Blue was six hundred and fifty-one years away from earth, but that figure was simply one of the constants he had fed into the terminal; mathematically, it made little sense as an answer. If the computer's response had been, say, somewhere around two thousand, he might have been able to relate it to the time of Marcus Flavius, and he would have a positive link between the seizures and the nightmares. But six hundred fifty-one only got him back somewhere into the early thirteenth century, which was meaningless. Either all of his computations were in error, or his unconscious had a recording mechanism as faulty as the one he once tried to use for dictation. Chad looked at the symbols and numbers scrawled across the blackboard, erased everything, and started all over. Writing the very first symbol, Γ for gamma, the chalk broke; Chad hurled it across the room and sat down, mad at himself, mad at Nils Lee, mad at the entire situation that had him doodling nonsense equations on his board.

Maybe all of them—Oeschlee, duBrul, and Nils Lee —were as crazy as he was.

"What the God damn hell are you doing?" roared the voice over his phone. It was duBrul, and Lee knew it was going to require a lot of stroking to keep him in line; charm could only go so far.

"I don't understand, Peter," Lee stalled.

"Seeing Lefferts is one thing—although you know damned well I wasn't wild about it. Telling him you're my associate and that we work together is something else. Jesus, Nils, keep this up and I'll be up in front of a Board of Examiners. I told you, Lefferts is a sick man."

Nils Lee felt a sudden surge of worry course through him. Perhaps, after he'd left, Chad Lefferts had suddenly decided that hypnosis was a crock; he'd certainly asked little about why Lee was using it. Lee shifted himself uncomfortably. He couldn't have Lefferts walk out on him now; neither could he tell duBrul what he'd discovered yet, although he was sure the psychiatrist was aware of what he was probably up to. Forcing himself, Lee concealed his concern. "Did he complain, Peter?" he asked casually.

"Hell, no. I wish he had. He thinks you're terrific. We spent most of his session today talking about you, dammit."

"I'm on to something, Peter. I really am."

DuBrul flared again. "Not with my patient, you're not. Jesus, I know the kind of crap you're probably feeding him. You don't seem to understand that between the nightmares and the seizures Lefferts is on the thin edge of total crack-up. All he needs is a dose of your psychic double-talk and he'll wind up in restraints, being dunked in alternating hot and cold baths."

"It'll help him. In the end, it will really help him. Honest, Peter."

One after the other, the experts Nils Lee had called earlier that morning called back. Their responses had virtually identical openings: "I don't know how the hell you knew about that, Nils, but I looked it up, and damn it, it's right."

Every location, every name, every building that Chad Lefferts had mentioned on the tape was in the process of being proved out. For this, Lee had turned to experts in archaeology and to specialists in the history of the period. The easy references they had verified on his first call, but many of the allusions were so obscure even the experts had had to dig into reference books or call colleagues around the country to check. Without exception, what Chad's Marcus Flavius had said on the tape was one hundred percent accurate. One building he'd mentioned—the temple of Agrippina Claudiae—described by Flavius as being "just below the Tarpean Rock, a disgraceful ruin of a building for the center of Rome, but one I understand they plan to rebuild"—had caused the noted archaeologist Dr. Vincent Machri to telephone a colleague in Italy.

"I had to, Nils. The fact that there was another, earlier, temple beneath the present one was only discovered about three weeks ago. I knew of it; Dr. Delacombi of the Italian Institute knew of it. He was the man who told me. But in the strictest confidence. The information was released to no one else; Delacombi was waiting for the annual archaeological conference to release his find. I didn't want him to think that I'd tipped his hand. How you found out about it remains a mystery to me; archaeology is a very closed-mouthed field—usually."

Nils Lee could feel his heart beginning to pound. In theory, all of the other references could have been dug out by someone with enough archaeological expertise and the time to do it. Even the obscure mentions of long-vanished buildings and minor historical characters could have been dug out of the footnotes of archaeological tomes. But the existence of the old temple of Agrippina Claudiae had been known to no one in modern times until Flavius. In answer to some question of Lee's, he had mentioned it on his tape.

It was happening. What Nils Lee himself sometimes dismissed as a hard-to-believe obsession was finally being proved in front of his eyes. Nils Lee sat back in his chair, wondering, *Why* Chad Lefferts?

"I've told you before. I don't know why, but that damned dress bothers me."

Lisa flared. "You're going to pick my wardrobe now?"

Not surprisingly, with their history of exquisite in-fighting, Chad responded in kind. "I could do better than you. *Anybody* could. That rag looks like something left over from Halloween."

Lisa minced across the room, burning inside. "Tell me, sweetie pie, do you do hats, too?"

"You can go shit in yours."

"Maybe your sideline in dress- and hat-designing is why you can't get it up anymore. If I was a boy, you might do better."

Chad stared at Lisa in disbelief. In these arguments, he knew just about anything went, but this was reaching so low for a comeback he was having trouble believing Lisa had said it. So was Lisa. "I'm sorry, Chad. I shouldn't have said that."

"I read in this morning's papers about some woman who killed a little boy out in Orange. Before she killed him, she tried to cut his balls off. Is that what you're trying to do to me, Lisa? Is it? *Castrate* me? That lady in the papers—she wore a long black dress, too."

"Chad, I told you I'm sorry I said it."

Abruptly, Chad's whole body began to tremble in a delayed reaction. This woman he loved—this woman who was supposed to love him—how could she have said what she said? Still shaking, Chad walked to her chair and stood over her where she sat; he could feel his face flushing and his eyes bulging. He had never, he thought, been so consumed by fury as he was at this instant. From his mouth, when he tried to speak, came only strangled sputterings. Lisa looked at him in alarm.

"I'm sorry, sweetheart. My God, it was just one of those things that pops out when we fight. I didn't mean it. You know that."

Chad reached over and took a small vase from Lisa's side table—it was something she'd picked up in Germany, a primitive attempt by medieval artisans to produce soft-paste porcelain—and hurled it as hard as he could against the stonework around the fireplace. Lisa winced; the piece was crude but really quite pretty. Chad spun, grinding the shards of porcelain under his shoe as he stalked out of the room.

Saddened by everything that had happened, Lisa painstakingly tried to assemble the pieces flat on the floor; she knew they could do remarkable things in reconstruction pottery at the Yale Museum of Art. But some of the pieces themselves—the ones Chad had deliberately pulverized with his shoe—were beyond reasonable recovery. Sadly, she got a dustpan and swept the shattered vase into it.

Over their years together, they had quarreled many times, yes. Their arguments had become almost an art form. But never before had Chad resorted to physical violence on objects; nothing had ever before been thrown, even in moments of the most extreme frustration.

By no standards could Lisa be described as dense. She realized full well that what Chad had really wanted to shatter was not a medieval vase, but her. Lisa shivered.

The light pulsed on and off like the eye of a malevolent demon. "I'm using a slightly different technique today, Chad"—they'd gotten on a first-name basis at the beginning of today's session, although Chad found he still tended to refer to Nils as Dr. Lee. "I will speak very little to you as you go under. To the pulsing light, I've added sound."

As Chad waited, Nils Lee pressed a small switch in front of him. The sound at first seemed slight, a thin, high-pitched beep that was in sync with the light— or possibly a fraction ahead of it. The longer he stared at the light, the louder the sound seemed to grow; just before his eyelids fluttered down, unable to stay open anymore, the beeping was a deafening roar that filled his ears and shut out everything else.

Nils Lee watched, then went over to Chad with a small, pointed instrument, scratching first the back of Chad's hand, then his cheek, to see if there was still any automatic nervous response. There was none. Chad sat, his mouth open a little, his hands resting loosely in his lap, as removed from the room as if he were dead.

Turning, Nils Lee nodded someone into the office. Dr. Li Soong moved quietly into a chair facing Chad. Soong was from the language department, a gentle man with a rare knowledge of dead languages long forgotten by the rest of the world. He was also a frequent guest of Nils Lee's at the Institute for Eastern Studies, and was a fellow enthusiast in Lee's private obsession. After the experience of the first hypnotic session, Lee wanted to have someone present who could speak colloquial Latin; he hoped to take Chad far back enough into the past so that he could *become* Marcus Flavius again. From that, he figured, they could learn much.

With a nod, Nils Lee handed Dr. Soong his first card. "Chad, Chad, this is Nils," read the linguist. "I want you to reach back through the years until you are a man named Marcus Flavius. Can you do that for me, Chad?" The deception—Dr. Soong playing the role of Nils Lee—was designed so that once Chad began to lapse into Latin there would not have to be a sudden change in the voice giving him orders and asking him questions.

"Yes, Dr. Lee. I can." Chad's voice, as it had been at this same stage of the first session, was as flat and expressionless as an automaton's.

"Good," read Soong. "Will you do that for me, Chad?" read Soong. "Go back through time, Chad, all the way back to the first century. . . . Think, Chad . . . let yourself float freely back to your life as Marcus Flavius. . . ."

A sudden scream came from Chad that startled

both men. His eyes, wild and terrified, fastened on them as if they were the soldiers of the Imperial Guard advancing upon him with their spikes and hammers to nail him to a cross. An anguished stream of Latin poured from him as he pulled himself flat against the wall, then suddenly darted to one side and pressed himself into a corner.

"He says, 'No, no, I am a nephew of the Emperor's,'" whispered Dr. Soong, translating Chad's Latin into English for Nils Lee's benefit. "'I have done nothing,' he says. 'You are mistaken.'"

Chad leaned forward slightly, apparently listening to one of the soldiers speaking to him. "'You are wrong, I tell you,'" translated Soong, his own eyes becoming as wide as Chad's. "'I am no Christian. Christianity is treason. Would a relative of the great Emperor Tiberius commit treason?'"

Chad listened again; Soong whispered an aside to Lee. "It is pure colloquial Latin—better than my own. It is difficult to imagine how he could have learned to speak it like that. I don't know what to say."

Chad had finished hearing the Imperial Guard's spokesman out. In a stance of arrogant disagreement, Chad contradicted something the man of the Imperial Guard had just finished saying. "'Your spies are wrong, Gaius. They lie to you for the money.'" Soong kept his whispered translations as short as he could and still gave Nils Lee the meaning of what Chad was saying. "'You should know better, my friend,' he is saying, 'than to trust your informers. You have my word: I am no Christian. The accusation is part of a plot.'"

Whatever the guard's reply, Chad's—Flavius's—expression changed abruptly. The scornful stance was replaced by an expression of abject terror; Flavius's voice became a series of hoarse grunts and cries as he struggled with the first two soldiers who reached him, flailing the air with a sword only he could

see. Over and over again, Soong told Lee, Flavius
screamed, "No, no! I am no Christian!" but the
soldiers, armed by their spies' information, would
not listen. Suddenly Chad stopped struggling and
fell on his knees, the tears running down his face
freely; his hands were clasped together and he turned
his face upward, lost in a sudden prayer of contrition.
"Oh, my Jesus," he wept. "I have denied you. For
the sake of my miserable self, I have denied you. Forgive me, forgive me. . . ."

In some ways, Chad looked ridiculous kneeling
there, crying like a small boy playing some part in a
children's play; but for the most part, the entire scene
was enormously moving. At one point Nils Lee swallowed hard watching Flavius suddenly turn repentant,
realizing that he had betrayed his Savior.

The moment of repentance did not last long. While
still on his knees, Flavius had apparently spotted an
opportunity to make a break for freedom. Shooting
to his feet as if tied to a spring, he tore through
imaginary restraining hands, raced across the room,
and sailed out through the window of Nils Lee's office. The noise of shattering glass and breaking wood
filled the room. Lee and Soong ran to the wreckage
of the window and looked out. They could see Chad,
farther down the building, hiding behind the bushes
of the foundation planting. "Chad . . . Chad . . ."
Lee called gently. There were people in the quadrangle of Davenport and he didn't want Chad to
come out of his trance and suddenly have to con-
front them, or he would have clapped his hands
and broken Chad's hypnoidal state then and there.

"Chad . . ." he called again, and helped by Dr.
Soong, began climbing out through the shattered
window.

Seeing him, Chad apparently thought it was the
Imperial Guard coming up behind him again, and
with a roar of fear burst through the bushes onto the

manicured grass of the quadrangle. Lee was left with no choice. "Chad!" he roared, and clapped his hands together as loudly as he could. Several people on the cement crosswalks turned to stare at Chad and him; they didn't know whether it was a game or whether something terrible they should report was taking place.

For a moment Chad stood stock-still on the lawn, shaking his head and struggling to focus his eyes. "What . . . what the hell?" he asked Nils Lee in a confused voice, one hand straying to his head as if to brush something away.

Gently, Nils Lee led him in through the front door back into his office. Lee had forgotten that Soong was unknown to Chad and had to explain him; Chad did not appear reassured by either the explanation or Dr. Soong's solemn promise he would tell no one of what he had seen.

After Soong had left, Chad asked again: "Why, Dr. Lee, was that man here?"

Nils Lee sighed. "He's a linguist, Chad. You see, today, as you did two days ago, you lapsed into colloquial Latin. I can't even speak academic Latin, much less colloquial. Dr. Soong can. He was here, at my invitation, to translate for me."

"*I* was speaking Latin?"

"Perfect Latin. Of a kind you couldn't learn at any school." Something was bothering Lee and he put it into words. "Did you ever study Latin, incidentally?"

"Only at the *amo-amas-amat* level." Chad looked at his scratched hands and at the remains of the window. "I was having one of my nightmares, I guess. Did you learn anything?"

"I am learning a great deal, Chad. More at each session."

"Like what?"

Nils Lee paused for a moment before answering. "I think it would be better if we had another hypnotic session before I go into that, Chad. I can tell you I am very convinced that I know the cause of your nightmares and probably the seizures as well. Just bear with me without specifics for a couple more days."

Chad shrugged. Lee's were the most promising words he'd heard in months.

CHAPTER TWELVE

With Robin at school, Lisa found her time increasingly free. This afternoon, she had hurried home from her session at the art school and picked up her camera. Robin was out somewhere with Mrs. Lafferty, and Chad was at his lab. It was getting dark earlier every day, and the weather at the moment was dreary and overcast, but she had a built-in strobe flash on her Canon AE-1, and there should be no problem.

Briskly Lisa walked around the block and slipped in through the same opening in the wall she had used before. She found herself wondering if the friendly Mr. Thomas had seen her go in; she supposed not. There'd been no sign of life at his house. It only took Lisa moments to find the first statue—the one that had initially terrified Robin so much—standing in the tall, waist-high grass. Walking in a circle around the wooden prie-dieu, she flattened the grass as much as she could with her feet to give her camera an unobstructed field. Then, from every angle, from every degree of long shot and close-up, Lisa took pictures of the ancient wooden figure, its hand raised in a silent benediction, its oversize eyes staring at her sadly. Lisa was satisfied. When developed, the pictures would provide a complete catalogue of everything one could see of the prie-dieu. The experts at the art school could go over them at their leisure, hopefully providing her with a date and a country of origin. Lisa began to move forward again, toward the arcade she'd seen in the rear of what had once been a garden, but stopped, turned around, and came back to the prie-dieu. Gently her fingers ran across the ancient wooden surface. Reaching into the camera's gadget bag, she pulled out a small, sharp knife—Lisa used it to trim the ends of the 35mm film she loaded into cartridges herself—and moved back to the prie-dieu. The wood that looked so soft and half rotten when you looked at it was surprisingly hard. It took her several tries and a good deal of sawing before she was able to cut off a respectable piece of it, taken from the base, where it would not spoil the statue's primitive beauty. This small section of wood, Lisa figured, would give the experts one important element that no picture could provide: a physical specimen of the wood they could study for signs of aging, grain, kind of tools used to carve it, and so on. It was carefully wrapped in a piece of Saran Wrap and replaced in the gadget bag.

Lisa glanced at her watch. The picture taking had taken more time than she had expected, and she still wanted to investigate the colonnade or cloisters she had seen that dreadful day here with Robin. She would have to hurry; Mrs. Lafferty was always obliging about staying with Robin, but Chad—he should be back from his lab by now—couldn't stand the woman. Leaving them alone too long was just asking for trouble, particularly with Chad acting increasingly more unreasonable as each day passed.

The closer she drew to the cloisters, the more fascinated Lisa grew. It was a long, low structure built entirely of stone. Thick columns—she suspected they dated from medieval times, with an attempt at the classic lines of Greek and Roman architecture, but with none of its grace. The sense of proportion necessary to provide this wouldn't appear until later, during the Renaissance. Lisa suspected the cloisters predated the prie-dieu, but not by much. Studying it, she could see the colonnade ran the entire width of the ruined garden, with a gently sloping half-roof typical of medieval architecture. Below were the stone floors of the cloisters. From the condition of the tilework on the roof, no attempt had been made recently at even a partial restoration. At one end of the stone path, still connected to the colonnade and sharing the same roof, was a small stone building. The entire arrangement was as fascinating as it was mysterious; it was rare to find such a building at the end of such cloisters, which usually turned a right angle at each end and enclosed a complete area. This design sprang from a cloisters' original raison d'être as a place that could provide shelter for the nuns or monks as they walked, deep in meditation or prayer, on their daily exercise tours. Usually the cloisters formed a hollow square and served not only to protect the monastery's sisters or brothers from the rain and snow during their mobile devotions, but also to allow them to move under cover from one building to another. Lisa looked for what she thought would have been the center of the enclosed area here, because that point ordinarily was graced by a religious statue. She wondered if the prie-dieu might serve that function, but she could see nothing, and the prie-dieu was much too far forward to be considered anywhere near the center.

Lisa pulled the Canon AE-1 from her gadget bag and changed the lens from her usual 50mm to a 28mm wide-angle; this would allow her to get the entire cloisters in one shot without having to move so far back she would lose detail. The curious building at

the cloisters' right end would have to be photographed
and investigated separately; she could see a small
slitlike door in the building's center and was impatient
to get through her distance photography so she could
move closer and see what was inside.

As she put the viewfinder to her eye and focused,
she had a strange feeling that she had picked up a
shadow of someone hurrying out of the building
along the cloisters. Startled, she took the camera from
her eye to get a better look. She could see nothing.
But when she raised the camera again, just outside
the viewfinder's eccentric focusing circle, the shadow
seemed to be moving again. This time she did not
lower the camera, but began shooting.

A sudden rumble above her shook the ground. A
rolling September thunderstorm had been muttering
in the distance for some time, but from its sudden
loudness Lisa knew the storm was almost upon her.
She glanced up at the racing black clouds and turned
back to her viewfinder to try to finish her shooting if
she could.

The first drops of rain came sporadically, but fell
with such force they seemed to have been hurled at
her by an angry sky. For a moment she stood there,
nursing an illogical hope that the rain would not
grow so heavy that she'd have to fold up her expedi-
tion for the day. Almost as if the sky had heard her,
the pelting turned into driving sheets of water. Lisa
swore, and jammed the Canon AE-1 into her gadget
bag before the rain could get to its expensive electronic machinery. Lisa had no raincoat with her and
could feel the water running down her face and neck,
and beginning to soak through to her body. At first
she had wanted to run through the overgrown garden and back to her house, but the memory of the
rotted well-cover that Robin had fallen through was
fresh in her memory; running, the same sort of thing
could easily happen to her.

Hunching her shoulders, Lisa picked her way carefully through the garden to where she could dimly make out, through the sheets of driving rain, the narrow opening in the wall. She cupped her hand over her eyes to try to keep the rain out of them, but her hair was so wet, the water kept running down her face and blurring her vision anyway. Above her, the thunder crashed about her ears. Damn, but she wished she could see better. Finally, finding the opening and once safely outside, she ran as fast as she could around the block to the dry safety of her own house.

Inside the small stone house at the right end of the cloisters, someone besides Lisa was having trouble seeing. Angrily, a pair of eyes peered out through one of the slitlike windows in the building, trying to understand what this intruder, Lisa, was doing. They had watched Lisa come in and now they watched Lisa leave, battling the same downpour that was making strange hollow noises on the building's tile roof. As Lisa got farther away, the narrowness of the opening made following her harder. Like Lisa, the owner of the eyes swore in frustration.

Watching the intruding figure grow dimmer, the eyes relaxed a little and allowed themselves to look away. For the moment, the stranger was no threat. Looking out through the slit again, the eyes watched Lisa slip out through the opening in the wall. An uncomfortable suspicion grew, however, that Lisa would be back.

There were things to get ready.

Dr. Peter duBrul was sulking and knew it. The fact irritated him; sulking was a regression to childhood behavior that had no place in the emotional repertoire of a psychiatrist. From every possible angle, he'd tried to analyze the possible motivations for his reaction. DuBrul could tell himself quite logically that Nils Lee was endangering his patient's taut mental state and almost believe it. Yet something more was bothering duBrul; his own reaction was far out of proportion, particularly considering that Nils was an old friend and that he should have been able to persuade him out of his hypnoidal sessions. Instead, he had allowed himself to become involved in an acrimonious battle with Nils, as if Chad were some prize to be won by the highest bidder. Stupid. Nils Lee had no ulterior motive, however wrong his behavior might be; it was that insane preoccupation of his with the psychic—something he had acquired in the Far East, perhaps—that was driving Nils on. Someday, when things between Nils and himself were back to normal, he must have a long, semidrunken talk with him and try to discover how such a bizarre preoccupation had ever gotten so in control of him. At times the man seemed virtually possessed by it.

Glumly duBrul got up from his chair. He could talk to Nils, but he already knew he wouldn't be able to shake his belief. Perhaps this single-mindedness of purpose—even if as grossly misdirected as he believed—was one of the reasons Nils had always fascinated him; duBrul didn't know. He *did* know Nils was a fascinating man.

The fascination that Nils Lee held for duBrul was not limited to him alone. Lee's beliefs and theories on a variety of subjects had reached out beyond the cloisters of normal academic circles and now had touched the general public as well. For the head of the history department at a university like Yale, the theories struck some people as curious; for the executive director of the Institute of Far Eastern Research, they began to make a little more sense. For anyone in the business of educating others, his beliefs were controversial, if not explosive.

The year before he had published a small book on a subject that had long fascinated and sometimes almost totally consumed him: *Plato to Patton: The Reincarnates*. Unlike most books published by university presses, his had sold well enough to reach stores outside academic communities, making him a sought-after speaker on the lecture circuit. A little baffled by the volume's success, Nils Lee saw it as a chance to open the minds of others to an area he considered long overlooked.

In his book, Lee described not only the religious, traditional views of reincarnation, but his own: "Unlike theists of the Eastern religions," he wrote, "modern Western views of reincarnation turn to physics for their explanation. According to the Law of Conservation of Energy, it is an accepted tenet that an energy mass can be changed in form and direction, but it can be neither diminished nor eliminated. Thus, the kinetic energy of a spinning wheel is not lost when the wheel stops turning, merely translated into the heat-energy of friction. Similarly, the complex of electric energy patterns that are the sum of our brains—our souls, or *karman*, to use the Eastern word for it—can be changed in form, but not diminished or eliminated. As with any other form of energy, the laws of physics require its continued existence, undiminshed.

"The totality, though, of a person's electrical brain-energy patterns—what G. B. Shaw described as the 'Life Force'—moves as a whole, or unit. As with all energy masses, the natural laws of physics governing it require it to remain in this form. To accomplish this, the brain energy masses seek out a home in a newly born individual, one whose own electro-energy patterns are not yet fully developed enough to resist it. Some people are aware of this presence within them—the sharing of their bodies with the energy mass of someone else's previous life—others are not. In some cases, the legitimate karman in the host-individual's body and the presence inside him of somone else's energy masses results in a lifetime struggle for dominance. Who is to be in charge? The energy mass of the previous lifetime, or the energy mass of the host-individual?

"In the Eastern religions, the same basic principles are called upon, but dressed up in the language of morality and the struggle for good. The laws of God replace the laws of physics. The different faiths—Hinduism, Jainism, Buddhism, and Sikhism—have only slightly different variations on the theme of the karman's struggle to reach *moksa,* which is described as a desirable state in which all desire has been extinguished. Picturing this progression as lives moving on an endless wheel, through birth and rebirth, the karman eventually hopes to reach *nirvana*—a oneness with God. Lest we dismiss it too offhandedly, remember that one quarter of the people on earth are members of one or the other of these faiths, and accept reincarnation as a matter of course. . . ."

To Nils Lee, the book was only a watered-down version of what he considered provable fact, not at all representing the strength of his conviction. To the public, the book was a fascinating excursion into a field of psychic exploration, redolent with astral spirits, earlier lives living on inside unwitting hosts, and even a bit deliciously frightening. To most of the academic community, the book raised suspicions that a once-valuable fellow worker had cracked under the strain; Yale had been sullied, their profession itself tarnished, by the publication of such utter nonsense.

To Chad Lefferts, once he was told of it, Nils Lee's book would begin by presenting a ridiculous face. With time, the concept would consume him as surely as one of Lee's energy masses looking for a new host-body to occupy would devour its later reincarnation.

CHAPTER THIRTEEN

Chad was reading *When We Were Six* to Robin. It was an unusual thing for him to be doing—usually he was so absorbed in mathematical abstractions he had little time left over for what the average father takes upon himself as one of his parental duties. Lisa stood in the hall, dripping onto the tiles, almost lulled into a childhood sleep listening to Chad read of Christopher Robin and Pooh Bear, Eeyore and Kanga, and Piglet and the Heffalump. Every time his father came to the name of Christopher Robin, of course Robin would whoop with delight; it was as if the book had been written specially for *him*.

Lisa tried not to notice the small pool of water that was gathering at her feet. Chad was a good reader, dramatic and able to effect sudden changes of voice that made the characters seem very much alive. She brushed the tangled wet hair out of her face and smiled softly. A shiver of cold ran through her, her drenched body reacting to the wetness and the sudden cold of their front hall. Reluctantly, she began planning some way to slip past the library door and up the stairs without being seen. In a very stern voice, after the incident in the garden where Robin had fallen into the well, Chad had already made his position clear: "Never take Robin in there again, Lisa. It's too damned dangerous," he had pointed out. "Matter of fact, I don't want you to go in there either. I'm not being arbitrary, but it's my misfortune to love you, and I'll be damned if I want you to kill yourself drowning in some stupid well."

"Well, you are being that. Arbitrary, I mean." Lisa had giggled. "What are woman's rights *for*, if a lady can't go get herself drowned when she feels like it?"

"I'm not kidding, dammit. I'm just telling you: stay out of that crazy place."

Lisa had shrugged. Because of Chad's unpredictable reaction to things since the seizures, she had not, to this day, told him the fascinating history of the place that Mr. Thomas had given her. She had merely stopped mentioning anything about how curious it was their house should have had its rear upper windows sealed. Mr. Thomas's account had provided more than ample reason for that.

At the moment, her major concern was to keep Chad from knowing she'd been there, and her drenched clothing and gadget bag were tip-offs she'd rather Chad didn't see just now. Carefully, she began tiptoeing toward the staircase, keeping herself as flat against the wall as she could.

"God have mercy, Mrs. Lefferts, where have you been, child? You'll catch your death, don't you know." Lisa hadn't heard Mrs. Lafferty come into the hall through the swinging door from the kitchen, and her bellowing voice shook her to the ground. She tried to signal Mrs. Lafferty to be quiet, but the woman was not easily stopped. "Get into a hot tub, child, and I'll bring you a nice cup of tea." As always, she pronounced it "cuppa tay." "Nothing like it, don't you know, to chase off a chill."

Lisa's heart sank. In the library, Chad's voice had

stopped. A moment later he appeared in the doorway. The argument she'd expected never materialized. "I got caught in it coming from the library," Lisa lied. "Wow, it came down like something."

"Instead of a 'cuppa tay,' maybe a glass of booze would work better." Mrs. Lafferty sniffed and disappeared back through the swinging door into her domain. Professors. Worse than priests, they were.

Lisa accepted the offer gratefully. If Chad had any suspicions—it would be unusual if he didn't—he was careful not to let them show. Robin was in the hall by now, giggling with delight at the sight of his thoroughly soaked mother.

"I'll take care of him." Chad laughed. "I'll bring you that drink—stiff—in the tub and read some more Milne to him."

Lisa smiled gratefully and sloshed her way slowly upstairs. Chad was being so normal, so kind, so thoughtful, it was difficult to remember he was the same man who could throw things around the room when he got mad. Or had seizures while driving cars that almost killed them all. Or left his son to do a balancing act on the tower battlements. Maybe he was getting better. A sudden thought struck her. Or maybe he was getting worse, and this would be his last rational moment before he shattered into ten thousand well-educated pieces. She didn't know, she didn't know. Chad had become as opaque and elusive as the dark, fleeting shadow in her viewfinder—and sometimes as ominous.

The small light pulsed insistently, blinking on and off at a measured pace like the eye of an angry demon. Today the light had been placed at an even more awkward angle, higher and to one side, forcing Chad to strain his eyes more than ever; the muscle strain became evident the moment Nils Lee told him to begin looking at it. The sound was also different from the time before, a muted bell-like ringing—the distant peal of bell changes in an old church.

Chad was aware that while Lee was talking to him, Dr. Soong was sitting quietly in a chair. The fact no longer bothered him. Nils Lee's explanation of why the linguist was necessary made sense after a fashion, although Chad kept stoutly denying he knew anything beyond the most rudimentary Latin.

He was almost in a trance and his eyelids were fluttering. From a great distance, he could hear Nils Lee speaking to him again.

"Moments . . . it will be a matter of moments, Chad . . . and I want you once again to take yourself back through time to your other life in Rome. . . ."

Nils Lee studied Chad carefully. Behind him sat Dr. Soong, studying his notes. Chad was in a cataleptic state, there was no argument on that point. His eyes were open and staring, looking at him but not seeing. His mouth had dropped slightly open and his breathing was deep and slow. But to the practiced eye of Nils Lee, there was something wrong that he couldn't put his finger on. Unlike his behavior in the previous trances—Chad was what Lee would have described as an "excellent" hypnotic subject—he had not yet responded to Lee's gentle order that he move back to his other life in Rome. This was both unusual and troubling. Nils Lee, a little more forcefully this time, repeated his suggestion.

"I want you to take yourself back through time to your other life in Rome. The life in which you were Marcus Flavius, leader of the Tenth Cohort, serving in the army of your great-uncle the Emperor Tiberius . . . back in time, Chad . . . Float . . . Chad . . . float back through time. . . ."

From the sound of Lee's voice, Dr. Soong could guess that something was not going according to plan, and lowered his notes to watch. Nils Lee was studying

Chad's every movement and made a gesture for Soong
to make less noise. Chad seemed to begin thrashing in
his chair; one hand remained on the arm of the chair,
but the other, his left, began to make small erratic
movements, lifting itself off the arm, clutching the air
as if trying to find something, then with a thud, dropping back onto the chair's arm. Chad's breathing, Nils
Lee noticed, had become shallow and more rapid; he
could see his diaphragm contracting and expanding
as if he were gasping for air. Lee turned to Dr. Soong.

"Try him in Latin," he whispered. "Quick, say what
I said to him in Latin."

Dr. Soong stood up and walked to one side of Chad,
giving the Latin translation softly but firmly to him.
Chad's head swung back and forth in a gesture of re-
fusal; both hands gripped the arms of the chair until
his knuckles grew white, almost as if they were tied
to it; his feet remained planted, held to the floor by
invisible shackles. Suddenly, Chad's body began swaying back and forth, then arched in a series of convulsions that lifted his chest and stomach away from his
chair, while his hands and feet seemed nailed to it. It
was like watching a man in the electric chair, his
arms and legs held to the chair by straps, his body the
only thing free to respond to the amperage coursing
through him. For the last few seconds, a low moaning
had been coming from Chad. Abruptly, it stopped. Dr.
Soong looked at Nils Lee questioningly. With a gesture of his hands, Lee expressed hopeless confusion.
Leaning back, he thought for a second, running what
had happened through his mind and searching for a
way to get Chad back under control and into his life
as Flavius.

The strange sound that had suddenly come from
Chad startled them both; it had the cadence of a
prayer, but the words were neither English nor Latin.
Without any change of his expression, Chad's voice
had shifted into a high register, the harsh guttural

words pouring from him in a paean of anguished complaint. The words ran together; the pitch of his voice remained high, but within its shrill, seemingly female register, varied up and down from deep to high; occasionally there would be an explosion of sound, as if Chad were cursing in a language only he could understand.

Nils Lee and Dr. Soong looked at each other. Noiselessly backing away from Chad, Soong leaned over to whisper to Lee. "What's happening, Nils? Those words—I think it's Frisian. Old Norse. No one has spoken it for centuries."

"What did he say?"

Soong shrugged helplessly. "It's an incomplete language, Nils. So much of it was lost. But I can pick out a word here and there—'God'—'verratough' for treason —'anklagich,' I accuse—'toteaugh' for kill—other words and phrases I remember. It's been some time since I really worked at Frisian. What is happening, Nils?"

"I don't know."

The words from Chad had subsided into a guttural muttering. But the thrashing in the chair had returned; Chad's head was thrown back against the back of the chair, and even from where they sat, Nils Lee and Soong could hear his teeth grinding angrily. One arm tore itself loose from the chair and began to wave wildly over his head. The force of his hand sent a lamp on the table beside the chair crashing to the floor; pieces of china and the shattered light bulb flew onto the oriental rug that graced the center of Lee's office. The shrill, rasping voice became suddenly audible again.

"Can you speak to him?" Lee asked Soong in a whisper. "Speak to him in Frisian, or whatever it is?"

"Not enough to make sense. It would take me a little time. I have my old reference books, of course, and with a few days to brush up—I could speak it once, you know, but no one else could, so I fell out of practice—but with a few days of study, yes, I probably could."

Lee wanted to continue. This sudden appearance of yet another life inside Chad was staggering in its implications, but they could get nowhere until Soong remastered the dead language of Frisian. Watching Chad twist and thrash in the chair, Nils Lee became worried that the man was on the edge of having another seizure. This would be something he wouldn't know how to handle. Reluctantly he clapped his hands to bring Chad out of the trance.

Chad returned to himself, standing there, looking confused. Questioningly, he looked toward Lee. "I was at it again, I guess," he said sheepishly, and smiled. "Back to wherever I was last time. . . ."

Nils Lee forced a laugh. "Not quite. Do you remember anything you said or did here today?"

Chad searched his memory. "No, I'm afraid I don't. At least I didn't go out the window this time. But my stomach. It feels sore. Like I'd been doing violent exercise or too many pushups."

"We'll talk about it tomorrow."

"Tomorrow? I thought our next session wasn't until the day after."

"Well, this will be a sort of extra one, just you and me. No hypnosis or anything like that; we can't have you doing so many pushups you get in better shape than you already are. Disgusting, being so young." Chad shrugged, his confusion still showing. His eyes fell on the lamp. "Did I do that?"

"Don't worry about it, Chad. Tomorrow what I want to do is talk to you—just talk. There are some things you ought to know. Perhaps it was unfair not telling you earlier, but at the time, it seemed wiser. Now it's time you learned about them."

Chad shrugged again; Nils Lee was being uncharacteristically mysterious, but possibly he had to be. "Okay, Dr. Lee, tomorrow."

"Good," said Nils. "Oh, Chad, there's something I'd like you to read before then, if you can. It's a book I wrote. Not very long; it shouldn't take up much of your time." Walking over to the bookcase, Nils Lee pulled out a fresh copy of *Plato to Patton: The Reincarnates*. Solemnly he handed the book to Chad, watching his eyes for a reaction.

Studying it, Chad appeared to have ignored the title, noticing only Nils Lee's name on the jacket. "I didn't know you wrote books."

"It didn't do badly. No best seller, of course, but all right. I'd like you to read it and think a little about what it has to say."

"Right."

A few minutes later Chad left, feeling, as he always did, far more cheerful and refreshed than when he arrived. Dr. Soong left less than five minutes later, hurrying to his office to begin getting himself up on his Frisian. It would not take him long, he assured Lee.

Left by himself, a sudden wave of conscience swept across Nils Lee. What had he done, my God, what had he done?

That night was a nightmare for Chad. Or more precisely, a night of nightmares; he figured he couldn't have slept more than one and a half or two hours during the entire night.

He had read Nils Lee's book before going to bed. The thing was beautifully written, with flashes of humor that were pure Nils Lee laced through the more serious exposition. But in the end he had reluctantly decided the book was silly. Nils Lee's preoccupation with something as farfetched as reincarnation both surprised and disappointed him. The man seemed so down to earth and rational. Too much time in the Far East, Chad decided.

With a sigh Chad switched off his light; he didn't

even bother to attach the electrodes of his anti-REM machine anymore. The damned thing had worked at first, but now that he had grown used to the alarm bell, it was totally ineffective. He fell asleep quickly, as he always did after one of Nils Lee's hypnotic sessions.

The nightmares were not far behind. At first they seemed harmless, but regardless, Chad would wake from each drenched with sweat, screaming. From them, the dim shape of a new character slowly emerged. A character who fit the second voice he had been hearing. A woman. He could barely make her out; she was hidden behind what looked like stone carvings whose centers had been cut out. The only light in the vast chamber she stood in was provided by stone torches stuck in fixtures along the wall, a wall made of great stones but intricately carved and decorated. The place seemed familiar to him, yet a place part of him was convinced he had never seen.

He heard a choir of boy sopranos and, turning, looked up. The boys were there in a sort of loft, and Chad knew they were wards of the church's orphanage.

This realization struck Chad as curious. How did he know this church? How did he know the choir consisted of orphans that were kept alive as one of the church's good works? Chad had no answer; at the moment, logical answers seemed unnecessary.

Regally, the woman emerged from behind the altar screen and pointed one long finger at him. The words she spoke were in a language he didn't know, yet he could feel his mouth move as she spoke. The other sisters turned and stared at him, their eyes showing they'd already condemned him. The woman—she had a gaunt, tired face that hinted at how old she really was—began speaking once more in her strange language, one that Chad could understand with increasing ease. Chad could feel his tongue move and his lips quiver as she spoke. As she moved to the center of the transept, the woman became easier to see. Observing her, Chad noticed she was dressed differently from the other sisters, wearing a long, flowing black robe of some sort. The black robe immediately seemed familiar to him, but it took a second for Chad to place it. Lisa's dress. Why was the abbess—how did he know that's what she was?—wearing Lisa's dress? The dress had always disturbed him; now he felt he knew why: the abbess was evil. There was no explanation for his believing this either; it was just something he knew. On command, the rest of the sisters rose from their knees and began moving toward him, their faces angry and determined. Chad turned and tried to run out of the church, but the heavy planked doors slammed shut in his face, their thick metal rings making a clanging sound as they began swinging from the sudden motion.

The abbess yelled at the sisters in his voice, urging them forward, her long bony finger still pointing at him. As they reached him, Chad could feel their impatient fingers tearing at his clothes.

Chad was awakened by his own screams. His mouth felt dry and he could feel his whole body tremble. In the bathroom, he looked at himself in the mirror— he was as gaunt and pale and old as the abbess. At the basin, he drank two glasses of water, knowing it was stupid; he would have to get up again later when they had worked through his system, but his mouth was so dry he had no choice. Back in his room, he sat in the chair by the window smoking a cigarette, looking out at a sparsely lit New Haven. At this hour, even the lights on Harkness Tower were off; when he'd been a student here, they stayed on all night, but that was before energy became a problem.

The dreams about Marcus Flavius had always drained him, but he could look back at them now as if they were nothing; he did not know why, but

everything the abbess did was so filled with violence
and evil, these dreams were far more exhausting.
He sat staring at the tip of his cigarette—it reminded
him, somehow, of Nils Lee's pulsing light—until he
began to feel sleepy. Maybe, he thought, as he felt
himself drifting into sleep, this time it would be
easier and he would dream of Flavius. Nothing evil
about him.

The abbess was arguing with a monk from the
Calian teaching order, a man Chad knew was the director of the abbey choir. He could hear her, in his
voice, yelling at him because the monk did not agree
with what she had ordered him to do. "I am in charge
here," she bellowed. The abbess's voice was firm;
once again Chad felt his lips move when she spoke.

"But, my Lady Abbess, the boy is only eleven.
Surely, you . . ." the monk protested.

"Yes, eleven. And in another year his voice will
change. He is our best soloist. That would be a terrible loss for us. The Vatican does it, why cannot
we?"

"It is cruel, it is wrong, it is—"

"I shall tell the bishop you consider the Pope to be
both wrong and cruel, Brother Septimus. Then we
shall see. . . ."

The monk turned pale. Wearily, he waved two
other monks toward him. Between them was a struggling boy of about eleven or twelve, who did not know
what was going to happen but was already terrified.
"Do as the abbess ordered," said Brother Septimus,
turning his back so he would not have to watch.

The abbess was not so squeamish. "Be careful not
to damage him any more than necessary; we need him
for Sunday's 'Ave.'" The two monks threw the boy
to the floor and pulled up his small cassock. One knelt
astride him, and with an extremely sharp knife quickly executed the abbess's command. The boy had begun
screaming when he was thrown on the floor; his voice

had turned to a shriek when the knife was produced. Now, as the knife did its work, an ear-splitting cry of pain rose from him, but quickly turned to a groan of pain so deep no scream could help.

Reaching behind him, one of the monks pulled a blazing torch from the wall and cauterized the wound. The boy began to shriek again, but the pain was too much and he fainted.

The abbess no longer had reason to worry about her best soloist's voice changing.

"Fader Oudre, der in Hefonium ist . . ." The nuns and novices stood motionless, chanting, their habits dim in the moving shadows made by the blazing torches along the wall. *"Allochne Desen Nomen Beyen . . ."* The chanting voices sounded hollow coming back off the dank stonework of the abbey, dark except for a pool of light around the candles on the altar.

Chad stared at them as they continued their prayer; once again, he could feel his mouth move with their words. It was the Lord's Prayer and he kept crossing himself as he prayed. When the prayer was over, there was a shuffling of feet, a sound magnified by the hollow acoustics of the abbey. From behind him came the peal of a primitive organ and sudden singing as the choirboys burst into the "Te Deum" in Latin. Chad could not help wondering if the boy soloist had recovered yet from his ordeal.

The abbess, gaunt, shrouded in her long, flowing black dress, moved slowly down the nave toward the transept, her hands wrapped around a large gold crucifix that hung from her neck; the monseigneur in front of the altar—Monseigneur Klough, Chad remembered—appeared to ignore her. Bowing his head and crossing himself, the priest genuflected deeply toward the altar before he turned to leave, his sandals slapping hard against the stones of the floor. For some moments, the abbess stood motionless, staring at the altar as if drawing strength from it. He was too far away for it to be possible, but Chad could see the ornate carvings on the front of the altar, bas-relief figures of the disciples of Jesus. Somehow, he saw what she saw; she saw what he saw. He had not noticed it at first, but Chad could feel the sweat pouring out of him, running down his sides beneath the dress in uncomfortable rivulets.

Finally, the abbess turned, halfway up the stone steps of the transept. She began reprimanding both the sisters and the novices, her voice strident and hoarse, telling them they were wicked because they had not followed the spirit of Jesus.

The abbess's voice rose in anger; he could feel himself shaking with fury. Slowly she raised her arm again, and one finger pointed, not at him, but toward the sisterhood before her. The pointing finger appeared to search briefly, then fixed itself on one of the novices. Haltingly, the novice stood up, swaying slightly from fear. The abbess's voice rose to an angrier and more accusing pitch, and Chad could feel the muscles of his throat tighten from the strain of shouting.

The abbess came partway down the steps beyond the altar rail, her finger still pointing, and gave a strident order to the two nuns nearest the novice. They seized the terrified girl and began dragging her up the steps, where the abbess waited, her arms folded. The novice screamed, trying to fight free of the two nuns, but they were stronger and heavier. He saw the two nuns throw the crying girl to the floor of the transept, and heard himself shrieking at her that she had defiled the Holy Order by thinking of things that were in themselves sins of the flesh, and that she must be punished . . . terribly punished. The novice shrieked, seeing the abbess advance toward her. . . .

His own yell woke Chad up. His bed had lost its

covers, the sheets and blankets lying in a heap on the floor. His entire body, as in the nightmare, was soaked with sweat, but felt more as if it had been plunged under a shower. Turning on the light, Chad could see that his thrashings had upset the water glass on his bedside table and that part of the water had spilled onto his bed.

Cursing, Chad gave up trying to sleep for what little was left of the night. In a way, this decision relieved him. Three times in a row he had begun this identical dream of the abbess and the novice; each time he had waked up before the nightmare could run to completion. He had no explanation for this— it was like seeing the beginning of a horror movie three times, yet never being able to work up the nerve to see the whole movie—but Chad knew somehow this dream must be terribly important to him. He would have to talk to duBrul about it. Or to Nils Lee. His face clouded; he was to see Lee at nine this morning and talk to him about the book Lee had given him to read. Silly nonsense.

For the rest of the night—it was about four—Chad Lefferts sat restlessly in his chair by the window, smoking too many cigarettes and watching the sky little by little lighten to announce the beginning of another day. That would hold what? he wondered.

CHAPTER FOURTEEN

"It's very interesting, my dear. The design is in a sense primitive. But it has been influenced, obviously, by the church-oriented statuary of the times. The artisans who worked for the church were, in turn, heavily affected by the remnants of the Graeco-Roman tradition. Not formally, of course. But the Romans carried their gods with them wherever they went, and their statues of deities and heroes remained long after the Romans had fled back within their shrinking empire." Tracey Neil, Sheffield Professor of Medieval Art, put down the magnifying glass he'd been using to study the details of Lisa's photographs and turned to her.

"These prints. Is it possible to make slides?"

"They *were* on slides. I had these prints made from them. That's why they're so damned small." Lisa giggled. "The price, my God, the price!"

"Slides are more convenient and are easier to study," said Neil somberly. He was not famous for his sense of humor.

"Can you date and place it?"

"Early German. Very early. Say, about the fourteenth century, I should think. It is not always possible to be exact about such things; the art styles were so derivative, you see."

Lisa picked up the slice of wood she had carefully brought back from the walled garden. "Did you learn anything from this?"

"Only as corroborating evidence. The wood was ash. The tools used were typical of German artisans of the fourteenth century, but, my dear, the tools they used hadn't changed much from what they were using several hundred years earlier, so it is impossible to be exact. What really excites me, though, is your account of the transplanted cloisters with a small building at one end. If authentic, it is highly unusual. Could you go back and get us some pictures of that in its entirety? From every angle, you understand, with perhaps a small piece of its stonework for authentication purposes."

Lisa was taken aback. "I should think, Dr. Neil, it would be far more valuable if you—the university— went back and examined it in person. I can take the pictures, but . . ."

The professor sighed, running the magnifying glass up and down one side of his nose to cover his embarrassment. "We have tried to gain access to that garden for years. The lawyers are following the gentleman—Mr. Oliver's—will to the letter: no visitors, no examinations, no pictures. I—anyone from the university—could do as you did and go inside without permission, of course. But there is a difference. You go inside as an individual. A student. If I or anybody from the university should do that, we would be breaking the law. Town-gown relations in New Haven are no different from those in any other college town; the city officials are always looking for something to jump on us for. The tax-exempt status of an institution like Yale infuriates them, you see." Professor Neil spread his hands hopelessly before going back to massaging his nose with the cool chromium rim of the magnifying glass. Then: "If you could get us some pictures, Mrs. Lefferts, not only I but the whole department would be much in your debt. . . ."

Lisa did not have to consider very long. Originally she had planned, herself, to take pictures of the cloisters. The buildings at one end still fascinated her but the sudden rain had stopped her the one day she had gone there with her camera. An uneasiness about the walled garden that she couldn't explain had made her hope the department or Professor Neil himself would obviate the need for a second visit. Neil's expression was somewhere between pleading and commanding. Lisa gave in. "Of course I can. I'll cover every inch of the place; no one ever seems to see me going in or leaving."

Neil smiled, gratified. "Particularly that little building. Most unusual, you see."

"I have a flash; I can take pictures of it inside and everything."

"Wonderful."

Lisa wanted to talk further to Professor Neil, but as soon as she had agreed to take the pictures, he appeared to lose interest in her, moving around in his chair, picking up and putting down various papers from his desk, and in general letting Lisa know their discussion, for the moment, was finished.

A few minutes later, Lisa left. Taking the pictures would be easy, even fun. But her sense of uneasiness about the walled garden remained with her, defiant and immovable. Maybe, she thought, Chad would go with her. No, he had forbidden *her* to go there. It was something she would have to do for herself.

"You didn't like it, then?"

"I thought it was silly. That's the only word I can use."

"I'll try not to cry."

Chad wasn't entirely sure how serious Nils Lee was

being. But it was possible his remarks had been a little too blunt and that he'd hurt Lee's feelings. He back-pedaled. "Well, what I mean is, the book isn't silly. I thought it was very well written. With just enough humor here and there to keep it moving right along. What's silly is the subject. Incarnation. I'm sorry, but that's something I just can't buy." Chad, sitting in a soft leather chair opposite Nils Lee, turned his pale-blue eyes directly on Lee's. "I can't believe you really believe that crap yourself." Chad hesitated a second, then: "*Do* you?"

"I've never been sure. I argued for it in the book, but in some ways, that was a sophistic exercise." Nils Lee looked down at his hands; they were clasped together on his lap, the fingers weaving an interlocked, constantly moving matrix, fiddling with the inevitable foul-smelling Sobranie. He raised his eyes to look at Chad. "It was an intellectual exercise; that is, until we started having our hypnoidal sessions. Now I believe in it entirely—fully and unequivocally."

Chad was stunned. He had expected Nils Lee to make a mild defense of reincarnation and then withdraw gracefully into the rational. For some reason, he found himself growing angry, as if the man had somehow cheated him. "Why?" he asked Lee.

"You are a physicist. Didn't my explanation built on the law of conservation of energy make sense to you?"

"The physics of it made sense, yes. The rest, no."

"What I was looking for was living proof. And now I have it. You. You are my proof."

"Oh, come on, Dr. Lee. You're putting me on."

Nils Lee sighed and got to his feet. "There's something, Chad, I believe you should see. We haven't discussed much of what went on during the hypnotic sessions; I have some videotapes that do it better than I ever could."

"Tapes can be doctored. Everybody knows that."

"Yes, but these *weren't*. You have my word on that. And I think when you see them you'll see why these particular tapes aren't the product of legerdemain, but of simple, straightforward recording. And if *they* don't convince you, Dr. Soong can tell you that they represent exactly what you said and did during the sessions."

"Jesus Christ." Chad got out of his chair and walked around the room, trying to dispel his growing anger. Nils Lee watched him. Chad's reaction was no more and no less than he had expected. He had suspected that a physicist was not going to surrender easily to anything as mystic as reincarnation.

"Would you like to see one?" Lee asked.

"All right, but it's not going to change one damned thing that I think." As a scientist, Chad knew this was a stupid, closed-minded approach to be taking. But the anger in him kept growing; he didn't know whether it sprang from a sensation that Nils Lee had double-crossed him, or whether he was mad because this man he respected so much had turned out to have an insane streak running through him, or whether he was mad with himself because he'd allowed this entire thing to happen.

At the very outset he should have realized there was some catch in Nils Lee's offer of help. He began sulking, exhausted from a night of practically no sleep, furious that he'd been taken in. He watched as Nils Lee walked over to his desk, sat down, and swiveled toward the bookcase behind him. The lower row of books turned out to be fake; when he pressed a button the entire row of books folded down on hinges. Behind it, Chad could see the black leather and chrome knobs and dials of an expensive tape machine—an Ampex, as Lee would later tell him. There were two separate amplifiers, apparently, two recording heads, and two reels of tape, as well as another two take-up reels already in position on the machine.

Above this, behind another row of false books on the next shelf, were the controls and screen of the videotape recorder. Nils Lee flipped a switch and the screen began to glow. The use of both a sound-tape recorder and a separate videotape track puzzled Chad, but he was in no mood to ask a question about it; this would involve talking to Nils Lee, something he found distasteful at the moment.

The sections of videotape that Nils Lee planned to play for Chad had been carefully selected; he wanted it to be enough to let Chad see himself under hypnosis, hear himself speaking Latin, and hear Dr. Soong's simultaneous translation of what Chad said. But at this point, he didn't want Chad to see the more traumatic moments from the tapes; they could frighten him so badly, he would never submit to hypnosis again.

Chad watched the gain-dials glow as Nils Lee flicked some switches; a single small light, a brilliant dot, glowed from the control panel of each of the amplifiers to indicate that the speakers were on. The television screen on the videotape machine flickered like a wind-tortured candle.

"Watch and listen carefully, Chad. I would like to play you just the beginnings of"—he looked down at the coding on the back of the box—"Session two E, nine fifteen A.M., September twenty-seven."

"You disappoint me, Doctor. I thought you'd at least do a few card tricks before you got to the main act." Nils Lee shrugged and turned back to the machine. He had expected hostility; he was getting it.

Chad indeed felt hostility: what he had expected to be bantering conversation during which Nils Lee would finally admit his book was a colossal hoax on the academic world, some sort of elaborate professorial joke, had turned out to be deadly serious. He felt betrayed, wondering what the hell he was doing sitting in this man's office, a lunatic quite seriously trying to convince him he had lived before—in the mid-first century A.D. Preposterous. Insane.

Nils Lee started the videotape rolling. Chad saw himself and Dr. Lee talking just before he went into a hypnotic trance for the first time. Like almost everyone, he hated the sound of his own voice; it sounded flat, nasal, and whining. His pose appeared awkward, as if self-conscious about the camera. Nils Lee looked and sounded exactly as Nils Lee always had. He heard himself being told to watch the small pulsing light, and could hear the beginning of the slurred tone his voice developed as the hypnoidal state began to overcome him. In the chair he saw himself begin to slump, fighting his closing eyelids. He could remember the effects of the pulsing light and the lulling sound of Nils Lee's voice so vividly, he caught himself on the edge of going under again as he sat there.

From the tape machine came Lee's voice asking a sudden question after a brief pause while he shuffled his notes. Then: "Good. For instance, as Marcus Flavius, you were living in Rome during the first century A.D. Right, Chad?"

"Right." Even Chad could hear the sudden new military crispness of his own voice on the tape. Awed, he watched himself answer questions about a Rome of long ago, things he had no way of knowing.

"For instance," Lee continued. "Can you tell me —I'm confused, you see—if I turned left from the Temple of Venus and Rome, is the Arch of the Emperor Titus on my right or my left?"

Chad sank deeper into his chair now, partly awed, partly convinced the whole tape must be a deception of some sort, and heard his own voice answer. "I know of no one named Titus, and certainly there has been no emperor of that name."

Lee leaned back and stopped the tape machine, fixing his eyes on Chad. "That was one of a series of trick questions that I used during the hypnotic session,

Chad. You see, there *is* an Arch of Titus in Rome, but it was not built until many years after the first century. At the time of your life as Flavius, Titus had not yet been born. . . ."

From Chad came the rattle of his throat being cleared. He was having increasing trouble believing what he heard himself say, but could not bring himself to admit it. Groping, he fumbled for some explanation. "Well, it's probably something I remembered from Groton or Yale. Something I was taught but had forgotten until the hypnosis."

Nils Lee smiled faintly. "Watch," he said. "I'd asked you precisely that question, and you answered it. . . ."

"Not at Yale, not at Harvard, not at prep school?"

Chad's own answer on the videotape shook him: "I am sorry. I do not understand you." The machine was turned off again. Nils Lee appeared to ignore Chad. On his pad he had the footage counts of the different sections of the tape he considered it important for Chad to hear today. Sections chosen to persuade without frightening. When he finished each section, Lee put the VTR on FAST FWD. and watched the footage counter until it reached the next section he wanted Chad to see. The squealing blur of speeded-up voices added an eerie undertone to the event. Nils was unaware of Chad's discomfort, since he was concentrating on his notes.

"Maybe you can explain this warning you give, Chad. It appears on the tape in several different places."

On the tape, Chad saw himself cowering behind the chair, saw his head turn, and heard his own strange warning issued in Latin: "Hide yourselves, hide yourselves!"

The look of fear on his own face panicked him further. The warning, sometimes half in English, then half in Latin, was hissed again. He saw himself as

Flavius dodging around the corners of Nils Lee's office looking for a place to hide. His whimpering became a Latin scream, and Chad watched Lee clap his hands, bringing him out of the hypnoidal trance and leaving him looking baffled and confused. As baffled and confused as Chad felt this very moment.

Turning around, Nils Lee stopped the Ampex and the videotape player. When he swung back to face Chad, he studied the man's expression. Confusion was etched across his face, confusion mixed with resentment, self-doubt, and an unspoken resolution not to be persuaded. "Well, Chad, does it make any more sense to you now?"

"It's not necessarily me doing all of that. There's all sorts of tricks they can play with tape. You know that, I'm sure. Boy, am *I* sure."

"There's a synch mark running through the entire audiotape. That's why I used the Ampex as well as the VTR. A synch mark is what they use to synch a film recording with a tape recording when they're making a movie. If the audiotape is edited, the synch mark is broken; a frequency meter—I'm sure the physics department has one in their audio lab—can prove that part to you: no editing."

"Well, you could probably hypnotize me into saying anything you wanted me to. Even in Latin, I suppose."

"Yes, it's possible we could do that. But let me tell you something, Chad. On a part of the tape I didn't play today—you can hear the whole thing any time you want—are spontaneously given details on buildings, places, and people. Many of them are so obscure I had to check with experts all over the country to authenticate them myself. One in particular—the Temple of Agrippina Claudiae—you described at length, including an observation that it was a disgraceful ruin of a building to have standing in the center of Rome. You added that you understood plans were under way to rebuild it. It didn't mean much to me, but in talking to Dr. Vincent Machri, an archaeologist of considerable standing, he appeared stunned, and immediately called a colleague in Italy. It seems that only three weeks earlier, the fact that there was another, older temple beneath the present one was uncovered for the first time during a dig for artifacts. Although the discovery of the older temple beneath the new one was a breakthrough, it was kept a close secret; the man in charge of the area for the Italian Institute for Archaeological Research wanted to surprise his colleagues at the annual archaeological conference.

"Only he and Dr. Machri were aware of the discovery. Now, Chad, if only two men in the present world knew that the older temple even existed—this one you mention on tape as a "disgraceful ruin," but one you believe is about to be rebuilt—how could *I* possibly know about it and put the words in your mouth for the tape? Answer: I couldn't. I'd never even heard of the Temple of Agrippina before you yourself mentioned it."

Chad found himself without an answer. There was no way to take issue with Nils Lee's facts and still make sense. Yet, he still could not accept even a suggestion that reincarnation was a valid premise; it became particularly offensive when applied to himself. He, Chad Lefferts, a first-century Roman soldier in the army of Tiberius, for Christ's sake. Out of hand he rejected all proof, including his own sudden ability to speak perfect Latin, a subject he had only dabbled with—not very successfully—and solely because Groton's curriculum demanded it. Unable to counter, incapable of even considering Nils Lee's premise, he took refuge in the only thing left to him: anger.

"I don't know how you did it, I only know that you did. This whole setup smells like some kind of con

game. And it's damned shitty that you're pulling that
kind of nonsense on me. Christ, I came to you for
help. I liked you; I trusted you. But that didn't make
a fucking bit of difference to you; you plucked this
reincarnation crap out of the air and beat me over
the head with it. Shit." For a moment Chad stared at
his shoes, blinking hard; the last faint straw left him
in his terrifying world of nightmares and seizures had
just vanished as he watched. His eyes rose to meet Nils
Lee's. "I don't know how to tell you how disappointed
I am in you. You're a real prick."

Abruptly, Chad stood up, straightening his shoulders. "I think I'd better go now. For good." He started
toward the door, stopping only when Lee's voice suddenly came from behind him.

"We have some distance to go yet, Chad. I admit
that. But I swear it's no game. I promise that it can
help. Why don't we discuss it tomorrow when we
have our regular session?"

"No. I won't be back. Ever."

"I'll leave the time open anyhow." Nils Lee winced
as the door slammed shut behind Chad. Christ, how
could a man *be* so dense?

CHAPTER FIFTEEN

As he parked his car in the faculty lot behind Yale's
science complex, Chad looked halfheartedly at the
imposing hulk of the Kline Biology Tower and then
suddenly smiled affectionately. It was comforting to
be back in this world of exact sciences, where atoms,
genes, electrons, chemicals, and viruses were tamed,
measured, and redirected. Inside the low windowless
shapes of the Electron Accelerator Lab and the Wright
Nuclear Structure Lab lay the sureness of rational
minds applying rational laws to the universe. To
Chad, they represented safety. A world of measurable
limits, far from the metaphysical purgatory of Nils
Lee and his anile premises. As he walked through
the lot toward his office, he could see the ugly Victorian hulk of the Peabody Museum of Natural History to his left, less exact, certainly, but still resound-
ingly solid.

Chad could not shake the sulk his meeting with
Nils Lee had produced. The man was mad. He had
trusted him and depended upon him only to discover
he had put himself in the hands of either a charlatan
or a totally unbalanced mystic.

Once in his office, Chad stared resentfully at the

cryptic equations still written on the blackboard.
Worked out because Lee had asked him to try to
correlate the nightmares of Flavius with the black
hole of Omikron Blue. That he had gone along with
Lee proved he was a little unbalanced himself. Spite-
fully, he took a piece of chalk and scrawled all over
the equations. They had proved nothing except that
however he came at them, they produced the senseless
number 651, a figure that was the same as the number
of light-years Omikron Blue was away from earth.
He supposed it kept returning, that number, because
it was the only hard fact he'd had to feed into the
computer terminal. Angrily, he turned over the little
sign that hung beside the top of the blackboard to
reveal its one-word message "WASH." These signs were
an invention born of desperation; the maintenance
men had long ago learned the risk of washing even
apparently discarded equations off this particular
building's blackboards: inevitably, the physicist or
mathematician would reappear in the morning—after
sleeping on the problem—and be livid to discover the
rejected scrawlings of yesterday had been washed away
by the maintenance crew. The signs kept everybody
happy—or at least with no room for argument.

Chad sat down in a chair to get back to his work
on a distant galaxy he had named Upsilon Termina;
he was very overdue to spend some time on what the
university was paying him for, rather than playing
with fainéant abstractions dreamed up by a border-
line mental defective. The moment he sat down,
though, he could feel the exhaustion behind his eyes.
In the anger of the moment, he had almost forgotten
that his total sleep from the night before only added
up to a couple of hours at most. The repeated nightmares about the abbess and the novice swam into his
consciousness. This was a dream chain he had meant
to tell Nils Lee about; suddenly he was glad he had

not. Instead of Lee, duBrul would be told. A little flaky himself, but light-years ahead of Lee.

The exhaustion was so pervasive, Chad moved across to the long leather couch that stood against one wall of his office. Ordinarily he was unable to nap, even in extreme circumstances. Today he was so tired, the idea struck him as not only feasible but desperately necessary. As Chad felt his eyes close wearily, a small smile flickered across his face. Dr. Koekeritz had been somewhat mystified at how little actual time his star addition appeared to spend in his lab. Koerkeritz had been far too professional to ask what Chad was working on, or why it required so little lab time, but Chad knew both questions must be piquing his curiosity. Today, Chad thought, Koerkeritz would abruptly turn up in his office and finally find his expensive protégé in his lab, sound asleep on his couch. Fuck him. He wasn't a union assembler, paid by the hour, counting the minutes while calculating his fringe benefits. The smile slowly disappeared; the mouth drooped slightly open; the breathing became deeper and more regular.

The abbess was screaming with his voice, yelling at the novice as the two nuns wrestled her to the hard marble floor of the abbey chapel. Chad was conscious, oddly, that what he was part of was a continuation of the earlier dream chain; it did not seem to disturb him. The novice wrestled and thrashed, but the nuns were both heavy and strong. To make sure they were entirely capable of overpowering her, the abbess—he could feel her looking at the rows of sisters, searching their faces until she found someone powerful enough—clapped her hands and told Sister Eugenix to come and help. From behind her came the continuing screams and pleadings for mercy from the novice; the abbess spun around, yelling at her to be quiet, that she had brought this punishment on herself by her many sins of the flesh. Chad, once again, could feel the strain on the muscles of his throat from the abbess's shouting.

The picture became a kaleidoscope of rapidly changing fragments: the novice's face, crying and screaming; the abbess, cold and detached, chanting an endless prayer; the faces of the choirboys, not wanting to watch but unable to make themselves turn away; the two older sisters, joined now by Sister Eugenix, their faces hard as they waited for a signal from the abbess. Chad's mouth moved as hers did, in the strange language, that was both foreign, yet familiar, to Chad.

"Now!" she yelled. Brutally, the three nuns tore the habit off the novice, leaving her naked before God and the assembled nuns. The underclothes, the shoes, and the cowl encircling her head, were ripped off and thrown to one side of the altar; the shaven head that marked all nuns gleamed softly in the candlelight.

"No, no, no!" screamed the novice, turning to the other sisters for help. "I have committed no sin of the flesh, I swear before Almighty God. It is the abbess. I refused her carnal lusts and she is punishing me for it. My sisters, my God, it is not *I* who have transgressed my vows, but . . ."

The novice's pleadings stopped abruptly. On the order from the abbess, the heaviest of the nuns smashed her heavy crucifix across the novice's mouth. Blood poured out. Fragments of teeth stuck out from her torn mouth like white marble pilings in a river of blood.

The abbess's face had gone white with fury. Chad could feel his chest rising and falling with her anger. "She lies," his voice roared. "I saw her smile at the head gardener. Repeatedly. A sister who smiles at any man goes farther when no one is about. In the cloisters. In the root cellars. Dear God, perhaps even in this holy chapel itself." The abbess leaned down to the struggling novice. "Because you are young and pretty you think you can fool the old abbess? Never. If you have such a need for your lusts to be satisfied, we will satisfy them for you—in God's name, with God's punishment."

Moving with surprising speed for her age, the long black dress fluttering behind her, its loose folds flapping wildly, the abbess seized the bishop's crozier that was leaning against the altar rail. It was always kept there, in case the bishop should arrive for some ceremony or inspection. Holding it above her head as if in performance of a ritual, the abbess carried it back to where the novice lay struggling on the chapel floor. It was a magnificent crozier, or shepherd's crook, fashioned of what appeared to be gold, inlaid everywhere with gems, and covered with delicate carvings in bas-relief. Barely pausing, the abbess shoved the straight end of the crozier between the novice's legs, which had been spread wide apart by the nuns to receive it. The abbess leaned on it, pushing it in as far as she could manage. Chad could feel the same sensual tingle he knew the abbess was feeling. The novice shrieked in agony, twisting her body in a desperate effort to escape, but held immovable by the three nuns.

"Sister Eugenix," commanded the abbess. "Help me." The two of them leaned on the crozier, ignoring —or perhaps savoring—the shriek of pain from the novice. "It is not enough," the abbess observed. Quickly she pulled out the crozier and reversed it, so that the hooked end was aimed between the novice's legs. The end of the crook was easily inserted. Then, standing upright, she called for Sister Eugenix to follow her as she moved toward the novice's head. Both of them pulled as hard as they could, leaning far back and putting their entire weight into the effort. Slowly, torn by the nuns' weight, the novice's tissue gave way, and the crozier ripped up from below through the wall of her lower stomach. The novice's shrieks had first subsided to groans; now there was only silence. The abbess fell to her knees, praying. On some signal the choir burst into the "Te Deum." Over the riot of sound Chad could still hear his voice pouring from the abbess, a succession of wild screams crying for more vengeance. Vengeance for the novice's sins against God.

Chad's eyes opened sleepily; he felt dizzy and disoriented, surprised for some reason that he should have been asleep at all. Gradually, he began stirring, trying to shake himself free of the torpor the nightmare had produced. But his body seemed unwilling to respond, and he gradually felt himself drifting back into sleep. And a further nightmare.

He saw the abbess move to the small, usually locked door of the high abbey wall. Or was it he himself who had his hands against the heavy paneling? Something made him quietly slide open the panel that covered a smaller door placed at eye level, so anyone using the door could first check the outside. Walking down the path outside the wall was another novice with one of the small children—a boy, Chad thought—from the abbey's orphanage walking solemnly beside her.

He reached up the flowing sleeves of the abbess's robe and pulled out the key, noiselessly unlocking the door of the abbey wall. The abbess waited until the novice and her charge were directly opposite the door, then threw it open, and with a scream Chad felt start deep down inside himself, fell upon the startled sister.

The struggling young woman looked upward, her eyes wide with fear; the little boy screamed and began to cry. "It is I, Sister Elevea," the novice cried. "My Abbess, it is Sister Elevea. I do not know—"

"I know who you are," spat the abbess in Chad's voice. "And I know what you are doing. The men you smile at—and, I suspect, far more than smile. That child you have with you is probably your own. Issue of the Devil's groin. . . ."

"No, no, My Abbess, no. He is from our orphanage. I have been with him to—"

"Silence!" Chad heard himself roar. "I know everything. You cannot hide your sins from me. And now you must pay for them."

The crooked dagger reappeared at almost the same time that the abbess tore the starched wimple and black hood from the novice's head, her shaved scalp looking grotesque in the sunlight. With a grunt, the abbess began plunging the dagger into Sister Elevea's body, while the poor girl shrieked in pain and terror, struggling, but unable to tear herself free from the abbess's iron grasp. "Whore! Whore! Lover of the Devil!" Chad heard his voice scream.

His voice was joined by another's. The little boy, terrified at first, was screaming as he beat his small fists against the abbess's head and neck, trying to stop the woman from killing Sister Elevea. The abbess turned and looked at the boy vacantly. He looks so like Robin, Chad thought, and, for that matter— But his thoughts were all jumbled up between his own and the abbess's and he could not follow them.

Pausing in her attack on Sister Elevea, the abbess spun around and plunged the knife into the boy. Chad could hear his voice as she snarled at him. "Spawn of Satan. You are as evil as your mother." The boy crumpled forward, falling into the rapidly spreading pool of blood that was collecting beside Sister Elevea. She was already dead, but the abbess continued to plunge the knife into her body, muttering and yelling at her. Then, with one quick movement, she pulled up Sister Elevea's long skirt and drew an enormous cross with the end of her knife on the young woman's body.

Chad heard himself crying out, thrashing on his couch. "No!" He forced himself fully awake. He tried to sit up—or perhaps this was still part of the nightmare—but was unable to. Suddenly his body went rigid. His back arched, his toes pointed, and the skin pulled back from his teeth. He heard the familiar groans coming from somewhere deep inside him and saw the same blinding flashes of light as his body was whirled into nothingness, far out into space. A moment later he knew he was back hurtling around the dim perimeter of the black hole near Omikron Blue. Inside the hole, he could hear the abbess's voice—or was it his own again, as in the nightmares, pitched higher but still undeniably his?—screaming at some man as she had screamed at the novice. The argument again. The terrible but familiar sensation of being pulled unmercifully between two powerful forces. And for the first time, the realization by Chad that it *was* he whom the fight was about; both the woman with the guttural voice and the man wanted to possess him for their own.

Chad Lefferts's fifth seizure since arriving at Yale dropped over Chad like a dark blanket as black as Omikron Blue's fearful orbit.

"It's the inflation, Missus, it's eating me up, it is."

These words were the opening guns of Mrs. Lafferty's sudden campaign for an operating subsidy. It had caught Lisa unprepared and about to go out, her hand on the knob of the front door. Finally freed, Lisa glanced first at her watch, then the sky. Her delayed departure made it much later than she had planned, but at least this time she would not be drenched by any sudden rainstorm; the sky was growing dark, but was absolutely clear. Damn Mrs. Lafferty. In spite of Lisa's obvious intention of going somewhere, the gadget bag and other equipment already in her hands, Mrs. Lafferty had been agonizingly difficult to escape. Money was the problem, she complained repeatedly. The university didn't pay her enough—and this in spite of her many years of loyal service to them. "It's a bloody, crying shame," Mrs. Lafferty declared, looking as if she might cry herself. Perhaps, Mrs. Lafferty had suggested, one eye on Lisa to test her reaction, she and Professor Lefferts would care to supplement her pay a mite. Of course they were under no obligation to, but she had had several offers from private employers and might be forced to accept one of them, don't you know. The discussion went on and on, Lisa battling not to give in, but worried that there might be some truth in the woman's veiled threats of other jobs. Robin adored her; she was hard-working and always willing to baby-sit for a little extra money. Finally it was left that Lisa would talk to her husband and see if something couldn't be worked out.

Mrs. Lafferty remained unsure and followed her through the door, still talking as she and Lisa descended the first couple of front steps, her face mirroring her uncertainty, torn between wondering if she'd said too much or not enough.

Lisa kept nodding her head and gave her a terminal wave when she reached the sidewalk; otherwise, she was afraid Mrs. Lafferty would continue her case while following her down the street. Lisa very much did not want to be followed. She was going back inside the walled ruin of the garden. Although the late September days were shorter and the light would be more subdued than she had planned, she was sure she could take clear enough pictures of the cloisters and the building's exterior to please the art department. Her flash would take care of the darker areas of the cloisters as well as the interior of the building.

Outside the wall, Lisa glanced at the threatening metal signs promising that trespassers would be prosecuted to the full extent of the law; they were nailed into the stonework of the wall at approximately every ten yards, and another was fastened to the heavy metal gate that glowered from the wall's center. Before, when she had slipped through the opening where the wall was crumbling, Lisa had thought nothing of it; after her meeting with Dr. Tracey Neil of medieval arts, she suddenly found that going through the tangle of sumac bushes left her with an overwhelming sense of guilt. Twice she had glanced up and down the street to make sure no one would see her go in; twice she had been able to reassure herself no one would. A prickly branch of some sort tore at her ankle and Lisa cursed; if the damned university wanted pictures of the garden and cloisters so much, why didn't they just send someone in themselves? Shaking her head, Lisa smiled. They *had* sent someone: her. Her feelings of guilt were stupid, product, she supposed, of the sinister feeling this place always gave her.

Carefully—the memory of poor Robin's plunge through the rotted well-cover was impossible to forget—Lisa made her way toward the far end of the garden, passing the prie-dieu with its solemn, enigmatic eyes, walking around the area with the well, and finally putting down her gadget bag in a small, flat clearing, perhaps twenty feet from the cloisters. From the gadget bag Lisa produced her collapsible tripod; closed, it was less than a foot long; open, it extended to three feet or more, and would give the AE-1 a good operating level from which to shoot. Her wide-angle 28mm should be able to give her the entire cloisters in a single shot, even including the curious small stone building at its far right end.

The small needle inside her viewfinder indicated she still had more than enough light for crisp pictures. She shot perhaps a dozen from here, then picked up the tripod and moved closer. Another dozen on film.

As she drew closer to the cloisters, she unscrewed the tripod, collapsed it, and placed it back inside the gadget bag. This part of her shooting would have to be done with her holding the camera herself. The darkness under the slanting tile roof of the cloisters demanded the flash; there were dense shadows along the whole area where the inside wall of the cloisters met the roof. As she studied some of the stonework, she was intrigued to discover that many of the pillars had intricate stone carvings at their tops. There were miniature gargoyles, demons, and succubae on the outer side, glaring forth evilly, as if to warn off anyone who trespassed into this sanctuary. Like herself, Lisa thought. On the inside, the carvings were more benign: cherubs, seraphim, and vaguely familiar religious faces. Lisa shot two rolls taking pictures of the detail work alone. Fascinating.

This left only the small building at the cloister's end to do. Lisa was tired, and it was getting increasingly dark, but this was the one part of the cloisters that had seemed to fascinate Dr. Neil the most. Wearily picking up her gadget bag, Lisa squeezed herself through the slitlike opening that had apparently once served as a door. She fumbled in her gadget bag and drew out a flashlight, glad she had brought it, even if by chance. The small building was almost totally black inside; the only meager light came through the slit of a door, and two small windows, also slits, in the far wall. Outside, the light was fading rapidly—a result of the early September sunset —and virtually no light was left to come through the narrow openings. Probably, she thought, what little light there was, was further dissipated by the slanting roof's overhang.

The flashlight showed a flat floor of solid stones

beneath her feet. The stones were beautifully laid,
strikingly even and flush, the work of a master stone
mason. But this masterful floor was littered with
paper and shreds of cloth. Vandals, Lisa supposed.
The single room of the strange house smelled dank,
partly because of its permanent state of semidark-
ness, partly because of the decaying bits of cloth
and paper that seemed to be everywhere. Lisa swore
she had heard the scurrying whisper of mice when
she first came through the narrow opening; once
she *knew* she saw the dim outline of a rat in one of
the corners. When she turned her flashlight on it, the
creature's eyes gleamed candescently in the brightness for a second, then it scurried away, its feet making a sinister rattling sound on the papers. Lisa
shivered.

On the far wall her flashlight picked out a large—
it must have been three feet in diameter—medallion
of stone. It was a woman's face, her stone eyes staring
vacantly from a face that had been savaged by the
years. Around the outside of this carving, the perimeter of the medallion was enclosed in a circle of stone
rope. Looking closer, she could see the rope was interrupted by smaller medallions, each bearing the like-
ness of a man's head. Dr. Neil would be ecstatic about
this discovery; to Lisa, the blank stone eyes of the
large central figure appeared to hold some hidden
knowledge of things she was forbidden to ever share.
With a sigh, Lisa reached into the gadget bag again
and once again began setting up the collapsible
tripod; it would be easier, considering the slow shut-
ter speed she would have to use, to do such detailed
close-up photography with something to steady the
camera.

As Lisa turned toward the gadget bag a sudden
wild, high-pitched screaming stunned her. The sound
rose and fell at a deafening level, reverberating from
the walls and almost physically painful in such a

small, enclosed area. Paralyzed with fear, Lisa didn't even turn the flashlight at the source of the screaming; even without it she could see the oncoming shape of a woman tearing across the room toward her at full speed. The details of the woman's appearance etched themselves in her brain as if on the emulsion of a negative. The woman was wearing a long black flowing dress of some sort, her head partly covered with what appeared to be a hood. Because of the dim light of the room in addition to the dark shadow cast by the hood, her face was impossible to make out. Automatically, her heart pounding with fear, Lisa stepped backward, tripping over her gadget bag. As her back hit the wall, the flashlight fell from her hands, lying still lit, on the floor. Then the woman was on her.

Two strong hands fastened around Lisa's neck. To the overpowering sound of the woman's shrill shrieks she added her own screams for help, simultaneously realizing that there was no one who could possibly hear them.

Raising her hands, Lisa tried to fend off the woman, hitting her as hard as she could in the face, clawing at her body with her fingernails, raising one knee as high as she could. But the woman—she was incredibly strong—shrugged off her blows and scratchings, shaking her body beneath its flowing black dress as if annoyed by no more than a persistent fly. The hands pushed Lisa's head back hard against the wall, then moved it forward, then shoved it back against the wall again. The jarring crash of her head against the stone took Lisa's breath away; her cries for help became as halting as they were useless, drowned out by the woman's insane shrieking. A cloud of red moved up across Lisa's eyes; through it she could still see the eerie light of the flashlight on the floor and could dimly see the savage face of the woman, her lips drawn back from her teeth, could hear her pant-

ing and grunting from the effort of repeatedly crashing Lisa's head against the stone wall. Slowly—clutching, clawing, crying—Lisa felt herself sink into un-
consciousness.

As Lisa crumpled toward the floor, the woman released her grip and allowed the body to slip completely out of her hands and collapse onto the ground.
For a moment she stood there panting, trying to ad-
just the loose, flowing sleeves of her dress so that her
hands would be free again. She dragged Lisa to the
center of the room. Quickly, she stripped her. From
one of her loose sleeves she pulled the razor she would
use to shave Lisa's head clean; from the other she
drew the twisted knife she would need to draw the
cross on Lisa's stomach. The woman should be
conscious for that part of the ceremony, she decided;
she need not be for the ritual of shaving the head.

Grasping a fistful of Lisa's long, glowing hair, she
cut it off with one stroke.

The woman was so intent on her work, at first she
barely heard the voice behind her. "What the holy
hell are you doing?" In the slit of a door stood Mr.
Thomas, the neighbor who had been so kind the day
Robin fell into the well. The woman looked at him
and snarled, like a wild animal protecting its kill.
Mr. Thomas, his eyes wide from what he was beginning to see in the dimness, started forward. The
woman leapt to her feet, brandishing the dagger at
him. He drew to one side, not sure what to do. The
woman made the decision for him. With another of
her unearthly shrieks, she tore toward the door,
bowling over Mr. Thomas with one outstretched
hand, like a quarterback stiff-arming a lineman. The
stunned Mr. Thomas slowly sat upright, hearing the
woman's shoes running down the cloisters and then
disappearing completely. A moan from Lisa put him
back into action. Crawling over to where she lay, he
slipped the gadget bag under her head and began

rubbing her wrists vigorously, something he seemed to remember as being the correct procedure in the case of an unconscious person. Lisa's eyelids fluttered. Suddenly they shot wide open, still filled with the fear she had felt when the woman was battering her head against the wall.

"Don't try to move, Mrs. Lefferts. Just lie completely still," said Mr. Thomas, remembering something else he had read about the injured: "Do not allow the accident victim to move or be moved."

"What happened?" mumbled Lisa, her face suddenly flushing an embarrassed red.

"Oh. Oh, my," Mr. Thomas gasped, realizing that Lisa had just become aware that she was stark-naked and that a man was bending over her. He had been so shaken by his experience and trying to revive Lisa, he only realized her nakedness himself when Lisa did. Turning, he grabbed her sweater and tried to cover her with it. It wasn't long enough. He had to take off his jacket and use that to cover her from the waist down.

"What happened?" repeated Lisa, struggling to sit up. Gently, Mr. Thomas pushed her back down on the gadget bag. "Please lie still, Mrs. Lefferts. It's better for you. Concussions can be tricky, you know."

"Balls," said Lisa loudly, which was perhaps the most startling thing Mr. Thomas later remembered about the whole event. "I don't have a concussion. That crazy woman just kept battering my poor head against the wall and choking me, and I guess I was so frightened I passed out."

Mr. Thomas started to protest, but Lisa was so firm he abandoned the effort. Solemnly he stepped outside the building, planting himself across the slit door as its guardian until Lisa could get back into her clothes.

Later, at his house, Lisa sat in the living room, sipping the strong drink Mr. Thomas had prescribed.

It was the only one of his first-aid suggestions Lisa had accepted. Leaning back in her chair, she lifted the glass to her mouth with trembling hands. "It's funny," she said. "I keep coming here to have a drink and be pasted back together, one disaster after the other."

Mr. Thomas did not smile. "Look," he said. "Do you want me to call the police, or would you rather do it yourself?"

A sudden panic swept across Lisa. The walled garden was a place Chad had twice specifically forbidden her to visit again. Under ordinary circumstances, she probbly would have told him to take his orders and go to hell, but he was strung so taut she didn't dare give him another reason to scream at her. "Neither," she answered firmly. "I am not going to call the police. I ask you not to as well."

Mr. Thomas was dumbfounded. "But that insane woman. She's a menace to society. You don't know who she'll go after next." He could see that his words weren't changing Lisa's mind in the least, and moved to strike a personal chord. "Hell, it could be your own son. Or you yourself again. You can't allow a woman like that to stay loose." Lisa's face remained set. "And what about those poor murdered children?" Mr. Thomas pleaded. "I've heard about the terrible things she's done to them on television. Sickening things. It *has* to be the same woman; she was just beginning to shave your head when I got there."

Lisa gave a little cry of alarm and ran across the living room. In a gold-framed mirror that she'd seen hanging in the center of the end wall she examined her head. He was right. She could see where some of her hair had been sliced off, but by combing in a slightly different way from her usual style, she thought she could arrange it so Chad would not realize anything had happened. When she came back to where

Mr. Thomas was sitting, she attempted to divert the subject from the police.

"How," she asked, "did you ever happen to get to me in time like that, Mr. Thomas?"

"I was sitting on my terrace. It's pleasant this time of day. Then I heard something. I had figured you'd be back, you see, so when I heard shrieks—they may have been that woman's, not yours—I guessed it was you. I thought you'd probably fallen into another hole; that old place is probably full of them."

"Lucky for me you were outside."

"Yes." Thomas paused; he was aware of Lisa's effort to change the subject. "But about the police. They just have to be called, Mrs. Lefferts. If you're embarrassed, I'd be happy to call them for you."

Lisa walked over, leaned down, and gave him her most winning smile. "I wish I could, but I can't. And it would be just as bad for me if you called. You see, my husband and I are having—well, difficulties— and he told me after the first time never to go into that garden again. I know it sounds silly, but learning that I disobeyed him openly might just be the final straw. For Robin's sake, Mr. Thomas, I'm asking you—no, I'm *pleading* with you—not to get the police involved. It could mean the end of my marriage."

Mr. Thomas was an old man, a widower. He was touched as he hadn't been in years by Lisa's pleading, by the confidence she'd revealed to him. All of his arguments about the police began slipping away from him. Who was *he* to hurtle a young boy into the world without a father? Who was *he* to drive this woman, obviously deeply in love with her husband, into a world of singles bars and leering suitors?

"All right," he said, and for a brief second held her two still-shaking hands between his.

CHAPTER SIXTEEN

"Yes," answered Raymond d'Attollo. "Yes, there is every indication we have the same kind of thing again. The major differences would be, of course, that in yesterday's killings, there were two separate incidents, separated only by a couple of hours. The second woman was older than the rest have been so far."

"The same mutilations, the same shaving of the head, and the same knife marks on the stomach?"

"With both of the women, I'm afraid so."

"You've given us the name of the younger girl—Hannah Dennis—but nothing on the older woman. Can you?"

"We have no identification of the older woman so far. She may not even be from around here."

"You haven't commented, Chief, that both of yesterday's incidents occurred in broad daylight. That's another difference, isn't it?"

D'Attollo sighed. "Yes, of course it's another difference. But when you remember that you have two women, both killed in the same grisly way within a few hours of each other it seems a little unimportant."

Chief Raymond d'Attollo of the New Haven Police

Force stood in his office facing a small group of newsmen. Station WTNH-TV (Channel 8) was the only television station on its toes enough to get a camera there, and d'Attollo was less than appreciative of their efficiency. He hated television cameras and could feel the sweat forming under his shirt as he looked at the camera's angry red eye, fighting to appear in control of the situation. He hadn't wanted the newsmen called in so early, but the mayor had decided that since a stringer from the New Haven *Register* lived in Derby and was already on to the story, the city had to face up to the situation promptly or be accused of not acting quickly enough. "In something like this, Ray," the mayor had told him, "it's better to release the news yourself, to be reasonably frank with people, and to admit what you don't know, than it is to try hiding from the mess. Otherwise, the papers and stuff scream 'cover-up.' People catch on pretty quick, see, and if we can control what they hear, bend it to our own sitution, sort of, we keep ahead of them. This damned thing is right on the edge of causing panic."

At the moment, it was Chief d'Attollo who was the nearest to being panic's first victim. His job, his future, and his life hung on how fast he could come up with an answer to the "Screaming Woman," as the murderer had been dubbed. Grudgingly, he'd gone along with the mayor's insistence on this news conference—"to beat the damned *Register* to the punch," as the mayor put it. It was an open conference during which d'Attollo told them everything he knew—with one exception. The marks carved on the victims' stomachs were public property, by now. That they were carved in the shape of either an X or a cross was known only to the police. That would remain a secret —if only to screen out the compulsive confessors. For himself, d'Attollo was convinced it was a cross, but couldn't prove it.

"The woman in black—the 'Screaming Woman'—did anyone see her as they did after the Cosaro boy's killing?" asked Roy Caraveth of the *Bridgeport Times*.

D'Attollo winced. "Yes, someone said she saw a woman like that getting into a car. Not far from the murder site. Yeah, she was screaming, all right. But the car was so far away and the woman—for obvious reasons, I can't give you her name at the moment—was so terrified—the little Dennis girl's body was damned near right at her feet—that she couldn't even give a description of the color of the car. Obviously, no license tag number."

"That makes five killings—all of them damned brutal—attributed so far to the Screaming Woman," Roy Caraveth persisted. "Do you think there were more? What I mean is, if there were others, would you tell us about them?"

"Damned right I would," snapped d'Attollo.

"Well, Chief, sometimes—"

D'Attollo was saved by a sudden question from Frank Harris of WTNH. He looked at the man gratefully, surprised that his archenemy, television, should come to his rescue. "Chief, can you tell us what steps are being taken to find this woman?"

The sigh slipped out of d'Attollo before he was even aware it was inside him. "It's a hell of a tough job, finding that woman. We don't know which suburb she lives in—or, hell, it could be right in New Haven—we don't know where she works, we don't know what she looks like. The only thing we got is her crazy screaming—the people who've heard it say it sounds like nothing they ever ran into before—shrill, kind of, but louder than hell. Mixed up with words no one's ever been close up enough to understand. The only description we *have* got is of the dress she wears—long and black and loose."

Frank Harris remained gentle in his prodding. "Okay, a woman might be able to get away with a dress like that at nighttime—like it's an evening dress —but how do you explain that she can walk around in an evening dress in the middle of the afternoon like she must have to kill poor little Hannah Dennis? *And* the unidentified woman."

"It's not really like an evening dress. It's got a great big hood of some kind that sometimes is up, sometimes down. But I agree—it's a pretty distinctive-looking rig. Day *or* night."

Roy Caravath came back into the questioning. D'Attollo shuddered. It continued like this for perhaps another half hour, the newsmen not coming away with a hell of a lot—not because the authorities were trying to hide anything from them, but because the authorities, like everyone else, simply didn't *know* very much themselves.

Back in his office, d'Attollo mopped his forehead. He'd change his shirt and maybe wash under his arms; he hated to feel the stickiness of sweat on his body. Maybe he'd even slip out for a beer—he could use something. He was standing there, shirtless, when the low murmur of voices from the room that was his private anteroom hit him. Shit. Mrs. Dennis, the kid's mother. A teen-ager—d'Attollo thought it was the girl's older brother—appeared in the door. "Chief," he began.

D'Attollo quickly put the damp, sticky shirt back on and buttoned it partway up. The beer and the whore-bath would have to wait; he had a duty, a lousy one for sure, but a duty. Walking into the anteroom, he saw Mrs. Dennis crumpled against another woman, her body shaking with sobs, the other woman trying to soothe her.

A pair of wet eyes rose to meet his. "Did they— did they—tell me, please—did they rape my little girl?" Mrs. Dennis shook with a new fit of sobbing, but kept her eyes fastened tightly on d'Attollo.

"No. No, Mrs. Dennis. The prelim examination

proves that much conclusively. They shaved her head, they killed her. But no, no one even *tried* to rape her."

The woman nodded numbly. It wasn't much, but it was something. Suddenly, a realization of how little it was appeared to hit Mrs. Dennis; she screamed and dissolved back into the other woman's arms, sobbing, wringing her hands, cursing the world. D'Attollo decided it would be kinder to leave them alone in their misery, wondering, as he walked back into his office, how much of his kindness was genuine mercy and how much was the need to get the hell out of that room with the dissolving mother and the accusing faces of her other children.

In the end, he went and had the beer without washing under his arms. One thing a good police officer learns is the importance of priorities.

In front of the mirror in his bathroom, Chad Lefferts looked at himself with a puzzled expression. He knew he had had a seizure at his office but couldn't remember how he got home. That he had driven here was certain; out of his window he could see the gleaming gray-tan Ford pulled into the parking circle of the driveway. Not to remember something like driving home was frightening. It was also a little strange. Even stranger was what kept him peering into the mirror to see; down his entire left side, his body was covered with scratches—long, deep scratches that reminded him of the ones he'd wound up with after that whore in Tokyo had raked him with her fingernails. As he took off his clothes, besides the scratches Chad could see his entire body was also covered with dirt. Where the hell did he get that? It looked like farm dirt, but he couldn't be sure. All Chad knew for sure was that the damned scratches hurt when he stepped under the shower. As the warm water flowed across him, he began remembering small pieces of the nightmare on his couch that had preceded the seizure. A sudden emptiness surged over him as he thought about the abbess's ripping the novice's snatch up her middle with the crozier. Christ, what a thing for a guy to dream about.

The strangest part of the dream, he supposed, was that for the first time he and the abbess, as with Flavius and himself, really became one person. He'd always had this strange feeling that it was his voice she used; he knew he frequently felt his lips move when she spoke. But in today's nightmare, toward the end particularly, he'd felt as if it went much deeper than that, and that he *was* the abbess. That didn't make any sense, of course. Thinking of himself, he was well aware he wasn't the world's most perfect person; he had admitted that frequently to Lisa. He was selfish, he was dogmatic, he was capable of being cruel.

But compared to the abbess, he was Little Nell. He shuddered at what Dr. duBrul or Nils Lee would think if they knew the kind of stuff he dreamed about. The abbess was not only fiendishly inhuman, she was degenerate. The novice had even said she was a lesbian. A butchering, sadistic dyke.

For a moment, the water stinging hard against his body, Chad lived again the sight of the novice's trim young body struggling on the floor to escape the abbess. The shaved head should make anyone look ridiculous, but the sexually charged picture of her flat, struggling stomach and trim pointed breasts in their convulsions on the floor quickly overcame the essential absurdity of a bald woman. Chad could once again feel the sensual tingling he'd experienced during the dream; he supposed it was what the abbess had experienced, too. He looked down his body, wondering if the fantasy and the stinging, running water might produce an erection—to an impotent man, the ecstasy of the first rain-shower after a long, searing drought—but nothing happened. Shit. Stepping out of the shower, he dried himself furiously. His scratches —deep as they were—weren't oozing blood anymore, but he decided he should put something on them: antiseptic. Band-Aids. Christ, he wished he could remember where he had picked them up.

It never occurred to Chad to ask himself how many terrible things—such as what happened to Mary-Jo Camero or Troop Leader Cosaro or Hannah Dennis, or the unidentified mother—were going to have to happen before the truth was realized by him.

"Christ, it's hot in here tonight. You could bake a mongoose by just letting it lie around."

Lisa looked up from her book; Chad sounded more relaxed and good-natured than he had in days. "Well, mongoose chefs don't wear ties when they're cooking. No wonder you're broiling."

Chad glanced away so he wouldn't have to look Lisa in the eye. "I just felt like a tie. Maybe it was a lousy idea, at that." Usually it was easy for Lisa to spot when Chad was being evasive; tonight, she didn't notice. She was too pleased that he sounded so normal. The fact was, Chad was wearing the tie so that he could keep his shirt buttoned; several of the scratches on his neck would be visible otherwise, and he didn't want—and couldn't have even if he *had* wanted—to explain the scratches to Lisa. As always after a seizure, he felt briefly euphoric. Calm, relaxed, a little tired, but at peace with the world.

When Robin came in to say good night, Chad picked him up and threw him into the air, catching him at the last second on his way down. This was a game that Robin particularly loved, and one that he'd missed for several weeks. "Do it again, Daddy, do it again!" he squealed, giggling and laughing so violently, it was hard for Chad to pick him up again. The game continued until Chad wearied of it and sank into a chair, feigning exhaustion. "You're getting too heavy, Robin. Much too big and heavy. Three tosses these days and I'm ready to drop."

Robin was not so easily flattered out of the game. "One more time, Daddy, please, just one more time."

Getting out of his chair like an old man, Chad gave him one final mighty toss that allowed Robin to tell himself he had touched the ceiling. He was about to start pleading for yet another, but Chad fixed him with a fierce look.

"That was nice, Chad," said Lisa, happy to see the interplay between him and his son. "Go get yourself some milk and cookies, Robin, then I'll come upstairs to hear your prayers." Robin scuttled happily toward the kitchen.

"Whew," Chad sighed, fanning himself with a magazine. "The heat and Robin together are too much. Crazy weather for September." Chad thought for a second and then laughed. "Crazy weather for your crazy husband; I ought to love it."

Chad was acting so like himself, Lisa decided it was time to give him an edited version of what she'd learned from Mr. Thomas about the garden. If he accepted that, she desperately wanted to tell him what had happened there this afternoon. "This house shouldn't be that hot with these high ceilings," she began, starting from left field. "Of course, those damned sealed windows keep it from getting the cross-draft it ought to have."

"Makes sense," said Chad pleasantly.

"Did I tell you I'd learned *why* the windows were originally sealed? From a nice old man, Richard Thomas. He lives just down the block from that crazy walled-in garden."

Chad fixed her with the same fierce look he'd just used on Robin. But with Robin it was part of a game, with Lisa it was not. "You haven't been back inside that place, have you?"

"No. Of course not," Lisa lied. She would tell him the truth as the story unfolded; there was no point in having an argument right at the outset.

"Good."

Lisa wasn't sure if he really believed her, but plunged ahead anyway. "Old Mr. Thomas said both our house and the walled garden used to belong to an Old Blue. Nuts like most of them, of course." Old Blues, as Chad had once explained to her, are a peculiar species of Yale graduate, afflicted with a mysterious disease that makes them believe they have never graduated from school. In its mildest form, the disease compels its victims to attend reunions every year, whether their class is holding one or not. In its more virulent form, the disease's victims buy houses in New Haven, attend every conceivable function, hold cards to the library, and visit their former fraternities or societies any night there's anyone there to visit.

"Anyway," continued Lisa, "Mr. Thomas says this particular Old Blue used to own both our house *and* the walled garden behind it. The guy had an old abbey imported from abroad and set it up, stone by stone, inside the wall. It was supposed to be so secret that when he sold our house to the university, he sealed up all the windows so whoever was living here couldn't see into his private abbey. Even after he died, his will stipulated that no one could set foot inside the place." Lisa studied Chad's face. It wore an expression of faint skepticism, enigmatic enough so that Lisa didn't know what he was thinking.

Lisa had misread Chad's expression. It was not so much one of skepticism as of muted panic. Too many different things were closing in on him. The nightmares about the abbess—particularly the one about the abbess killing the little boy and the novice that had reminded him so of Robin and Lisa. And now, a reconstructed abbey directly behind him. Marcus

Flavius. The seizures and a growing realization of their relationship with the nightmares. The black hole beside Omikron Blue. The convergence of these different coincidences and forces seemed to be closing in to suffocate him, conspiring to destroy him. Abruptly, his earlier euphoria disappeared, replaced by a sullen need to strike out at the world. As the person nearest him, Lisa became the target.

"Shit." Chad's voice was a grunt seething with fury. "All that crap about an Old Blue and you really expect me to believe you haven't been back inside the garden. You lied, damn it. You looked me right in the eye and lied."

"Chad! Chad! It wasn't a lie. It was just—"

"I should be used to your lying by now. No wonder you were so damned anxious for me to go to the hospital. I bet you couldn't wait to get it on with this guy. Any prick in a storm. You and Thomas. I'd ask you more about it, but you'd just lie again."

"Chad . . ."

The hatred was still surging through Chad. A hatred that was the only escape valve available to his fear of a world that had stopped making sense. He didn't mean what he'd said, he knew that. Poor Lisa. None of the things that were destroying him were things he could tell her about. If he could have, she would have become his staunchest ally, he knew that, too. But he couldn't, and she became the surrogate victim of his mushrooming panic. "Fucking whore, that's what I married. A goddamned go-go girl who drops her pants for anyone who'll have her."

"Chad, Chad," Lisa stood over his chair, the tears running down her face. "Tell me. I know that wasn't you speaking. Tell me what's happening."

Chad reached for her hand, but abruptly snatched it back as if the hand were charged with electricity. The panic was rising inside him again; his reason dissolved. Shaking, he got up out of his chair. Some voice out of some other life formed and spoke the words. "All through our marriage, the other men, that's what's happening. Tell *me* about that, Lisa. Don't you know it's against God and the church to commit adultery? Sins of the flesh, damn it, that's what it's about."

The words startled Chad as much as they did Lisa. They were familiar to him, those words, words that the abbess had screamed at the novice in his nightmare. Why was he saying them? How had such old-fashioned phrases suddenly poured out of his mouth? It was as if he had been seized and possessed by something out of another lifetime.

Backing away, her face mirroring her shock, Lisa stared at her husband. "God and the church . . . sins of the flesh . . . adultery?" She looked at Chad as if he were a sudden stranger standing before her. "You can't be serious, Chad. My God, you can't. . . ." The growing self-righteousness Chad had demonstrated several times before cast a new and bewildering shadow across their familiar arguing, a kind of communication they had once actually delighted in.

To Chad, it was as if the whole world were spinning around him, moving faster by the second. With a terrible groan, Chad raced out of the room and upstairs to his own. Lisa stood in the center of the living room, watching him run blindly upstairs, listening until she heard his door slam shut behind him. Robin had apparently been witness to the last minute or so of Chad and Lisa's argument, and came into the room with a frightened, tentative look. Lisa put her arm around him and tried to think of something to say. Instead, Robin spoke.

"I had the cookies, Mummy. Can I stay up a little and watch television?"

Lisa knew what Robin was doing. He had been witness to something he wasn't supposed to, something that had happened that his mother and father shouldn't have allowed to happen, and was using her guilt to blackmail her into a special privilege.

Lisa forced a laugh. "No, sweetheart. Go upstairs and brush your teeth and get all ready for bed. I'll be up in a minute to hear your prayers and tuck you in."

"But, Mummy, I—"

"Scoot."

As a blackmailer, Robin gave in too easily; later, Lisa knew, he would learn the art of making the unspoken threat stick. Sadly she looked around the room. All of the artwork, so lovingly arranged around the fireplace wall, suddenly seemed silly. Maybe her passion for medieval art was silly too. Some of it, looked at objectively, was almost ugly.

But this room, no matter how it had been decorated, would have been ashes in her mouth now. Too much had happened here. Like the artworks, Lisa's whole life seemed suddenly ugly.

CHAPTER SEVENTEEN

The door opened quickly, as if someone had been standing just inside waiting for it to be knocked on. "I thought you might come today; in fact, Dr. Soong and I had a bet on it," Nils Lee said pleasantly. "He just lost." With a smile, Lee stepped back and welcomed Chad into his office. Dr. Soong, in spite of having been on the short end of the tote-board, shrugged sheepishly and smiled himself.

Chad almost turned around and walked out. There was a smugness to Nils Lee's assumption that irritated him. Yet the events of yesterday and his argument with Lisa had drained him of will. Slouching, he walked across the office, nodded to Soong, and took a chair. "Why?" he asked. "What I mean is, what made you think I'd show up?"

"I believe we're reaching a crisis. The convergence of many individual factors that have been battering you. I could spot it yesterday. I assumed the factors would approach a critical state after you left here. A seizure, perhaps. An ultimate nightmare, possibly." Chad knew Nils Lee was watching his eyes, waiting for some indication of which had happened. He finally had to make an admission.

"Both."

Lee shrugged. "It's not unusual."

Chad flared. "The whole thing is damned unusual to me." He was aware that Lee was only being objective and that he shouldn't let it upset him. But Chad's irritation with Lee because of the tacit assumption about his arrival today had grown and exploded with his suddenly casual tone about yesterday's happenings. The only thing he could thank Lee for at the moment was that at least he wasn't pushing the reincarnation nonsense this morning. "I came to you for help, not to be told that my problems are run-of-the-mill. If that's conceited, I'm sorry. But that's the way I feel."

"You're quite right, Chad. The remark was insensitive of me. Of course your problems are unusual. If they weren't, I wouldn't be spending all this time trying to get to the bottom of them." Nils Lee laughed. "There. *That* is *my* conceit."

"All right. Let me see if—"

Nils Lee held up his hand. "I think it would be better if we had one more hypnotic session, Chad, before discussing yesterday. What you dreamed, what lay behind the seizure, will probably play back during the session anyway. And I would much prefer to get to it before we've spent any length of time talking about it."

"All right," he said lamely, and settled back in the chair. The pulsar light was produced, and dimly he saw Lee opening the shelf of phony books to start the Ampex and the videotape recorder. Today it took practically no time at all; he was so conditioned by now that he could feel himself slipping into the trance almost the second the light and the electronic beeper were activated.

"Hand me that, will you." Lee whispered to Soong, and the linguist reached for a small, shiny probe lying on top of his desk. Carefully Nils drew the pointed tip of the probe first across the back of Chad's hands, then his neck, then the side of his cheek, pressing hard enough with it so that anyone not in the deepest state of trance would react, but not so hard as to leave marks. There was no reaction. "Under. Really under today," said Nils Lee in a normal voice. "It always amazes me how quickly subjects become increasingly vulnerable to hypnosis and go under more easily and deeply with each successive session. I suppose, in theory, you could carry that to a point where you could get a subject to stop his heart from beating."

Soong looked alarmed. "Nils, you're not—"

"No, of course not," Lee answered. "Just a fascinating speculation." Lee adjusted the dials on the Ampex, placed the microphone nearer to Chad, and turned to Soong. "All yours. I'd start with the Latin. Then try the Frisian. I don't know if we'll get anything there this time or not."

The questions Soong had prepared today about Rome were exhaustive and filled with little-known minutiae. Dr. Machri in Rome had cooperated—without knowing why—adding some verifiable detailed questions of his own. Lee hoped to keep Chad away from too deep an involvement with Flavius and his fear of crucifixion, and on more productive areas that would help him establish his hypothesis of Chad Lefferts as a full-blown, provable reincarnation. In the Frisian area, neither he nor Soong had any idea of what Chad's time frame was—except within the limits of when the language was spoken—or of who was talking in this long-dead language, or even, for sure, of the sex of the speaker.

Soong took Chad back in time, speaking to him entirely in Latin, and posed his questions. One after the other, Marcus Flavius answered them calmly and exhaustively. It was when Soong mentioned the Temple of Mars and Minerva that the state of tranquility

suddenly evaporated. Chad began stirring restlessly
in his seat, his hands rising from the chair's arms
and dropping back with listless, dead looseness; his
whole body began to shake and he had trouble staying
in the chair. Prompted by Nils Lee, Soong asked Chad
what was happening.

"It is the guard again. The Imperial Guard," Soong
whispered to Lee in a brief translation of Chad's
frenzied burst of Latin. "They have me cornered.
This time they will catch me, I know they will catch
me. My God, I will be crucified." Chad ignored them,
continuing to scream in Latin. Abruptly, he sprang
from the chair and hid behind anything he could
find in Lee's office, pressing himself into corners, trying to crawl under the furniture. Suddenly he knelt
on the floor and prayed God for forgiveness for his
frailty. But his eyes apparently saw the guard coming again, and he dashed to the other side of the
room, whimpering. "No, no, no! I am close relative
of our Emperor Tiberius," he screamed. "I have done
nothing . . . you must leave me . . . I command you
to leave me in the name of the Emperor. . . ." Chad
turned around and once again groaned his curious
warning to unseen others behind him. "Hide yourselves, for God's sake, hide yourselves."

Responding to Lee's whispered advice, Soong talked
quickly to him in a dizzying outpouring of colloquial
Latin, assuring Chad that the guard had left, that
they had seen someone else and gone running after
them. Dr. Soong tried to find out who the people
Chad was warning were, but could get no response.
Chad stood in the middle of the room, blinking. "I
have denied our Lord again," Soong translated for
Lee. "My faith is frail. Christ, dear Christ, forgive me
for my weakness."

Gently Soong talked Chad back into his chair. Lee
told the linguist to let him rest for a few moments; it
was important, he said, they not have to waken him

now. Soong nodded. They both watched Chad sitting in his chair; his breathing became deeper as he went deeper into the cataleptic state. To make sure, Nils Lee turned up the volume of the electronic beeper. They could see the shaking and twitching slowly drain out of Chad's body; he appeared to be a man in a deep state of benign repose. Nils Lee gave a gentle laugh. "Someday I'm going to have a word with that damned Imperial Guard. They keep lousing things up." Picking up the shiny chromium probe once more, Lee moved toward Chad to see how deep a hypnoidal state he had achieved.

Then it happened. For a moment no one was sure what was going on. Nils Lee, his eyes fastened on the probe he was about to press into Chad Lefferts's cheek, first felt himself thrown violently backward—so hard he tripped and landed on the floor, painfully twisting his left wrist—and then saw Chad dive across the room. The sound coming out of him was unearthly: a high-pitched scream, piercing, but guttural, that tore at the air around it; its frequency was so rapid, it sounded almost like a woman's scream, but a woman filled with a passionate hatred of the world.

Dr. Soong had risen from his chair, his mouth open, unable to move as Chad's body hurtled straight at him. From somewhere Chad had pulled a knife—it was a short, ugly, twisted affair—and, still screaming, had raised it high in the air to plunge it into the still motionless Dr. Soong.

Nils Lee's instincts reacted faster than his logic; he tore across the office and began wrestling with Chad from behind, trying to pin his arms. He was stunned at Chad's strength; if Dr. Soong hadn't been able to raise the clipboard he was using to hold his notes in front of him, the twisted dagger would have ripped him down the middle. Again and again the dagger tore through the air, each time deflected by Soong's clipboard, which he kept moving in front of him like a shield. It struck Nils Lee that Chad's strength might not be diminished by the hypnoidal state—in fact, he wondered if it hadn't increased—but that his ability to cope with changing situations *had*. Three times in a row now, Lee had noticed Chad strike almost the identical spot on the clipboard, like an automaton following the orders of some unseen commander.

Lee increased his efforts to pin Chad's arms. Chad had changed from his earlier screaming to a chain of furious shrieks, words in a language that Nils Lee could not understand. Dr. Soong could. He yelled at Chad in the same tongue, lashing out, trying to get through to him. In spite of Nils Lee's injured wrist—it hurt like hell—he was finally able to pull Chad halfway around and off Soong. Screaming the terrifying high-pitched scream again, Chad threw himself at Nils Lee instead, the twisted dagger flashing in the air above him.

What should have occurred to Lee some moments earlier finally did; until this moment, the confusion and surprise had overwhelmed the logical. Shouting Chad's name, Lee clapped his hands loudly, three times—the pain this produced in his left wrist made his face contort—and brought Chad out of his hypnoidal state.

Chad stood stock-still in the center of Nils Lee's office, his eyes blinking as if each blink were an excruciatingly painful process; slowly his eyes saw the strange dagger in his hand, and his expression, already one of childlike bewilderment, turned gradually to one of stark comprehension.

Soong and Nils Lee, panting from their struggle with Chad, exchanged glances of relief. Lee even essayed a weak joke. "Just now, the Imperial Guard looks like a pretty tame outfit."

Shaking himself, Soong slowly sat down in his chair, examining the back of the clipboard; he was stunned by the realization that the deep gouges in the wood had been intended for him.

"That dagger, Chad—or whatever it is—do you know where you got it, Chad?" Nils Lee asked.

Chad's speech was still slurred, the words coming out of him in thick clots of language, almost whispered, incoherent, and very difficult to understand. "Lisa—it's Lisa's—part of her collection—don't know—don't know why I have it—medieval art collection—on the wall—living room—doesn't make sense . . ." Uncertainly, Chad stared at the dull bronze-handled weapon in his hand, shaking his head as if in an effort to clear it.

"May I see it, Chad?" Lee asked gently.

"Oh. Of course. It's a funny-looking thing. But Lisa—Lisa said it was very old." A recollection of something swept through him and he looked at Lee. "I remember now. I was going to drop it off at the Art Museum for her. She said they'd agreed to try and tell her exactly when and where it was made." The sudden note of brightness faded from his voice, replaced by a tone of inner sadness. "It was always on the living-room wall. She had some other *objets* hanging there, too. Medieval stuff, all of it."

"I tell you what, Chad. Dr. Lansing of the Peabody is an expert on medieval weaponry. It's a hobby of his—almost a passion. He can give you a complete run-down on it for Lisa. Leave it with me, and I'll get him to look at it for you."

"That would be very kind of you." In the circumstances it was an inane answer, and Chad knew it. His answer had been so overly polite it sounded like part of a conversation snatched out of the heart of a faculty tea. He corrected himself, aware as he did, that he was only making things worse. "What I mean is, that's great. Thanks."

"Chad," began Nils Lee. "I know you must be exhausted. But I want to go into what happened here quickly, while the experience is still on the top of your unconscious. I'm going to make us some coffee— or would you rather have a drink?—and then we can discuss some things that are overdue to be gone over."

"A drink," Chad answered miserably. "Scotch?"

Nils Lee nodded and disappeared into the small kitchen to one side of his office, pulling Dr. Soong after him with a look. "That language he was yelling in. Could you make anything out?"

"Old Norse. Frisian, as I said before." Soong smiled thinly. "Frankly, I was a little too busy keeping myself from being sliced up to be able to give you a verbatim, but in this manifestation he is definitely a woman. I can tell, you see, from the word endings; as with many Slavic-root languages the masculine and feminine genders of the same word are frequently completely different. For instance, the word for 'high' in the—"

"Did you get anything of what he *said*?" Lee demanded impatiently. The professorial approach to things frequently maddened him.

"It was difficult," answered Soong, a little taken aback, "the dagger and everything. But he—she—was yelling at what seemed to be a novice. A sister in training. A provisional. I shall have to check the words out carefully, of course, but I think I'm correct in that. In any case, she was screaming at this novice. Again, I'll have to check his words against my memory. You made a sound tape?"

"In the morning. I'll give it to you in the morning." Dr. Soong was almost pushed out the side door of the office by Lee; Soong appeared baffled, but Nils Lee did not want Chad and the linguist to get into any discussion that would interrupt the rhythm of the session.

Back in his office, Lee handed Chad his drink and set his own on the small table beside his chair. Gleaming dully at them from the corner of the desk, the

bronze handle of the twisted dagger stared nakedly at
them like a gesture of reproach. Covertly, watching
Chad pull on his drink, Nils Lee glanced at the Ampex
to make sure there was still plenty of audio tape left
to go. Because the machine was only running at 1 7/8
IPS, there was. Nils Lee exhaled in relief; to put a
new reel on now could have upset everything. The
videotape was still good for three hours.

"Chad, this last hypnotic session adds a completely
new element to things. New to me, anyway. Tell me,
these nightmares of yours, have you been having a
different kind recently? Ones in which you play the
role of a woman?"

Chad's mouth fell open. The new series of nightmares was something he had kept wanting to tell Nils
Lee about, but something else had always come up.
The fact that Lee already knew of them startled and
upset him. "Well, yes," he fumbled. "I meant to tell
you, but—"

Quickly Lee tried to put him at ease. "Nothing to
worry about, Chad. Would you like to tell me about
them now?"

A long, deep sigh rose from Chad. He was unable
to decide why telling Nils Lee of these new nightmares
made him feel so uncomfortable. That he wanted to
tell Lee of them he was sure, yet something repeatedly
kept frustrating his efforts each time he tried. Chad
knew enough about psychology to realize such con-
tinually failed attempts meant he was deliberately
searching for excuses not to. DuBrul had put his
finger on it yesterday: "You want—but do *not* want—
to tell me about these new dreams. It is difficult to
imagine what could be in the nightmares that makes
you so reluctant to talk about them. Consider: violent
things, dirty things, disgusting things—there's probably
nothing I haven't already heard from one patient or
another. . . ."

Nils Lee appeared to be reading his mind. "You

know, Chad, there's nothing to be embarrassed about in what you may have dreamed. Hell, if a man were judged by his dreams, my God, we'd all be frying in hell." He paused, about to inject a thought but wanting to be sure he could gauge Chad's reaction. "However evil, of whatever sex, a dream is a dream is a dream. Telling me just might help in our investigations here if I knew about them."

Chad wasn't sure he agreed with Nils Lee, or that he believed him. His instinct was right. For years Lee had struggled in his own mind with the problem of how responsible a man should be held for his past actions during earlier lives. Is, for instance, a well-meaning, benign reincarnation of a sadistic, evil Torquemada going to be influenced by his earlier life as the Inquisition's cruelest examiner? Or conversely, is the reincarnation of Dr. Albert Schweitzer necessarily a pure, almost saintly jungle physician as a result of his earlier karman as Schweitzer? Sometimes Nils Lee could feel, looking at Chad, the tortured goodness of Flavius, and, more recently, could feel the evil of the new violent woman's life in his past. Lee became suddenly aware of Chad, still sitting slumped in his chair, his tired-looking eyes searching Lee's face. "Anyway," said Lee suddenly, "those dreams—those nightmares—of yours, Chad. We might just make a great step forward if you could bring yourself to talk about them."

Reluctantly, haltingly, Chad surrendered. He told Nils Lee the entire frightening story of the abbess, the choir, the *castratol*, and the novices, even the gory details of the bishop's crozier. "They really got to me, those nightmares. Even worse than the ones about Flavius. He was a scared man. Frightened, but basically good. The abbess was so evil, so incredibly evil.

"And I could see what she saw and she what I saw; she spoke with my voice and I with hers; it was like she *was* me."

"In a way, she was."

Chad snorted, but the sound lacked conviction. He could hear it himself: little by little, particularly under the pressure of his experiences as the abbess, Nils Lee's thesis of reincarnation, something at which he had scoffed so thoroughly at first, was beginning to take possession of him.

"Do you know the abbess's name, Chad?"

"No. I don't remember the sisters calling her anything but 'Abbess.' I have a feeling—I can't explain it now—that it was a name like Helen or Ellen—anyway, something like that."

"Do you know where this abbey was?"

"There is some carving on the floor of the narthex that—"

"Narthex?" It was a curious word, one unfamiliar to Nils Lee, and he wondered if Chad was beginning to lapse into Frisian.

"The narthex. It's a sort of vestibule, a place where the penitents and the unbaptized have to stay instead of coming into the church itself." Chad thought for a second. "It's pretty dismal there—people are moaning and pleading to be let in the rest of the way."

"I see." Lee did not press the point, but this obscure bit of ancient church custom could be part of Chad's experience in only one way.

"Anyway, in the narthex of the abbey chapel there is this circular design carved deeply into the floor. It's some sort of squared-off cross, with ends that suddenly grow larger. And around the cross are the words 'Given to the Glory of God in Augsburg.' I'm not sure how big Augsburg was, but it seems to me it was a good-sized town or city."

"Quite a large one. In Bavaria. Very, very old. If I remember, it was founded as a fort by the younger brother of Tiberius, later the Emperor Nero. Chad, can you describe the town?"

Chad looked at him as if he were crazy. "Me? Good

God, Nils, I've never been there. Or anywhere in Germany."

Lee moved quickly. "Then how did you know about the carving on the floor of the abbey?"

"I—I—Jesus, Nils, I don't know how." An expression of confusion mixed with bitter resignation settled across Chad's face. What Nils Lee had been trying to get him to accept these last few days, what he had scoffed at, what he had heard of himself as Flavius on the tape, had shaken but not really persuaded him. He had been able to cling to the belief that somehow what Lee said was untrue. That it was the product of some sort of psychic legerdemain. An illusion. A con game. His own description of the narthex in Augsburg—what the hell was he doing talking about something like a "narthex" anyway? It was a word he'd never even been aware of until he himself used it— but his description of the outcasts in the narthex pleading for admittance and his detailed recollection of the carving on the floor had rattled his conviction as nothing else to this point had. There was no possible explanation, unless—the hypnosis. That was it, the hypnoidal trances. Post-hypnotic suggestion. Nils Lee had deftly planted the description of the carving, the wailing petitioners in the narthex—all of it—in his unconscious.

"What about the new tapes?" he demanded of Nils Lee, almost savage in his anger.

"Let's talk about some other things first, Chad. These new tapes—well, they're going to shake you up a bit. And they'll make more sense if I outline what I think is happening to you first."

Chad gave a derisive hoot. "You mean you thought you had everything rigged to sell me the idea of an earlier life as Flavius. Now somebody else—someone out of the nightmares, for Christ's sake—has loused up your plan. Tough." His arrogance was born of desperation, and Chad knew it. So did Nils Lee.

Crossing the office, Lee picked up Chad's glass and made them both another drink. He was trying to re-cast the situation and get Chad into a more relaxed, receptive state of mind before he went any further. For the next few minutes, Nils Lee struggled to change the subject entirely. In desperation he even resorted to talking about the World Series, a phenomenon he had a nodding acquaintance with only because Dr. Soong—an improbable fan if ever there was one—talked of games behind and batting averages and pitching streaks and designated hitters *ad nauseam*. Looking at Chad's expression, it was clear that Chad had as little interest in baseball as he himself did.

Chad's head rose. His eyes were drooping and the conversation was making him increasingly sleepy—product, he suspected, of his Lee-induced catalepsy. The words came out with difficulty. "The new tapes . . . I want to see the new tape."

"In a minute, Chad. First, let me explain some-thing. Ordinarily, someone who has lived before—a reincarnate—has only one karman inside him. If there are two, they share the cyclic electric brain energy with the host body—the reincarnate. For some reason, in your case, both of these previous lives inside you are struggling for dominance: Marcus Flavius on one hand, and what you refer to as the abbess on the other. This is highly unusual. The only explanation I can come up with is that they are struggling for the phys-ical possession of your present manifestation, presum-ably so that they will be the first of the karmans to go on to another life when you die. . . . Somewhere I've read of such a phenomenon before, but I confess I—"

Chad, drawing slowly on his drink, only heard part of Nils Lee's explanation. It made sense if you *be-lieved* what Lee believed, but the entire subject seemed terribly removed from himself at the moment, and, besides, he was too tired to argue about any-thing. Slowly, he let the exhaustion creep over him, a deep, numbing paralysis of the will softly lulling him toward sleep. Nils Lee's voice had grown softer and dimmer, and finally Chad couldn't hear it at all.

A gentle noise made Lee look up in mid-sentence. The sound had been a soft snore; Chad was dead to the world, his head drooped forward, one finger of his left hand occasionally twitching as he sat motionless in his chair. Nils Lee sighed. He knew Chad had been awake at least partway into his exposition; he hoped it had been long enough to let him make his point. Gently he shook Chad and talked him into going home, an errant child who refuses to surrender to bedtime. Sleepily Chad finally agreed.

Nils Lee watched him leave and then, checking his watch, made a call to Munich. Dr. Erich Schwarz, an old friend, was a splendid historian and would be able, possibly without resorting to reference material, to tell him all about the abbey in nearby Augsburg. If anything was known about an abbess with a name "something like Ellen," a violent woman who existed during the days when Frisian was still spoken in this part of Germany, Schwarz would know of that, too. Usually reaching Europe was easy; today the long-distance circuits to Munich seemed to take forever before they finally stopped their electronic chattering and put him through.

CHAPTER EIGHTEEN

Mrs. Lafferty kept trying to help, but repeatedly found herself rebuffed. Not even very politely. "I can do it, damn it. I can do it fine, Mrs. Lafferty," Chad kept repeating.

"But that's *my* kind of job, Professor, don't you know. It needs a little more water and a lot more elbow grease—not to be suggestin' you aren't putting your back into it, Professor. But it's woman's work and—"

"I will do it myself, Mrs. Lafferty, and that is that."

The sharp edge to Chad's voice let her know that the professor's mind was not to be changed; nor did Mrs. Lafferty miss the note of irritation and impatience that laced it. Behind his back, she threw her hands in the air and settled for watching him struggle at the sink. Pride. For the love of God, men had such stupid pride. She was standing in her gleaming kitchen while Chad, bent over at an awkward angle, tried to polish something in the stainless steel flower sink. On the draining-board were arrayed all the chemicals and brushes and cloths man had ever invented for the cleaning and polishing of metal, but for something like this, with so many years' accumulation of tarnish and

time, it needed a professional. Such as herself. Th
professor's grunts and curses finally chased her fro
the pantry, and Mrs. Lafferty, shaking her head sadl
walked slowly out through the swinging door into th
dining room. There were, after all, many things in th
house that could use a good polish, and the sight c
the professor's lack of expertise set Mrs. Lafferty t
collecting them. After he was done playing, she woul
show him how the job was *really* done.

Lisa arrived home in high spirits. Her latest phote
graphs from inside the walled-in garden—the one
showing the detail work on the columns, the complet
views of the cloisters, and a series of spectacularl
clear shots of the curious building at the cloisters
right end, had produced considerably more excitemen
than her first set. Members of the department hac
clustered around the prints, pointing out one feature
after another, excited as children at their first glimps
of the sea. The praise was lavish; the commendation.
flattering. Lisa had left the museum feeling both ap
preciated and fulfilled.

Deliberately she had not mentioned that in taking
the pictures she had almost gotten herself killed, o
mentioned the crazy lady with the high-pitched shriek
who had attacked her there. She knew the university':
position in letting her do what they themselves did
not consider legally permissible was tentative; to include an attempted murder in her recital would have
ended any future expeditions there.

Stepping inside her front door, Lisa immediately
felt something was wrong. She could not put her finger
on it, but some inner voice was whispering in her ear
with ominous clarity. As she crossed the front hall her
eyes glanced into the empty living room. She stopped
abruptly, unable to believe what she saw. The Roman
soldier's breastplate, stolen from Pompeii, hung in its
usual place on the stone fireplace wall. But someone

had polished it to an unbelievable shine, its ancient surface burnished as if on a polishing wheel. Two thousand years of history had been polished off the breastplate in the process; instead of its former dark, almost black color—the oxidation and aging that proved its antiquity—it now gleamed like a cheap brass doorknocker on a split-level. Lisa stared at it, still unbelieving. The breastplate was Chad's pride and joy, the one piece of artwork he had ever seemed genuinely interested in; Lisa swore, preparing herself to skewer Mrs. Lafferty for so stupid a transgression.

Mrs. Lafferty got to Lisa before Lisa could get to her. "He spent near two hours on it, you know, mumbling, sort of. I tried to help but he was rude, quite ugly, about it. Not like him. It isn't my position to say, of course, but I thought that an antique was *supposed* to look old; the way he shined it up, it looks like the handle of a chippy's handbag, don't you know."

Lisa turned her stare from the breastplate toward Mrs. Lafferty. "The *professor* did that? Are you sure, Mrs. Lafferty? He's ruined it."

"I watched him, m'um. Right out in my flower sink. For hours—scrubbing and rubbing and swearing as if the Devil hisself was in the dirt."

Mrs. Lafferty had many failings and could be irritating beyond belief, but Lisa had never known her to vary from the truth by so much as a word. "I still can't believe it, Mrs. Lafferty. I thought it had to be someone else." She paused and forced a laugh. "To be perfectly honest, I thought *you'd* done it to make it look better."

With an expression somewhere between shock and wounded pride, Mrs. Lafferty swallowed hard. "*Me,* m'um? Never. I worked around university folks too long to tamper with their stuff."

An apology was called for and given.

Mrs. Lafferty could sense she had Lisa on the defensive and used the opportunity. "Could I ask you—mind you, I know you could take offense at my meddling—could I ask you a personal question, m'um?"

Inside Lisa something fell like a heavy weight. She could guess what Mrs. Lafferty's question would be; she also didn't know how to answer it. "Of course, Mrs. Lafferty. You're almost one of the family," she said numbly.

"It's the professor, m'um. Is he all right? What I mean is, the man's changed so since I first came here. Solemn and all. And I don't understand too much of what he's talking about anymore. Is Professor Lefferts sick, m'um?"

The question. Innocent. Unanswerable. Well-intentioned, but eviscerating. Lisa fumbled. "Well, no, Mrs. Lafferty, no, he isn't. Just a little tired. His work—all this change—new responsibilities—new people—everything all at once . . ." She looked at Mrs. Lafferty, aware her answer had been both too long and highly unconvincing. Part of her wanted to break into tears, to tell this relative stranger the private hell she was living in, to ask her what to do. The other part was busily building a high wall around her emotions: to confide in this woman, even if she was desperate to share her problem with someone, with anyone, would be self-defeating. Mrs. Lafferty wouldn't know what she was talking about. Mrs. Lafferty would tell the other ladies of the domestic's underground and it would be all over New Haven by morning. Mrs. Lafferty was too ignorant, too simple, to grasp even the perimeters of her agony. Lisa felt herself closing tight, like a disturbed clam.

For a moment Mrs. Lafferty studied her, then: "That's what I thought."

Lisa panicked. "That's what I thought" *what*? That she herself was too ignorant to be told what Lisa thought was going on, or that, well, yes, Mrs. Lafferty, yes, Professor Lefferts was sick as hell and she didn't know what to do about it? For the first time she could think of, Lisa wished she had been gifted with a sister or a brother—or even that she had a near-by close friend—to whom she could talk and be re-asssured. Mrs. Lafferty remained planted in the door-way, finally clearing her throat to remind Lisa she was still there. Lisa stumbled on a solution that avoided any further temptation to talk. "You know, Mrs. Lafferty, I was thinking on the way home. You've been working awfully hard here and doing all that nightwork as baby-sitter, too, and I was thinking you really ought to take more time off. Why don't you start today, and, you know, just go home or shopping or whatever you like."

"It's only noon, Mrs. Lefferts."

"I know. But you could go to the movies or some-thing. . . ."

Mrs. Lafferty argued, Lisa persevered. Grumbling, Mrs. Lafferty finally left. As Lisa heard the front door close, she did something she practically never did. She mixed herself a stiff drink and collapsed into a chair in the library. As the drink reached her, she could feel her eyes filling with tears. How sick *was* Professor Lefferts? My God, didn't *anyone* know the answer to that question?

Chad, without benefit of drink, was, like Lisa, sit-ting in a chair staring straight ahead of him, feeling a little like crying himself. Nils Lee had never played him the tape; he didn't have to. From his experience with Flavius and what he'd heard himself say while in the hypnoidal state, he could imagine all too well. The tapes showed that, in catalepsy, he acted out the nightmares of his life as Flavius. He could assume that, in the last session with Nils Lee, he had, for some reason, suddenly begun acting out the nightmare of his life as the abbess. Chad shuddered.

Slowly he let his eyes rise to his blackboard. It was

clean, washed by the maintenance man and empty except for a large "651"—the persistent number the computer kept feeding back to him, representing, in one extrapolation at least, the number of light-years away that Omikron Blue was from Earth. That is, if someone with an electron telescope could focus their lens on the star, what they saw would be what was happening there six hundred and fifty-one years earlier. Conversely, if someone could stand on Omikron Blue and train their electron telescope on Earth, what they would see happening would be what had happened six hundred and fifty-one years earlier.

That would be the year A.D. 1327. It did not escape Chad that that was also the approximate time that Nils Lee and his experts had fixed as the era of the abbess. More interesting, around the black hole near Omikron Blue were two concentric discs, representing areas where, over the years and as the power of the black hole's awesome gravity slowly diminished, enough light had escaped the gravitational field to give a faint dark-gray aura around the black hole's lightless center. Written beneath the magic "651" was a smaller "X2.97." In his earlier calculations Chad had discovered the gravitational field of the outermost of these discs to be an inverse 2.97, or .3367 of the gravity field at its center. If you multiplied the abbess's 651 by this constant, 2.97, you arrived at the figure 1933. Subtracting that number from this year's date gave you A.D. 44, a date fixed by Nils Lee and others as about the time that Marcus Flavius had been hounded around Rome by the Imperial Guard.

In an insane, obtuse way, it was all beginning to fit together. Chad had never said as much, but the experience of seeing himself on tape—speaking freely in Latin, a language with which he had had only the remotest acquaintance, had made a tremendous impression upon him. So had Lee's apparent knowledge of the abbess and Augsburg, something the man could only have obtained from the latest tape. What he had so long avoided accepting was becoming increasingly difficult to shrug off; his own figures and permutations were beginning to add a quasi-scientific base to Nils Lee's beliefs. It was something he had never admitted to Lee, nor could he; he had trouble enough admitting it to himself.

This unwillingness to accept reality—albeit an insane reality—was why he had pretended to be asleep when Nils Lee outlined his explanation of the two separate karmans living inside him—Flavius and the abbess—locked in a deadly battle for possession of him. He had only closed his eyes to *appear* asleep, avoiding the need for any comment or reaction on his own part. Chad Lefferts sighed. He wished it were as easy to close his eyes and shut out the whole crazy mess.

On the surface, he pretended he didn't really give a damn who wound up in possession of him, but this, he knew, was a pose. If someone had to win, he very much wanted the winner to be Flavius, a weak man, perhaps, but a well-intentioned one. Like himself. For the abbess to win was unthinkable—but possible. A sudden question crossed his mind. If he should suddenly die—kill himself, for instance—who then would have possession of him?

Chad shook himself and stood up. He was nowhere near ready for suicide yet.

The return call from Munich didn't come until almost ten thirty that night. Earlier, Nils Lee had spoken to Dr. Schwarz and learned what he had expected: yes, there had once been a seal carved on the floor of the abbey such as Chad had described, but the entire place had been floored over again sometime during the fifteenth century when the abbey was upgraded by the Church hierarchy. But he seemed to remember, Schwarz had added, references to the seal in early German ecclesiastical writings.

To learn about the abbess herself, Schwarz had had to do some quick research, which is why it took so long for him to return Lee's call—and when he was already home for the day. "This abbess you mention—with a name like Helen or Ellen—is probably Elua of Schrobenhausen," Schwarz added. "She was every bit as violent and cruel as the woman you describe. At the time, her reputation was such that she was referred to locally as 'The Mad Abbess of Augsburg.' We do not have a great deal of reliable information on the woman, but it seems strange that Elua could survive in even the brutal church of that time. For instance, she frequently castrated the best boy sopranos in her orphanage to keep the choir in good voice. Granted, the Vatican at the time had its own *castrati,* but it was unusual for a local abbey to use such a practice. The writings suggest she probably enjoyed the castrations.

"You see, Elua was obsessed by the wickedness of sex. She constantly believed her novices were carrying on behind her back, and her punishment of them was violent and brutal. Some were torn apart on Elua's orders, others she stabbed to death personally. All of them, once the abbess had decided they were guilty, were mutilated. There are several accounts, Nils, of how she carved a ritualistic cross on the stomachs of the novices before she killed them; it was, she said, her way of proving to God that she was punishing them for their sins against Him.

"We have no accurate account of how she died, Nils. Except one can assume her cruelty didn't catch up to Elua until she was a very old woman. Through her family, she had connections with the local bishops, you see. We do know that she was burned to death— apparently on the orders of the Abbot Christian of Munich. And that, I'm afraid, Nils, is about all I could find for you on such short notice. If you want me to search further . . ."

Nils Lee assured Schwarz he didn't, and that what

he'd already given him was more than enough. He allowed the conversation to drift into other areas, not really listening to what Schwarz was saying, and then ended the call almost abruptly, thanking Schwarz for a job that had obviously taken him well into the small hours of morning, Munich time, and hung up.

For the last few minutes of the call, Nils Lee hadn't been listening at all. A terrible suspicion was raging inside him; it had passed through his mind once before, but what Schwarz told him had given his fleeting suspicion a new and ugly solidity.

Oddly, his first question to himself was whether or not anything he had done could have made matters worse. For a man who believed what Nils Lee had come to believe over the years, the question made little apparent sense.

"I don't really know. And I'm very afraid, even if I did, I couldn't say anything. I have to be guided by the canon of ethics, certain rules, you see, that govern privileged communications."

"But in a case like this. How can I know what I'm supposed to do? What I'm supposed to think? It's a nightmare."

Peter duBrul nodded in agreement, trying to ignore the clammy sweat he could feel beneath his shirt gathering in tiny rivulets and running down his sides. In front of him, her face drawn, her eyes lined with sleeplessness, sat Lisa Lefferts. Her request to be told what was happening to her husband, Chad, seemed entirely fair and reasonable. The poor woman had every right to know; her life, and that of her child, were as deeply concerned as his patient's. It was why duBrul had agreed to this unusual Saturday-morning meeting.

Yet, without Chad's permission—and Chad had made it enormously clear that under no circumstances was Lisa ever to be told anything he and his psychiatrist discussed—his hands were tied. If he violated that trust, the APA—the American Psychoanalytical Association—could, quite literally, take away his license to practice.

DuBrul's position was made more eviscerating for him by the fact of his original disclosures to Nils Lee about Chad. The APA would have glowered at him for that, certainly, but at least it could be partially explained away on the basis of a professional consultancy. Inside, duBrul groaned. Even seeing Chad's wife in these circumstances was unethical. He searched frantically for something to say.

"I wish I could be of more help, Mrs. Lefferts. And while I'm barred from saying anything to you about your husband's condition, there's nothing to stop you from telling me what *you* feel, of what you know about the situation, and anything you know of that's been happening in your husband's life. I realize it isn't what you came to see me for—or anything near it—but I might learn some things from you that your husband —perhaps unintentionally—has not told me. In a sense, we would work together, and perhaps help your husband, even if professional ethics do not allow me to comment in any way on what I personally know."

Lisa bridled. This man was virtually asking her to inform on her husband. But almost at the same moment, she realized that she knew absolutely nothing of what was going on in Chad's life at the moment, and that that was the principal reason she had come to see Dr. duBrul. "You know, I'm sure, of his"—the words were hard for her to force out of herself—"his—his—"

"Impotence? Yes."

"And about this strange Dr. Nils Lee? He seems to spend a great deal of time with him. In some ways, Doctor, I think it's made him worse."

This was an area duBrul very much didn't want

to get into. But Lisa's last words left him no choice. "Worse in what way?"

"I can't explain it, Dr. duBrul. Moodier. More distant. A good deal more frenzied. It's impossible to put it into words."

DuBrul gave one of the noncommittal nods that are standard ammunition in the analyst's arsenal. Lisa could sense it; duBrul could feel her tighten up. From this point on, their conversation never rose above a strained, impersonal level. Lisa learned nothing from duBrul; duBrul learned nothing from Lisa—except perhaps that Chad's exposure to Nils Lee had affected him negatively, at least in the opinion of the man's wife. It was a piece of information duBrul savored, and one he would use later on Lee.

As she left, Lisa turned to Dr. duBrul, shook his hand warmly, and looked duBrul squarely in the eye. "I know this has been hard for you, Doctor, and I appreciate your seeing me. We were both trying to talk without saying anything, and that's always tough. But thank you very much anyway."

"Thank you very much for *what*, Mrs. Lefferts? I haven't done a damned thing for you. I couldn't answer a single question you wanted to ask me. I realize that—I hope you realize the reasons I couldn't—and I'm sorry. It's just the way things are."

Lisa nodded and walked quickly out of the psychiatrist's office. DuBrul watched her leave and then moved to the window to let his eyes follow her slowly down the path. The poor woman, the poor suffering, tortured woman. And he had been no help. Damn Nils Lee for bringing his psychic nonsense into the picture anyway. And damn himself for ever telling Lee about Chad in the first place. If the situation was too much for him, a qualified psychiatrist, how could it be anything but much too much for a psychiatric layman like Lee?

CHAPTER NINETEEN

The air around him was alive with whisperings and chantings; he saw the crude blazing torches flaring along the abbey walls, but they kept going in and out of focus, replaced by the fire burning in a sacrificial altar in Rome.

The men gathered around the brazier were simple people, dressed, most of them, in the plainest of tunics or togas, some quite ragged. There was only one other soldier besides Flavius, who himself stood on watch at the door.

"Oh, Lord," Chad heard the leader of the group say in Latin, "forgive us." The leader's voice barely rose above a whisper; the man was very old and bearded, as was the custom with Roman aristocrats of the day. "Forgive us miserable sinners for worshiping Thee in this pagan temple, but we know of no better way to avoid the spies of the Emperor than to worship Thee and Thy Son, Jesus, than by pretending to worship *their* gods in *their* temples. We are not denying Thee, O Lord Jesus; we are trying to avoid death at the hands of the Emperor so that we may continue to spread Thy word. Have mercy upon us."

A chorus of "Amens" rose from the small gathering of Christians.

"Let us join in the Lord's Prayer," intoned the leader. Awkwardly, shyly, as if still embarrassed by what to them was a new ritual, the group sank to its knees. Chad kept his eyes on Flavius, kneeling now by the door, still frequently glancing outside as his mission required. As always, Chad could feel his own lips move as Flavius's did, softly reciting the words of the prayer. "Our Father, who art in—"

Flavius suddenly turned toward the leader; Chad could feel the soldier's terror. "Hide yourselves, hide yourselves!" Flavius hissed.

The leader shook his head angrily, refusing to let the prayer be interrupted, and beginning again. "Our Father, who art in Heaven,/Hallowed be Thy—"

Flavius had risen to his feet, his face a mask of terror. Chad felt himself try to warn the people in the room again, but no one seemed to hear him.

A piercing shriek filled the room and scattered the worshipers. It was the abbess. She raced into the room in her flowing black robes, screaming at the people in Chad's voice. The startled group drew back against the walls. Mixed in with the worshipers in their tunics, Chad suddenly saw the novices and the nuns and the choirboys, one of the boys holding the bishop's stained golden crozier high in the air between his outstretched hands. The abbess, still screaming her terrifying scream, had almost reached the group's leader. Flavius drew his shortsword and planted himself between the abbess and the leader. With a sudden move that was so fast it seemed only a blur, the abbess seized the heavy crozier from the choirboy and began swinging it at Flavius, who tried to defend himself with his Roman shortsword. With the crozier so much longer than his sword, he had great difficulty, and Chad could feel the blows on his own body each time the crozier struck Flavius. He could hear his own voice screaming as the abbess screamed; he could hear his own voice yelling as Flavius ordered her to surrender.

For several moments they fought, shortsword against crozier, like men dueling. With an incredible screech, the abbess flung herself on Flavius, hurling him to the ground by the suddenness of her move. They wrestled back and forth on the floor, screaming, shouting, cursing, groaning. The glowing pagan brazier was knocked over as they rolled by it and scattered burning coals across the straw-covered floor. Almost instantly the entire room seemed to become filled with a dense, choking smoke. The group of Christians began praying in Latin; the nuns and novices and choirboys started their expressionless chant, *"Fader Oudre, der in Hefonium ist . . ."*

As they wrestled for their lives on the floor, sometimes the abbess appeared on top, sometimes Flavius. At one point, Flavius, choking on the thickening smoke, finally seemed to have the abbess pinned to the ground, but Chad heard his own voice screaming to her charges; the nuns and novices and choirboys rushed to her aid, beating Flavius with their fists, their heavy golden crucifixes, and the bishop's crozier. Flavius had to release his grip on the abbess to protect his face from the blows, and a moment later they were back rolling in their death wrestle on the floor. At first, both seemed oblivious to the flames that rose higher and higher around them, but the abbess's long robe began to smolder and suddenly broke into flames. The abbess's shriek was so loud and piercing, Chad could feel the muscles in his throat ache from making the sound. The abbess had leapt to her feet and kept beating uselessly at the flames on the robe, her screams now not of anger but agony, while Flavius stared at her, his shortsword hanging limply from his hands.

It had been a curious battle, Chad realized. Himself *against* himself. Himself as Flavius, himself as the

abbess, struggling, he supposed, to see who would seize
control of his karman and take the next place on the
wheel of life when he died.

Suddenly Chad felt his body swaying and saw that
the earth was beginning to spin. It was not a new
sensation. A few seconds later he was hurtling around
the intense void of the black hole near Omikron Blue,
the abbess's voice still screaming from the agony of
the flames. In the far distance Chad thought he could
hear Marius Flavius calling to him, warning him,
pleading with him. (Fainter because of the X2.97
lapsed gravity factor? Chad didn't know.) He wanted
to answer, but his voice was drowned out by the abbess's shrieked orders to him.

And Chad knew she had to be obeyed.

She wasn't going to let him. Not tonight. For
Christ's sake, did Petey think she was a whore? Rose
Pitano stared moodily out of the window of the car,
watching the reflections of the passing cars as they
traveled across the glass like fast-moving ghosts. For
the moment, neither she nor Petey were saying anything; Petey's mind was racing ahead, searching his
mind for the right place to park, Rosa's building a
case that would allow her to refuse again without losing him as a boyfriend.

The car turned off onto a secondary road, and Rosa
squirmed in her seat. She wanted to say something to
discourage him, but for the moment couldn't decide
what. She had used a mythical period only a week
ago; that easy avenue was closed to her. A headache?
So trite it was almost a joke. Moral scruples? If she
was so goddamned moral, why had she let him do it
before?

"Here we go," said Petey, sending the car up the
steep drive that would bring them out a little past
East Rock. There was a wooded area nearby, and if
crazy Rosa didn't pull something funny, he'd be home

free. At the top of the road, Petey pulled up the car in one of the parking insets, where they could look down on the lights of New Haven stretched out below them like a sequined blanket. Rosa braced herself. She would have to stop him now or she would never be able to.

"Petey," she began. Rosa didn't get any further. Petey had shot across the narrow seat of the Volks Beetle and had his mouth pressed into hers, sucking so hard he seemed to be trying to draw out her soul between her teeth, savagely exploring the inside of her mouth with his tongue and sending small, involuntary shudders through her whole body. Struggling, she tried to push him away enough to speak, but his hands were inside her T-shirt and rubbing her nipples until they became turgid and hard. She tried one more time to say something, but one of his hands had freed the zipper of her jeans and was inside her panties, the fingers rubbing the hard, bony mound above her vagina. Two fingers moved inside, first touching, then pressing, the spot that always drove her crazy. In some dim recess of her mind, part of Rosa was still resisting, and she tore her mouth away long enough to speak. "Petey, we *can't*," she said desperately. "Not in the Beetle. Last time I hurt all over for a week."

Petey straightened up and started the engine with a roar. "Hang on, sweetcheeks, I got it all figured."

Rosa watched Petey jam the Beetle into reverse, turning around quickly and shooting further down the road. Perhaps half a mile beyond where they'd been parked, he suddenly turned off onto a narrow dirt road and pulled up in a clearing surrounded by the scrub pines that cluster on East Rock. Rosa was still quivering, but her resolve was returning; she could, she thought, still fend him off. Petey was very businesslike, unfolding a blanket he'd had on the back seat and smoothing it out on the ground. He lifted his head to look at her through the open car door, his face an unspoken invitation.

"No, Petey. Please, no. It's cold up here. Someone will see us. I'm scared."

Petey walked over to the car, grabbed her by the arm, and pushed her forcefully down onto the blanket. His fingers went to work again, on her breasts, inside her, everywhere. "No, Petey—please, Petey—Christ, Petey—oh, Petey, Petey, Petey. . . ."

Gradually she stopped trying to speak anymore because the will was drained out of her and she didn't want to protest any longer and she let him pull the T-shirt up over her head and the jeans down off her hips without a word, shaking all over with the excitement of it. Her panties ripped when he pulled them off, and she swore angrily, but the words were lost inside his mouth; and when he started to take off his own clothes, she found herself helping him, her hands rubbing hard on the bulge in his jockey shorts until he finally took them off. She screamed only once, when she felt him go inside her; it was not a scream of pain but of ecstasy; the thrusts were deep and slow and long, and she beat her hands against his naked back from the pure pleasure of it, digging her nails into his smooth buttocks until he groaned because it hurt so much at the same time that it felt so good.

The terrible screaming came at them out of nowhere. For a second Petey thought it was maybe a new kind of police siren, but he couldn't turn around very well because he was so far inside Rosa. She managed to twist her head to one side and saw the woman rushing straight at them, something long and black flapping behind her. The screaming woman had something in her hand; suddenly Rosa recalled the headlines she had read in the papers about the screaming woman and she began screaming herself. Petey seemed unable to move, staring at the woman for a second, his eyes bulging in horror, and then he pulled himself violently out of Rosa and tried to turn over.

The heavy stick the woman had in her hand crashed into the back of his head without his ever realizing she had it; he collapsed flat onto the blanket. Hurling herself, the woman fell on Rosa, pinning her arms to the ground while Rosa yelled for somebody—Jesus Christ, anybody—to help. Nobody answered. From her chain belt, the woman yanked some lengths of leather thong, and before Rosa was even sure what was happening, had her hands and feet tied and trussed up like a chicken. Roughly, the woman turned Rosa onto her back and stuffed something in her mouth to keep her from yelling anymore. Rosa watched as the woman —she kept muttering, but Rosa couldn't understand what she was saying and couldn't even tell if the woman was speaking English or some foreign language —took more of the thongs from her belt and tied up the unconscious Petey in the same way.

Turning back to Rosa, the woman reached deep into the pockets of her robe and laid three items neatly out on the blanket beside her: a large pair of scissors, a dagger with a twisted end like that of a corkscrew, and an old-fashioned straight razor; her grandfather had one like that. Kneeling, the woman muttered something that sounded a little like a prayer Rosa used to say at Mass, but in the same mumbled, foreign words so she couldn't be sure. Finishing, the woman kissed the golden cross that hung loosely around her neck and crossed herself. Rosa writhed and struggled, but the woman paid no attention, leaning forward and cutting off as much of her hair as she could with the scissors. With a flourish, she held the razor high for a moment, then shaved her head clean. The corkscrew dagger was lifted the same way, and Rosa, unable to speak, could only groan as the woman, chanting now, pressed its sharp point against her stomach and carved something Rosa couldn't see. She wanted to scream, she wanted to argue, she wanted to cry out at the cruelty of what this crazy woman was doing, but all Rosa could manage was more thrashing and a strangled moan.

Abruptly, the woman turned away from her toward Petey. He was beginning to come to, and his eyes couldn't believe what he saw or accept the fact that somehow he had been hit on the head and tied up like this. He wanted to pee badly, but he was afraid of what Rosa would think. Above him loomed the dark shape of the woman, the razor in her hand. Carefully she leaned down, and chanting something he couldn't make out, shaved off all the hair on his lower stomach, leaving him looking as he hadn't since he was about twelve—six years ago.

Rosa tried to signal Petey with her eyes, pleading for him to do something, but he apparently was so terrified he was unable to move. The razor was still in the woman's hand. With another of her sudden shattering screams, the crazy woman leaned down and grabbed roughly what Rosa had treated so gently just a few minutes before. The razor swung through the still night air, making a thin, hissing sound. His face frigid with terror, Petey tried to scream, but the razor had reached him, the blood gushing forth. Petey fainted. Like the abbess's favorite boy soprano, he had just received the ultimate purification.

Rosa almost fainted herself from the sight of what had happened. The woman was standing upright now, and walked briskly over behind a tree. When she came back, she was carrying something that Rosa couldn't figure out until the fumes from the gasoline she was pouring over both of them reached Rosa's nose. It was a five-gallon jerry can. Rosa tried to roll away, but the woman kicked her back into place beside Petey each time she tried. Once more the crucifix was kissed and the sign of the cross made over them both. Rosa did not see the match the woman threw onto the gas-soaked blanket until she, Petey, and the blanket all burst into a brilliant, burgeoning ball of orange-blue flame. Somewhere beyond her, as the terrible pain of the fire engulfed her, she heard the woman's voice chanting. For the first time the words were clear, even if they made no sense. *"Fader Oudre, der in Hefonium ist . . ."* That was all Rosa heard, and all she would ever hear.

The moment she heard Chad's car leave the driveway, Lisa was wide awake. For perhaps an hour she had lain in bed trying to go back to sleep, but found she was too worried and upset to. Turning on her light, but keeping her eyes half closed so the glare wouldn't get her any further awake than she already was, Lisa fished around in her bedside table until she found the Tuinal bottle. The little capsule, one half of it brilliant red, one half a cheerful blue, seemed wrongly dressed for a sleeping pill; but Tuinal usually worked for Lisa, and she was in no mood to counter with *House & Garden*'s Color of the Month. The coldness of the water in her water glass wasn't ideal to bring on sleep, either. But Lisa was determined—he had never left in the middle of the night like this before that she knew of—not to let Chad's illness destroy her, too. There was Robin to think of.

Turning over, Lisa had settled down carefully in a determined effort at sleep. Every time a troubling thought would enter her mind, she would dismiss it summarily. A sexual fantasy about Chad had also been dismissed; she remembered reading somewhere that such thoughts could keep you awake. Counting sheep was passé, but she could understand the theory behind it. As a modern electronic substitute, she kept her eyes focused on the small red dot that blinked once a second on the face of her Corbus Time Cube, at the same time counting backward from one hundred every even second and forward from zero every odd second.

Trying to keep the numbers in order would keep her mind off anything else. She had no idea of how similar her system was to the routine followed by Nils Lee to bring Chad to a cataleptic state.

In theory, her system was fine, but the agonies of the mind that were torturing her seemed immune to mind blanking and barbiturates and autohypnosis. Small traffic sounds from the street kept intruding on her; animals rustled the dry leaves of trees and ran across the roof; the mattress seemed suddenly lumpy; the pillows developed hard spots and sags where there had been none before. The problem, Lisa finally realized, was that no amount of trying to trick her mind or sophisticated sedation could eradicate listening for one simple sound she was desperate to hear: the soft purr of Chad's car pulling into the driveway.

Angry at herself more than at Chad, she looked at the time cube; she had been struggling toward sleep for almost an hour. To continue was an exercise in futility. Turning on the light, she lit a cigarette and walked down the hall to check Robin: sound asleep, curled up in a tiny ball to protect himself from the alien night. Downstairs, she went into the library and settled down to wait. For a few minutes she tried watching television, but the fare at three A.M. was less than inspiring. On the cable, she finally thought she'd found a half-decent movie on Channel 2 from New York, but the picture turned out to be about a woman who had moved into a new house only to find herself driven into screaming fits of terror by the ghosts and demons left behind by its last tenant.

It was too close to be bearable, and Lisa switched off the set, feeling self-conscious and embarrassed to be so easily rattled. In the silence she was amazed to discover how painfully their own house creaked and groaned at night; the old wood complained endlessly, like the timbers of some crewless schooner under full sail.

Lisa had been half asleep—this time without conscious attempt—when she heard the door of Chad's car slam shut in the driveway. All of her woke at once, like a small animal. Listening to his footsteps on the outside stair, she moved silently across the room toward the door that opened into the front hall. Chad would have to be faced; she could avoid it no longer.

The door opened and Chad walked in, carrying something—it looked like a bundle of black cloth wrapped round and round itself—beneath one arm. Crossing the hall, Chad appeared to make no effort to be quiet; it was as if it were a perfectly normal thing for him to come home at three thirty in the morning, and that he therefore had no reason to be either secretive or stealthy about it.

Within Lisa, accumulated anger, worry, and frustration came to a head; for the moment her sympathy for Chad and all his troubles evaporated in the heat of her sleeplessness. "Damn it, Chad, where the hell have you been until now? I'd think there was another woman, except that I, of all people, know better."

Chad appeared not to hear her. He took the car keys out of the pocket of his jacket and carefully placed them in the small tray on the narrow credenza, the place where both his and Lisa's car keys were always kept. As he turned toward the stairs, he stumbled once on the edge of the needlepoint rug in the center of the hall, but quickly recovered his balance.

"Chad!" Lisa began again. "Chad. I asked you where you've been."

He walked past her, standing planted in the doorway, as if she weren't there. Not even his eyes acknowledged that she had called to him.

"Chad, damn it, Chad!"

His head never turned. He continued on, untouched by her insistent calling and even her below-the-belt insult, walking like a man in a trance. Standing at the bottom of the staircase, she tried calling to him once more. His step never faltered, his progress never slowed, there was nothing to indicate that he had heard her, or if he had, that he had made any effort to answer. His figure slowly receded up the long, graceful staircase and disappeared as she watched, leaving behind only a faint, familiar odor that Lisa finally recognized as gasoline. A second later, she heard the door to his bedroom close and the key turn in the lock.

CHAPTER TWENTY

The distant voice that Chad had heard coming faintly from beyond the periphery of Omikron Blue's black hole grew louder and less distant during the second seizure.

"Help me," the voice said. "Help me, for I am weak and our Lord Christ cannot overlook my cowardice in denying Him." The voice belonged to Marcus Flavius; for the moment, spinning around the terrible circumference of the black hole, Chad was surprised that the abbess should remain so unusually silent.

"I can't help you," Chad told Flavius in Latin, lying. "I don't know what you want or who you are."

"I was you. Help me . . . help me. . . ." The voice trailed away into nothingness as Chad's thrashings on the bed grew less violent. In the distance he could hear traffic moving outside his room as the chirping of the late summer birds mixed with the first of the winter ones to arrive, impatient for their warm-weather brethren to leave and surrender the territory to them.

Chad got out of bed, looking at his clock. Ten. He still walked like a man in a trance, as he had the night before when Lisa had seen him come home.

Going to the closet, he slipped out of his shorts and into a curious-looking pair of brief skirtlike trousers festooned with long, pointed strips of heavy cloth. He had bought them earlier in the week from a costume company on Whalley Avenue.

Downstairs, he walked into the living room. Robin, still in his pajamas, was sitting on the floor playing with some blocks, oblivious to his father. A cough shook Chad's body and Robin looked up.

"It's an airport, Daddy. Look at my airport. See, the hangars are over here, and I have my little gasoline truck here, and—"

Chad stared vacantly at Robin and ignored him. Robin was oblivious to the lack of reaction and too youthfully unknowing to realize that Chad was in the "walking stage" of a seizure. He began racing around his father's feet, holding out his arms and making airplane noises that grew louder as he tightened the circumference of the circles.

"Come on, Daddy," Robin shouted. "You be the control tower and I'll be an F-15 and you tell me which runway to land on and where I should taxi to when I'm down. Come *on*, Daddy." Robin began tugging at Chad's left arm, trying to get him involved. "Silver 127 to tower, Silver 127 to tower. . . ."

Robin stumbled over Chad's bare feet, but Robin was undeterred. "Turbulence, tower. Please instruct . . ." He tugged at Chad's arm again.

Roughly Chad shoved him away. The thrust was so hard, Robin was knocked over and landed hard on his bottom. His eyes filling with tears, Robin sat there and watched with wonder as his father moved across the room. Carefully Chad took the burnished breastplate off the stone wall and slipped his arms through it. Almost running, he went over to the couch and pulled out a two-edged Roman shortsword from beneath it. His eyes darting, he began creeping around the room, peering behind one piece of furniture after the other, looking for any evidence that the Imperial Guard might be hiding nearby.

The sight revived Robin's spirits. It *was* some sort of a game his father was playing; the cruel shove had not been in anger, but, like the funny clothes and the creeping around the room, was a part of the same game. Happily, Robin began creeping alongside his father, imitating his searching and his occasional sudden thrusts with the sword. For the first time, Chad suddenly appeared to notice him. Roughly he grabbed Robin by the neck and forced him down on his knees alongside him. He folded his hands and made Robin do the same. He was speaking some kind of crazy language and Robin began to get frightened; it was a pretty stupid game, anyway. *"Pater Noster, qui in hevonium est . . ."* Chad intoned, lowering his head in prayer.

Infuriated that Robin did not join him in the prayer, Chad suddenly pressed the tip of his short-sword against Robin's neck and repeated the opening line of the Lord's Prayer. *"Pater Noster, qui in—"* Stumblingly, confused, beginning to be completely terrified, Robin tried to repeat the words after his father, but the language was strange to him and he couldn't get any further than *"Pater."* "Please, Daddy, take that funny thing away from my neck. It hurts, Daddy. *Please,* Daddy. I don't know what you want. . . ." Robin began to cry.

"Pater Noster, qui in hevonium est," Chad began again, the tight-lipped fury showing in his voice. A sudden sound from outside made Chad's head jerk toward the window. The sword moved away from Robin's neck long enough for him to run screaming from the room. Chad seemed not to notice that he had left, but continued his prayer, kneeling and lifting his eyes toward the ceiling as he repeated the same words over and over as if it were some magic spell.

Out in the hall, a startled Mrs. Lafferty gathered

the crying Robin to her and comforted him. What he was saying didn't make much sense, but then, what had been happening in this house for the last few weeks didn't make too much sense either. She wouldn't have been here at all on a Saturday morning like this, but Mrs. Lefferts had asked her to baby-sit Robin while she went to see some doctor or other, and, after the sudden extra time off she'd been given yesterday, she'd felt obliged to say she would. Worried, she put Robin behind her and walked to the door of the living room.

The second Chad saw her, he crouched behind a chair and cried, "*Loquisti! Loquisti!*" at her. That he was afraid was obvious. The shortsword in his hand clattered to the floor and he tore off the breastplate, leaving it in a heap. Without looking at them again, he dove out through the French windows, picked himself up, and disappeared. Mrs. Lafferty stood stunned, staring at the shards of broken glass as if they were pieces of Chad.

"Mary, Mother of God," she said, crossing herself quickly. Behind her, Mrs. Lefferts had come through the front door and stood beside her, her face torn with anxiety.

"It was Mr. Lefferts, m'um. Something's wrong. Terribly wrong. Scared the young 'un half out of his wits, he did. . . ."

Haltingly, Mrs. Lafferty tried to tell Lisa what she knew of the incident. Robin, clinging to his mother, was quickly moving from terror to excitement. "And, Mummy, he held that sword against my neck and tried to make me say something. In a funny language. I was scared, Mummy, but I was brave. I only cried at the end, didn't I, Mrs. Lafferty? Tell Mummy, Mrs. Lafferty, how I didn't cry until the end."

"He was a real brave boy, m'um."

A funny look had come over Robin's face. "What's

wrong with Daddy, Mummy? He's all funny. Will
he be back like he was?"

"Of course, Robin," said Lisa, wrapping an arm
around him. "Of course he will. We just have to be
patient." Lisa cringed. The lie didn't fool Mrs. Lafferty, the lie didn't fool herself, and Lisa wondered if
the lie even fooled Robin. Lisa felt like crying, but it
wouldn't be fair in front of Robin. Like him, she
would have to be brave and not cry until the end.

"I lied to you this morning. I don't know why; I
just did." She had finally reached duBrul by phone.

"I see. Well, everybody lies to a certain extent.
Would you care to tell me what you lied about? Only
if you want to, of course."

Dr. duBrul's voice sounded calm and reassuring.
To Lisa, this in itself was a great help; Mrs. Lafferty
only made things worse by painting the grim kind of
pictures only the Irish can conjure forth. Getting hold
of him again this morning had not been easy. Saturday was not a day he was usually in his office, so when
she'd tried to call him there, an answering service had
explained he was not in. Nor was he expected. When
Lisa had asked for his home number, the answering
service became evasive; the best they could do, they
explained, was to take her name and number and tell
the doctor she called when he checked them for mes-
sages.

"But it's an emergency," Lisa had cried. "I already
saw Dr. duBrul this morning, but things have happened to my husband since then that he has to know
about."

A psychiatrist's answering service is inured to patients who demand to talk to the doctor, inevitably
couching it in terms of an emergency. But the tone of
panic in Lisa's voice, the fact that Dr. duBrul had
come in on his day off to see her earlier this morning,

and that she was not a patient but a patient's wife, finally moved them. They would call the doctor at home, they had said, and Dr. duBrul could call her back. The implied "if he wants to" did not escape Lisa, but it was the most she could expect, she decided.

Almost minutes after Lisa, sitting on her bed and smoking one cigarette after the other, had hung up, duBrul called her back. Dr. duBrul had asked if she would care to tell him what she had lied about. It was time, Lisa decided, very much time.

"I lied this morning by *not* telling you things. Last night, for instance. Chad went out. For hours. Without telling anyone. I saw him when he came back, and he was like a zombie. Walked right past me like I wasn't there. And smelled of gasoline or something. Then, this morning, while I was at your office . . ."

Trying to ignore the quaver in her voice and the urge to burst into sobs, Lisa told duBrul what had just happened. Of how Chad had put on the breastplate and scared Robin half to death by making him pray at the point of a sword. That he'd screamed something at the housekeeper and then dived out the window. . . ."

"I could come over, and I will, Mrs. Lefferts, if it would be any help to you. I'm glad you told me about last night, but, frankly, I'm more concerned about what just happened. Is he still wearing that Roman getup?"

"He tore most of it off just before he disappeared, Doctor. Where do you think he is?"

"I don't know. But let me talk to Nils Lee. He may have an idea on it. You see, your husband's acting out part of a nightmare. And he's probably had a seizure and, in a medical sense, *is* a zombie for the time being. He's in a trance. Nils Lee has gone farther into these Roman actings-out of your husband's than I have. Let me call him. I'll get back to you."

"I feel so damned helpless," Lisa said, feeling the precarious grip she had on her self-control slipping steadily away.

"We're *all* helpless, Mrs. Lefferts. I'll get right back to you."

The urgency in the way duBrul repeated this statement told Lisa that he was as worried as she was. But, my God, Chad was just a patient to duBrul; to her, Chad was a husband, a lover, a close best friend, and father of their only child—one he had come, once again, perilously close to injuring or killing this morning.

The injustice of the whole thing was too much for Lisa. Unwillingly, hating herself for her weakness, she surrendered to a flood of panic-stricken and almost hysterical crying.

"Yes, gasoline. They were doused in it. Tied up like that, those kids didn't have a chance."

"Did anyone see her this time?"

"No. No one."

"But you're sure it was the 'screaming woman'?"

"Positive. We have ways of making sure. Certain marks known only to us and the killer."

Chief d'Allotto once again could feel the sweat gathering beneath his arms. These press conferences were killing him, even though he knew he was developing a secret taste for them. As the "screaming woman" had become more and more of a media headliner, his audience had grown. Not only were there local newsmen and television cameras present; the networks, wire services, and national press and news magazines were jammed into the room as well. Every detail he gave was held up, examined, and analyzed for evidence that elements of the story were being held back. The mayor had been right on that score; the city of New Haven was better off revealing as much as it could and being cooperative with the media than

holding back and facing the charge of a cover-up.
Particularly when they finally found the "screaming
woman"—d'Allotto assumed this even to be inevitable,
even if the prospects appeared dim at the moment—
there could be no charge that they had produced some
convenient half-wit to be scapegoat for the crime. Too
much would have been revealed in advance. She
would be nailed.

"I realize," the stringer from *Newsweek* said somberly, "that you're looking for a needle in a hay-
stack. But can you give us any idea, Chief, when you
think you may hit pay dirt? What I mean is, have you
developed any real, solid leads yet?"

"Yes. Finally, we have." For the first time, a murmur
rose from the newsmen. D'Allotto was glad someone
had asked the question; if they hadn't, he would have
volunteered the information. With his repeated exposure to these press conferences—although they still
made him break into waves of nervous perspiration—
he'd begun to master some of the elements of basic
showmanship.

"This," he said dramatically. With one hand he held
up the dagger with the corkscrew point. "This was
found this morning a few feet from the charred bodies.
Forensics indicates it was used for the ritualistic draw-
ings on the victims' stomachs. I can't pass it among
you—it's court evidence—but the dagger will be available for photographing at the end of this meeting.
You will note the brownish stains—dried blood."

The newly emerged showman in d'Allotto was
pleased by the stares of wonder the dagger in its
plastic envelope had produced among the newsmen.

"Was this the same weapon that was used to—to
castrate the boy?"

"No. That was apparently done with a razor. Or
an extremely sharp scalpel."

"Where do you think this new piece of evidence—

the dagger—will lead you, Chief?" asked the local man
for CBS.

"We don't know yet. It's an extremely unusual
dagger, though; experts have told us that just from
hearing its description over the telephone. Two professors from Yale are coming over later this morning
to give us an idea of how to trace its owner, if that's
possible. The thing is, there apparently aren't too
many like it."

The buzz rose from the newsmen again. D'Allotto
decided it was time to bail out now, while they were
still impressed. He announced that that was about all
he had to say for the moment, but that Sergeant Lu-
plaski would help them get their shots of the weapon.
He strode out of the room and back to his office with
the air of a man who had everything under control
and was fully confident in where he was heading.

Once inside, the pose evaporated and d'Allotto sank
into a chair. One lousy antique dagger was all he had
to go on. That was going to deliver an insane mur-
deress? Shit. Show biz certainly asked a lot of a guy.

The telephone in Nils Lee's office rang repeatedly,
a desperate sort of ringing that mirrored the mood of
the man calling. When it finally stopped, unanswered,
it rang again only a minute later. The caller was making sure that he hadn't misdialed. The same desperate
ringing then took place in Nils Lee's home, the same
stopping, the same redialing. There was no one to
answer at either place.

Impatiently Peter duBrul put the receiver back on
its cradle. There was nothing to do but wait.

It wasn't until half an hour later that Nils Lee
walked into his house and heard the phone ringing
like an enraged animal. He was stunned by duBrul's
opening gambit.

"Where the hell have you been, Nils?"

Lee answered automatically. "Over in the library stacks. I was looking for—some archive stuff on Augsburg." The rude tone of duBrul's question and the assumption that where he spent his own time was any of duBrul's business caught up with Lee abruptly. "I don't know why I told you that. If you don't mind my being blunt, Peter, since when do I have to account for my comings and goings to you?"

"Since you started meddling with one of my patients. I asked you not to get mixed up with that poor, sick bastard, but you went right ahead anyway. Since you started filling one of my patients' heads with your usual crap about reincarnation. Telling him he'd lived before, for God's sake. He believed it so much, he began acting out the role. Chad Lefferts, the first-century Roman soldier. Christ. Even his wife says he's been worse since he started seeing you."

"I don't want to be too hard on you, Peter, but you had only seen him once yourself when, as you put it, I 'started seeing him.' So maybe it was *you* that made him worse, not me. I'm not sure that believing in reincarnation is any crazier than believing in Freud."

DuBrul suddenly remembered the urgency behind his having called. "Look, Nils, for the moment let's skip the recriminations. We've got a problem."

Briefly and quickly he sketched the outline of what he'd learned from Lisa earlier on the phone—Chad's disappearance into the night the evening before, Chad's sudden reemergence this morning dressed like Marcus Flavius and forcing Robin to pray with him. "My real question, Nils, is, Do you have any idea where the guy could be now? He went out through a window in his house and no one knows where the hell he is now."

"No, I don't. He could be anywhere. But I'll tell you. I'm going to go over to my office and see if he shows up there. It's not too much of a possibility, but it *could* happen."

"All right, I'll try and calm down Mrs. Lefferts and then maybe I'll join you over there. We've got a lot of talking to do. Mrs. Lefferts didn't tell me a lot of what's been going on, and I have a suspicion you haven't either. It's no time for games. This guy could hurt himself—or someone else—pretty easily. He came close with his son already today."

"Okay. Call me there if you hear anything new."

Nils Lee knew his parting remark was a stupid one. Obviously, duBrul would; he would have to. For a moment he sat in his chair, still smarting about du-Brul's charge that Chad was worse since he had begun exploring his other lives. His own comment had been correct; it could just as easily have been Peter who made Chad worse. Slowly, his mind moved on to wondering what the chances were of Chad's showing up in his office. Slim, he decided. Still, the fact that the acting-out episodes under hypnosis were still in his unconscious might draw him back. Perhaps he would return because, as Flavius, he had been able to communicate there with Dr. Soong in Latin. Or, as the abbess, in Frisian. For a moment, he debated calling Soong, then decided against it.

With a resigned sigh, he pulled himself together and headed for his car. It was a hell of a way to spend Saturday.

DuBrul's phone rang only a few moments after he had hung up from Nils Lee. It was Lisa, and she was crying.

"I just got a telephone call. Chad. I don't know where he was calling from or anything, but it was Chad. His voice was all funny, and I couldn't get him to answer anything, but there is no question: it was Chad."

The strange way Lisa kept repeating the phrase about Chad—as if saying it often enough would make it true and bring her husband back—worried duBrul.

Lisa was getting very near the edge. "I see. Can you remember anything he said, Mrs. Lefferts?"

"He only said one thing, Doctor, over and over. I'll never be able to forget it as long as I live. Not a word of it. He kept saying, 'The black hole. The black hole of Omikron Blue. I should never have fucked around with it. It doesn't belong to me, it belongs to Flavius and the abbess, and they're fighting to see who gets my next life. I don't know who's winning, dammit. . . .' That's all it was. He said it three times. The same each time. I tried to get him to answer me, to tell me where he was, but he never answered." There was a long pause and duBrul could hear Lisa struggling to bring herself under control. Then: "He just hung up. And that was it."

DuBrul tried to think of something comforting to say. Again he offered to come and see her at home, again she refused, and the best he could do was to say he would call her the instant he heard anything. She put down the phone in the living room and stared at the display of medieval *objets* and paintings grouped around the fireplace. Carefully, not knowing why she was doing it, she hung Chad's prized Roman breastplate back where it belonged. The display seemed to mock her; what she had been so proud of only three weeks ago now was a monument to a destroyed husband. Something, she noticed, was missing from the display of *objets*, but she was too distraught to figure out what.

As she sat down again to wait for duBrul's call, she had an eerie feeling that she was being watched, that somewhere an unseen eye was studying her with intense malevolence. From the kitchen came the busy sounds of Mrs. Lafferty doing dishes and simultaneously entertaining Robin.

But there was another sound, too, one at first she wasn't sure she had heard. It was the sound of footsteps over her head, coming from Chad's room, followed by the peculiar groan his door always made when opened slowly. Lisa slipped toward the pantry and stuck her head into the kitchen. "Mrs. Lafferty, quick," she whispered. "Take Robin outside. *Now*. Don't argue. Take Robin outside." Blinking, trying to understand, Mrs. Lafferty let the door swing shut in her face and, gathering up Robin, grudgingly shepherded him toward the back door.

Inside, Lisa looked out through the open front door and checked to be sure Chad's car was still in the driveway. It was. Biting her lip, she stood anxiously in the front hall at the bottom of the stairs, waiting for Chad to come down. Today, now, whatever it was would have to be faced.

CHAPTER TWENTY-ONE

Nils Lee drove East on I-95, oblivious in large part to the traffic he saw moving on either side of him. Not so much by design as out of habit, he kept to the center lane of the three-lane eastward flow, causing anger among those who wanted to go faster and frustration among the cars who wanted to stay below 55. The result was a fistful of horn-blowings and resentful stares from the Saturday drivers, both those passed, and those who passed him.

So far today, things had been going badly. He hadn't been able to find the material he wanted in the Sterling Library stacks, and now he was having to make a second trip into town. DuBrul had called him at home in Branford and been unpleasant, and Chad's behavior of the night before, as related to duBrul by Mrs. Lefferts, had once again stirred up the terrible suspicions that had been growing inside him about Chad.

The string quartet on his car radio seemed to stop abruptly. A smooth voice—one more used to Mozart than mayhem—was interrupting with a news bulletin. Reaching forward, he turned up the sound a little. Another of the "screaming woman" murders. Two kids out by East Rock—it had already been dubbed lovers' lane by the media—tied up, mutilated, and set on fire. The worry in Lee grew. But then a recording of Chief d'Allotto's voice came on, talking of the first piece of solid evidence that the police had: the antique dagger with the corkscrew blade.

As suddenly as it had come, the suspicion drained out of Nils Lee. Yes, Chad Lefferts had a dagger like that—or rather, his wife did—but this time the dagger ruled Chad out as a suspect. The curious weapon still sat on the corner of his office desk. In spite of his promise to Chad, Lee had not yet called his friend about it; he had seen the knife there last night, just before he went home. Nils Lee began to whistle, feeling suddenly relieved. It had probably been stupid of him even to consider the notion that Chad was responsible for the chain of killings outside of New Haven. He himself had been misled by the coincidence of the nightmares and the actual killings. That Chad acted his nightmares out in his office was one thing; for him to go out and commit the terrible crimes that were being pinned on the "screaming woman" was something else.

Without remembering to use his signal indicators, Nils Lee turned off at Exit 47 to make his way through New Haven's light Saturday traffic and go to his office. A violent blowing of horns let him know his sudden unannounced turn was not appreciated, but Lee paid no attention; he rarely did. He was still feeling good. The suspicion about Chad that had been haunting him was at last laid to rest. Five minutes later, he pulled up in front of Davenport College and walked through the gate toward the inner courtyard, where his office was.

Almost immediately, Nils Lee knew something was wrong. A campus cop stood outside one of his ground-floor office windows, gesturing to Lance Whittemore, a graduate student who doubled as Lee's personal assistant. Even before he got closer, Lee could see that one of his windows had been broken and the window then opened; the curtain flapped forlornly outside the window in the brisk fall wind.

"Oh, Professor," said Whittemore, "I was just about to call you at home. Someone broke in last night; Sergeant Worth here noticed it and called me." He studied Nils Lee's expression and added quickly, "But it's all right, Professor Lee. They didn't take anything. I let myself in and checked around. Everything's there—they didn't even try to swipe the Ampex or the VTR. Nothing's missing. It's crazy."

"I'd think maybe it was some student who got liquored up and broke the window by mistake, except whoever did it really wanted to get in. They used the hole they made in the glass to reach inside and unlock the window," Worth noted. "Your man Whittemore here says you always keep them locked. So I don't know what to think."

Nils Lee did, but said nothing. Even before he moved inside with Whittemore and Worth, he knew what he'd find: the ornamental dagger with the cork-screw tip that had been lying on the corner of the desk would no longer be there.

"Oh, it would be a big help, believe me. I'll pick him up as soon as I find out what's going on, don't you know." Mrs. Lafferty smiled appreciatively and turned Robin over to the black housekeeper who worked in the house to the right of the Lefferts's; the woman had worked for the university almost as long as she had, and although her opinion of blacks was not in general a high one, she'd known Violet so long she felt safe leaving Robin in her charge. Mrs. Lefferts's whispered orders to her earlier to get Robin out of the house had upset Mrs. Lafferty; the poor lady was beside herself with worry, and that crazy husband of hers was capable of anything. She might need help.

"I'll be right back, Robin. Now, be a good boy and do whatever Miss Grallup tells you," she said, and scurried back toward the Lefferts's house.

Inside, Lisa still stood waiting at the bottom of the stairs for Chad. No one came down the winding staircase; she could hear no sound at all from the second floor. The piercing, wavering shriek, when it came, seemed to start somewhere directly above her. Lisa had time only to raise her head before the woman in the strange black robe stepped off the balcony, hurtled through the air with her robe flapping behind her, and landed directly on top of her. She crumpled to the floor under the woman's weight, simultaneously realizing it was no woman at all; it was Chad. The whole picture snapped into focus in her head even as she struggled to stay alive. It had been Chad that day inside the little building at the end of the cloisters who had knocked her down and tried to scalp her. It had been Chad who bowled over her rescuer, Mr. Thomas, and disappeared into the night. It had been Chad, she supposed, who had committed the string of sickening killings she'd heard about on television. Chad. *Her* Chad. She was having to fight too desperately to ask herself *why* Chad was behind all of these things or why he was dressed as a woman, then and now.

She thrashed and struggled, but Chad was a strong man and she was no match for him. His only problem seemed to be the sleeves of the flowing black robe he was wearing; they kept getting in the way of his hands and he had to keep pushing them up constantly. "Chad," she managed to gasp, "my God, Chad, *why?*"

At first he had been holding her arms outstretched on the floor and kneeling on her chest, but now he had moved up and was kneeling on her arms, holding her down with his body. His fingers tightened around her neck and Lisa was unable to say anything more. She could hear him muttering something she could barely make out, pushing the heavy crucifix dangling in front of the robe away impatiently. Lisa heard a strange mumbling coming from him. Over and over again he crashed her head against the tile floor, trying to knock her senseless. Finally she heard the words he was muttering clearly enough to make them out; they made no sense. *"Fader Ouder, der in Hefonium ist . . ."*

The fingers tightened closer around her neck; her head crashed against the floor again; she could feel a distant buzzing inside her skull and realized she was beginning to lose consciousness.

Only dimly was Lisa aware that something heavy had just been crashed over Chad's head. And that someone else was screaming as loudly as Chad, in the same pitch, but a genuine woman's voice. Mrs. Lafferty. She had barely gotten inside the kitchen when Chad had hurtled from the balcony on top of Lisa. The housekeeper grabbed the first thing she could find in the kitchen as she raced out into the hall—a heavy bowl of cake batter. She knew, even as she charged toward the robed woman assaulting her mistress, that she should have stopped and picked up a knife or a meat cleaver, but she was acting out of instinct, not out of any carefully thought out plan.

The blow of the heavy bowl splitting over his head momentarily stunned Chad, and he turned in surprise. From the umbrella stand by the front door Mrs. Lafferty grabbed the only thing she could see: a pneumatically operated umbrella that Chad resorted to in extremely rainy weather. With it she beat Chad across the face as hard as she could; the pneumatic device abruptly opened the umbrella, and Mrs. Lafferty shoved it forward at him with all her weight. "You fiendish creature!" she screamed. "You she-devil. Trying to kill good people as is in this house. Wait'll the po-lice get their hands on you, you screaming bitch!"

Chad blinked at her, his eyes still vacant from the

trance. Absently, one hand reached up and felt his scalp, coming away red from the deep gash Mrs. Lafferty's bowl had made in his head. With a shrill snarl, he grabbed the end of the umbrella, tearing it from Mrs. Lafferty's hands. Staggering to his feet, he looked as if he might attack them both again, but shook his head and ran out the front door, still muttering in the strange foreign language that seemed to be all he could talk. A second later Mrs. Lafferty heard a car start and roar down the driveway.

By then Mrs. Lafferty was on her knees beside Lisa, helping her to sit up. "Are you all right, dear? Are you all right, Mrs. Lefferts?"

Lisa wore a dazed look and nodded her head numbly. She watched as Mrs. Lafferty dashed into the kitchen and reappeared with a wet cloth, which she put on Lisa's forehead. "I'll get you some ice in a minute, Mrs. Lefferts." She studied her anxiously. "Are you *sure* you're all right? That crazy woman had the strength of a she-bear."

"Robin?" asked Lisa, slowly looking around her.

"Next door with Violet. She'll take good care of him. I knew something was very wrong here, m'um, and I didn't want the boy with me when I came back."

Lisa nodded again as Mrs. Lafferty helped her walk unsteadily to a chair. "Thank you," Lisa said, her words still slurred. "Thank you for everything. I guess you saved my life, Mrs. Lafferty."

"Anyone else would have done the same thing, m'um," Mrs. Lafferty said with a self-deprecating shrug, but shaking all over from pleasure at Lisa's statement. "But I think, soon as you're feeling a mite better, we should call the po-lice, Mrs. Lefferts. She could have killed you, that woman. And I think she stole the professor's car; I heard it start up a minute ago. . . ."

"In a minute, in a minute. If you'll help me into the library, Mrs. Lafferty, there's a call I've got to make first. And something to drink. My throat hurts. . . ."

"No wonder, with that woman trying to squeeze the life out of you." She looked at Lisa strangely as she helped her into the library; she could feel the woman trembling all over from her terrible encounter. Yet, instead of the police, she wanted to call someone else first. Out of their minds, these university people, clean out of their minds.

It took Lisa three tries to dial the number; her fingers kept missing and pressing the wrong buttons. The phone answered almost the second it began ringing, as if someone on the other end were waiting to answer it. Dr. duBrul sounded stunned when he heard Lisa's story, but his first question was not about how Lisa was at all. "Have you any idea where Chad went? Where he is now?"

"No. I should have told you about that woman attacking me in the walled-in garden, I suppose. But at the time, it never occurred to me there was any connection."

"I'll be right over, Mrs. Lefferts. Just don't stay there alone. Lock the doors. I'll get hold of Nils Lee and we'll be right over. Keep that housekeeper in the same room with you; I'd leave your son where he is, until"—duBrul paused, trying to find the right words but unable to—"well, *until*. And try to stay calm; everything's going to be all right."

"Everything's not going to be all right with Chad, though, is it? Ever."

Peter duBrul did not answer Lisa's question.

The three of them sat in Lisa's living room, trying to affect some degree of normalcy. In the kitchen, Mrs. Lafferty could be heard banging around, making them sandwiches; all of them, for some reason, were suddenly hungry. The police had still to be called, and Mrs. Lafferty was somewhat scandalized that her advice on this point was being ignored; instead of the house being full of New Haven police and state troopers, these two unfamiliar men had arrived and closeted themselves with Mrs. Lefferts.

"And that's the story, Mrs. Lefferts," Nils Lee said softly. "I know it's difficult to accept at first, but those tapes of your husband are just about impossible to explain in any other way." Lee had brought a portable tape player with him and exposed two of them—it was the first exposure of any tapes to either duBrul or Lisa—made when Chad was in his hypnoidal state. Briefly he had then explained the theory—both his own hypothesis of reincarnation and the Far Eastern religious version—to them.

Lisa stared at him as if the man had gone mad; duBrul, for the first time, was appalled to find himself beginning to agree with Nils Lee. There was no other explanation. At a total loss, Lisa floundered. "It's all so new, so crazy-sounding to me. I can't believe it. And why should this happen to Chad? These two awful people—well, one of them's awful anyway—fighting each other to get his next life. I mean, I've read about reincarnation, of course. But why Chad?"

Nils Lee sighed. "There's no answer to that, Mrs. Lefferts. Or at least, none I know of. But what you heard on the tapes—the voice that was talking—that *was* your husband's, wasn't it?"

Lisa bit her lip. "Yes, it was. I still can't believe your explanation, but yes, it was."

"The other voice on the tapes, that is Dr. E. Y. Soong, a highly respected linguist at the university. He handled the interpreting for me. I had to call him in when your husband began speaking colloquial Latin as Flavius, and later, when he started in with Frisian—Old Norse—as the abbess. Your husband told me he had never been deeply involved in Latin, or Roman history; as for Frisian, no one has spoken it for several hundred years. It's a dead language, you see."

"Well, Chad was lousy at Latin. I remember his telling me that; he used to joke about it. As for Frisian, I don't know how he could speak it; he can't even handle German. But that still doesn't mean—"

For the first time, duBrul began talking. "Mrs. Lefferts, you have to understand that, like yourself, I didn't believe a word of this whole thing when Professor Lee first talked to me about it. I thought perhaps it was done by some sort of post-hypnotic suggestion, and that your husband might be suffering some sort of multiple personality disturbance. It's still a possibility, but a very faint one. There are some things that all our science doesn't know yet, I'm afraid. This is one of those things. For myself, I am reluctantly persuaded by details such as Chad's knowledge of the temple in Rome that no one else knew about. And the wealth of detail he's familiar with as far as Augsburg and its abbess are concerned. It's a very difficult thing for a psychiatrist to accept—all of this—and yet, I'm beginning to find I *do* accept it. As Professor Lee points out, there is no viable alternate explanation."

"I don't know, I just don't know," Lisa said miserably. "And I'm not sure that even if I did, it would help things at the moment. Chad, what do we do about Chad?"

"Eventually," said Nils Lee, "the police will have to be involved. I'm sure you realize that. Your husband will probably be judged insane"—Lee looked at duBrul, who nodded grimly—"and while that's a terrible idea to have to accept, it's probably better than having the courts decide he is *sane*, and therefore responsible for all these killings around New Haven."

"I can help on that score, of course," added duBrul. "Expert medical opinion—all that kind of stuff." The pained look on Lisa's face made him explain further. "I should think trying to prove that he was not responsible for the killings because he was acting under the control of another, earlier life was just about impossible. That's a point you might want to discuss with a lawyer, however. For the moment, in any case, it would seem the best step would be first to find Chad, and *then* call the police."

Lisa nodded. The whole thing was too much for her. First the outlandish acceptance by two highly intelligent men of something as hard to believe as reincarnation, then this same reincarnation they *believed* in being used to prove Chad insane so he could avoid being held responsible for the terrible chain of deaths. "I don't know what else I can say but yes. It's all so weird. Sometimes it makes me feel like I've gone crazy myself."

"Have you any idea where Chad might be hiding?" asked Nils Lee again.

"None."

"I have my assistant—Lance Whittemore; he's a graduate student who works with me—sitting in my office in case Chad shows up there," Nils Lee said, and then turned around to duBrul. "Is there anyone who can cover your office, Peter?"

"He's been seeing me—when he showed up—at the university medical center. There's a receptionist on duty there. Even on Saturdays, I'm pretty sure. I'll call and check." While duBrul was talking on the phone, Lisa turned to Lee with a pleading look.

"There's no other way? I mean, without the police?"

"I've had my suspicions about Chad ever since the abbess emerged during that session you saw on tape. But I put them aside," Nils Lee noted. "I probably should have said something to the police then. Now that we're sure, there isn't any way to handle it *except* by telling the police. For one thing, that dagger of yours will eventually be traced to you. It's a very un-

usual piece. And I gathered from Chad you'd shown
it to some people at the Art Museum, trying to pin
down its period. It's only a matter of time."

Lisa looked up and studied the stone wall around
the fireplace. Earlier, she'd known something was
missing; now she knew what it was. "I see," she added
limply.

"All fixed up. The receptionist will call me here if
Chad shows up in my office," duBrul told them, trying
to fan the foul-smelling smoke from Nils Lee's Sobranie out of his nostrils. There was a painful silence,
finally broken by Nils Lee. Gently, he turned to Lisa.

"Did Chad ever give you any idea of where he went
during any of his seizures?"

"No."

"Has he ever said anything that might have given
you an idea?"

"None that I can think of."

"Damn," duBrul said. "He must have a hiding
place, some secret refuge he keeps going back to, someplace he can act out the role of the abbess."

The idea was so simple, Lisa couldn't believe it had
been right there in front of her all the time. She
hesitated, part of her not wanting to tell them, part of
her knowing she *had* to. "Well, the one time I did run
into him dressed as that crazy woman—not counting
today—was in the cloisters of the walled-in garden behind us. I didn't know it was him, of course. But
maybe . . ."

Both duBrul and Nils Lee were standing up. They
exchanged a long glance and began adjusting their
clothes to leave. DuBrul broke the silence. "You say
right behind this house?"

"Yes. There are signs all over the wall saying no
trespassing. The place is deserted, and the gates are
locked. But there's a small opening in the wall, to
the left of the gates. I used it myself to go in and out.
Do you want me to come along and show you?"

The glance was exchanged again. "I think it would be better—and safer—if you stayed here," Nils Lee said firmly. "Keep the doors locked and your housekeeper in the room with you. That mother and her son he killed yesterday. Symbolically, you and Robin, I'm afraid. It would be very dangerous for you to be here alone . . . he might come back."

"But you. What if he . . ."

"There're two of us, Mrs. Lefferts. We can handle him. Just try not to worry. I realize that's a lot easier to say than do. We'll be back as soon as we can."

Lisa stood up, suddenly grabbing duBrul's arm with her fingers; the grip was so tight he felt himself wince. "Please," she pleaded. "Please, whatever happens, don't hurt him. None of this is his fault. Please don't hurt him."

DuBrul and Lee nodded and were out the door before Lisa could say half of what she wanted to.

CHAPTER TWENTY-TWO

"Where the hell is it?"

"To the left of the gate, she said, to the left."

"Looking in at it from the street, or out from the inside?"

"Good question."

Peter duBrul and Nils Lee were not having an easy time of it. The opening in the wall Lisa described had so far eluded them. They had discussed going back and getting her—or at least getting more definitive directions as to precisely where the opening was—but both agreed this would only upset her further. Finding the walled-in garden itself had been simple; driving around the block, they had immediately seen the thick, ugly wall and the garish, Day-Glo metal signs fastened to it every few feet, warning that it was private property, that no trespassing was allowed, and that violators would be prosecuted.

"I've heard of this place," Nils Lee commented. "Some Old Blue bought it a generation ago. The university has been trying to buy it for years."

"They're welcome to it."

For a moment they had stood outside the heavy twin metal doors in the center of the wall, testing them to see if they might open, even though heavy padlocks were visible hanging from their hasps. In spite of their searching, however, the opening in the wall seemed to have disappeared.

"Wait a minute," said duBrul suddenly. "Right down there. Isn't that a break in it?"

"Where?" Nils Lee followed duBrul's pointing finger, but could see nothing but more wall.

"There, damn it," said duBrul impatiently. "Behind that sumac bush. See? It looks like a narrow slit in the wall where the masonry's caved in."

They almost ran to the spot. DuBrul was right. Behind the yellowing sumac leaves, an opening could just be made out. Nils Lee, being slim, slipped through easily; duBrul, cursed with the occupational hazard of all psychiatrists—an overly generous midsection—had considerable difficulty getting through. "Have you thought of the Pritikin Diet?" asked Lee, acidly.

"Oh, shut up."

Both men were affecting a lightness they did not feel; it was insulation against the depressing emotions that were sweeping through them. Inside, they looked at the almost head-high grass, brownish from the fast-advancing fall. Beyond this, they could barely make out the long, low tile roof of the cloisters. "There's a rotted-through well-cover somewhere along in here," noted duBrul. "Lisa mentioned it."

As they walked carefully forward, Nils Lee in the lead, they searched the ground tentatively with their feet. If there was one such mantrap in this overgrown garden, there could well be others.

"The place could use a gardener," said Lee, still trying to keep up a bright front.

"Lefferts may not be here. There could be another place he hides himself."

It was as if the abbess had heard duBrul and was

answering him. Nils Lee stumbled over something; there was a sudden snapping sound, like the explosion of a small firecracker, followed by a much louder crack and a sudden *whoosh,* as if something had been shot through the air. Something had. The body of a man, suspended head down by one leg, had shot skyward as the trigger released the bent sapling, and hung there, springing up and down like a rubber spider at the end of a latex thread.

Nils Lee had staggered backward when the trip wire snapped, stumbled, and fallen into duBrul; both of them landed on the ground, staring at the body hanging in front of them. Richard Thomas's head had been crushed. The device that suspended him so grotesquely in the air showed that the abbess had not forgotten the method of execution that tore the head out of Ronnie Cosaro's body.

For a moment, after they had gotten back on their feet, both duBrul and Nils Lee stared at the body.

"Who is it?" asked duBrul, moving toward the body that was still gently moving up and down from the springiness of the sapling.

"I don't know. He must have seen Lefferts go in through the same opening we used and come in himself to investigate."

DuBrul examined his fingers where he had touched them to the wounds. "It wasn't long ago. The blood's still fresh, even a little warm."

"Then he's probably still here somewhere."

Standing up, duBrul stared at Nils Lee anxiously. "I think maybe we should get the police involved right now, Nils. I don't know—*you* don't know—what he's apt to do when he seees us."

"The police will shoot him, sure as hell. If we find him and bring him in, they won't dare. Too much publicity."

"You're right, I'm afraid. But this damned place is

a setup for an ambush. He could be lying in wait in a hundred different spots. He knows the place; we don't."

"Just keep your eyes open and stick close to me. We'll be okay."

Slowly they started forward, side by side. DuBrul remained anxious. "We're no match for him when he's acting out his role as the abbess. Look at his wife. Look at that poor bastard back there," said duBrul glumly.

"Scared, Peter?"

"Damned right. I've had patients throw things at me; one even slugged me once. But usually they just *wish* me dead. This guy . . ."

"Watch it," said Nils Lee suddenly. Ahead of them, looking as eerie as ever, was the bleached statue of the prie-dieu, its unseeing eyes staring emptily into space, one hand raised in a mocking benediction. DuBrul and Lee gave the prie-dieu a wide berth, afraid that Chad might be hiding behind it. Slowly and carefully they made their way toward the cloisters; as they neared them, they could see the decorated columns that supported the slanting tile roof. Finally they could make out the small building Lisa had told them of at the far right end of the cloisters and sharing the same roof.

Once on the stone paving of the cloisters, they breathed a little easier. They could see clearly in either direction and there was less chance that Chad could spring at them from some hiding place in the tall grass. DuBrul suddenly felt Nils Lee grab his arm.

"Look. Look down there, Peter." Following Lee's pointing finger, duBrul saw the slit-like doorway into the small building. Outside, flanking it like sentinels, were two wire mannequins. On one, a purple-fringed toga was draped; a Roman shortsword on a leather belt hung across one of its shoulders. The other mannequin was dressed in the long, flowing black robe of Elua, the Mad Abbess of Augsburg. Some sort of wire inside kept the hood in an upright position, as if a pair of eyes were staring out at them from its black interior.

DuBrul sighed. "What do you make of it?"

"I don't know. Those clothes—they're Chad's costumes, I guess. They represent the two earlier lives that are struggling for possession of his karman, and—"

"Oh, shit, Nils." Nils Lee looked at duBrul with surprise; he had thought he'd made a convert. But while duBrul could go along with the theory of reincarnation up to a point, he wasn't prepared to go this far. He changed the subject adroitly. "I suppose we should go in. Lefferts is probably in there. But, Christ, it's going to be dark with just those tiny windows . . ."

From his pocket Nils Lee produced a flashlight. "Picked it up in Mrs. Lefferts's hall closet when I got my hat," he explained sheepishly. "I didn't know where we might wind up having to look."

Cautiously they moved toward the slitlike door. From outside, Lee shone the flashlight around the building's interior, but couldn't see very much. "Do you think he's in there?" duBrul asked.

"I'm not sure. If he is—and if he's still playing the abbess—we're in trouble." Nils Lee thought for a second. "On the other hand, he left her costume outside, so I don't think he is. He must have come out of his trance."

DuBrul moved up alongside him and leaned toward the door. "Chad!" he called. "Chad, are you in there? It's Dr. duBrul and Nils Lee. You can answer if you're in there. We're not going to hurt you, Chad."

There was no answer except the echoes of duBrul's voice ricocheting off the walls, and the sound of small feet scampering across what sounded like old news-

papers. Mice or rats, duBrul decided. "Chad!" Nils
Lee called inside. "This is Nils Lee. I'm coming in. Is
that all right?"

There was still no answer. Lee turned to duBrul.
"I'm going in. If you hear a scuffle, run like hell and
get the police. But I don't think anything's going to
happen."

"Be careful, Nils."

With a deep breath, the flashlight held in front of
him, Nils Lee stepped inside. The gasp he gave was so
loud, duBrul heard it even outside the building,
where he was standing. "Peter, Peter, come in quickly.
Peter!"

Squeezing himself through the narrow opening, du-
Brul forced himself inside. "Nils, are you all right?"
Then his eyes followed the beam of the flashlight
and duBrul gave his own gasp. On the same wall as
the door, Nils Lee's flashlight had not picked it up
until he was inside. From a crude wooden cross nailed
into the wall hung Chad Lefferts's naked body. On
the floor below it lay the hammer he had used. His
legs were nailed to the bottom of the upright and
one hand had been nailed through the palm of the
hand to the horizontal. The other hand had been
tied with a knot and slipped over the other end of the
horizontal, then, apparently, yanked tight so that its
slipknot would prevent Chad from changing his mind
and trying to escape from the cross. The death Marcus
Flavius feared above all others had been acted out to
its final conclusion: crucifixion.

"Jesus," groaned duBrul. "What do we tell Mrs.
Lefferts?"

"What do we tell the police? Or, for that matter,
what do we tell ourselves? It's incredible."

Nils Lee's question was largely a rhetorical one. He
knew exactly what to tell himself. Granted, Chad
Lefferts's self-crucifixion came as a shock. But thinking about it now, after the fact, it made a crude, if

horrible sense. In the struggle between Flavius and the abbess for possession of Chad's karman, Flavius had won. It would be Flavius who died in possession of Chad's karman, and therefore it would be Flavius who would take the next turn on the wheel of life. The abbess would have to wait a little longer.

Chad's so often repeated "Hide yourselves, hide yourselves" suddenly returned to haunt him. Originally, he had thought that Chad had been trying to warn Lisa and Robin; now he wondered if possibly one part of Chad hadn't been warning the others inside of him to hide from the abbess. Chad was so many people at the same time, so many lives fighting for their freedom, it made a certain sense. Trying to explain any of this to others would be impossible; for the moment, it would have to be a secret even from duBrul. Blankly, Nils Lee stared at him. "I suppose we have to—"

"Yes, I'm afraid we do. Shit."

Dreading it, the two men walked out of the building, through the tall grass, and out onto the street. The world outside appeared strangely harsh and banal, the traffic sounded unusually loud, and the children playing in the street were a mockery.

Slowly, Nils Lee and Dr. Peter duBrul walked around the corner and headed for the Lefferts's house. Neither of them spoke a single word. Both were struggling to think of some way to tell a woman that her husband had just crucified himself in the pursuit of a better eternal life. It would not be easy.

L'ENVOI

Every afternoon, when the sun hits the rim of the water and begins to disappear, a thick black fog rolls off the Pacific and blankets Carmel, California, as if God had reached out and turned off the lights. A short time later, the fog lifts once more and you can drink in the golden afterglow of its long amber rays flickering across the water.

It was a sight that never failed to excite Lisa. Every afternoon since she had moved here, she watched the interplay of fog and sun, making almost a ritual of standing in front of the sliding glass doors that looked out over the cliffs and onto the Pacific. Her new home was completely different from the house the university had installed them in in New Haven—or, for that matter, any other home she had ever lived in before. It was as different, inside and out, from the gloomy showplaces where she had used to display her medieval art collection as California was different from the cold, wintry East Coast.

Inside, the same difference would have been noticed by anyone who had ever seen any of Lisa's previous homes. Gone was the collection of priceless medieval paintings and *objets*, replaced by the abstractions of unknown modern artists. Against the bleached oak walls of the living room, they seemed as completely at home as Lisa did. Another difference: the entire house was ultramodern, a long white-washed stone affair all on one floor. Expanses of glass were everywhere to take advantage of the ocean view; outside every window, a profusion of flowers that seemed to bloom all year around punctuated the blue of the Pacific with their bright splashes of tropical excess.

The house, the view, and the tiny patch of land that surrounded all three seemed perfection. It also seemed—and was—a very expensive setup for a university professor's widow. There was an explanation. Lisa's medieval art collection had turned out to be worth far more than she had ever dreamed; Yale's Art Museum had bought several of the paintings themselves, paying, possibly because of the circumstances, somewhat too much. The rest, sold at public auction, had done almost as well; in an inflation-frightened market, paintings of such venerable and provable antiquity brought a premium. For herself, Lisa had not kept a single reminder of the collection.

The victim of a past mild stroke, Lisa's mother had succumbed to a major attack while reading about her late son-in-law's suicide and the crimes with which he would have been charged had he lived. To Lisa, her sole heir, this brought a further influx of money. And Yale itself had helped. The entire incident was one of great embarrassment to them. That one of their senior faculty had killed himself was bad enough; that he had killed himself in such a bizarre way had made it a front-page story. Their embarrassment was heightened by the fact that a Yale-affiliated psychiatrist, Dr. Peter duBrul, had been treating the man during the entire time he was efficiently killing teenagers all over the New Haven suburbs. As a final blow to their position in academia, another Yale professor, Nils Lee, head of the history department, had written

an article claiming, from personal knowledge, that
Professor Chad Lefferts of the physics department
was the victim of a struggle for his soul between two
previous lives he had led, a Roman named Flavius
and an abbess from the thirteenth century. Ridiculous! If both duBrul and Lee hadn't had tenure, they
would have been terminated promptly. As it was, all
that the university could do was withhold any possibility of advancement, make life as unpleasant for
them as they could, and hope they would go quietly
away.

What terrified Yale most was that Lisa, unless well
provided for, might be forced into doing some writing
of her own, or allow herself to be interviewed on television talk shows, or lend her permission to a book
and movie about her husband. With this in mind,
Yale quickly saw that Chad's pension was increased,
that his university insurance was paid in spite of the
suicide, and provided her and Robin with security
guards and free moving expenses to wherever they
wanted to go. On her own, Lisa had also secured a
job editing art writings; she refused to cover one area
only: the medieval.

Outside, the evening's show was about over. Robin,
already in his pajamas, was racing around the living
room in tight circles, playing as he always seemed to,
F-15. After his original question about his father had
been answered, he never mentioned Chad again. The
turmoil, the reporters, and the faculty callers had
initially provided a source of excitement, but the
hushed tones used to talk to his mother told some
part of him something was wrong. To him—at least,
on the surface—it was as if Chad had never existed.
Lisa sometimes worried about this, but had never felt
sure enough of her own emotions to bring Chad up
herself. Very quickly, to her, too, as to Robin, it was
as if the man had never been the focus of their lives;
he was part of something they had known one bleak

New England fall, and their lives were now here, in the ceaseless sunshine of the West Coast.

The phone rang stridently from the small den. Lisa got to it and picked it up while Robin continued his jet flight, following his mother into the tiny paneled room. "Oh, hi, Lionel. Tomorrow night? Well, if I can get a sitter, I'd love to. No, I'm not putting you off; I'm sure I can. Hold it just a minute, Lionel." Lisa put her hand over the mouthpiece and told Robin to get ready for bed, not to forget to brush his teeth, and to get his own glass of water for his night table. "I'll be up in a minute, sweetheart, to hear your prayers." With a look of irritation, Robin zoomed down the long hall to his bedroom. "Robin," explained Lisa into the phone. "If there's one thing he hates, it's going to bed." More plans for the following evening were discussed, and with a vague, satisfied smile Lisa hung up.

Lionel Asher was not much; she knew it. Worse, Lionel was aware of it himself. But what Lisa wanted for her second husband was a quiet, steady man who would make a good surrogate father for her son. Lionel was in insurance, a quiet and steady enough business for anyone. In his profession Asher was extraordinarily successful, and while he had none of the genius or flair or piercing humor of Chad, he had none of the mercurial weaknesses Chad had had either. If someone suggested reincarnation to Lionel, he would laugh in his face. Lisa neither liked nor disliked the prospect of becoming his wife. That she would be asked, she was sure; it was as inevitable as Lionel's actuarial charts.

After drawing the living-room curtains for the night, Lisa walked calmly down the hall toward Robin's room. Standing in the open door, she saw that Robin had started his prayers without her. He heard her, looked around, and began again. Lisa smiled slightly. It was the classic Norman Rockwell pose: little boy kneeling beside bed, hands clasped, head supported on them. The picture had everything Rockwell loved except, perhaps, the falling down rear door in the Dr. Dentons. As a finishing touch, Lisa heard the gentle vesper chimes from the Mission of San Luis d'Osorte roll across the peaceful hills.

But as she listened to Robin, the smile on her face suddenly froze; Lisa went ashen and sagged against the door. It was impossible.

"Fader Oudre, der in Hefonium ist . . ." piped Robin, the harsh guttural Frisian sounding more evil than ever breaking through his small, musical voice. *"Allochne desen Nome Beyen. . . ."*

The abbess had already found a new home.

THE WILD ONE

by MARIANNE HARVEY

bestselling author of *The Dark Horseman*
and *The Proud Hunter*

Proud, beautiful Judith—raised by her stern grandmother on the savage Cornish coast— boldly abandoned herself to one man and sought solace in the arms of another. But only one man could tame her, could match her fiery spirit, could fulfill the passionate promise of rapturous, timeless love.

A Dell Book $2.95   (19207-2)

Cry for the Strangers

John Saul

author of Punish The Sinners

A chilling tale of psychological terror!

In Clark's Harbor, a beautiful beach town on the Pacific, something horrible, violent and mysteriously evil is happening. One by one the strangers are dying. Never the townspeople. Only the strangers. Has a dark bargain been struck between the people of Clark's Harbor and some supernatural force? Or is the sea itself calling out for human sacrifice?

A Dell Book $3.25 **(11869-7)**

Comes the Blind Fury

John Saul

Bestselling author of
Cry for the Strangers
and *Suffer the Children*

More than a century ago, a gentle, blind child walked the paths of Paradise Point. Then other children came, teasing and taunting her until she lost her footing on the cliff and plunged into the drowning sea.

Now, 12-year-old Michelle and her family have come to live in that same house—to escape the city pressures, to have a better life.

But the sins of the past do not die. They reach out to embrace the living. Dreams will become nightmares.

Serenity will become terror. There will be no escape.

A Dell Book $3.25 **(11428-4)**

Dell Bestsellers

At your local bookstore or use this handy coupon for ordering:

Dell **DELL BOOKS**
P.O. BOX 1000, PINE BROOK, N.J. 07058

Please send me the books I have checked above. I am enclosing $_____
including 75¢ for the first book, 25¢ for each additional book up to $1.50 maximum
postage and handling charge.
Please send check or money order—no cash or C.O.D.s. *Please allow up to 8 weeks for
delivery.*

Mr./Mrs._____

Address_____

City_____ State/Zip_____